THE RISE OF GREG

THE RISE OF GREG

— Book Three of —
AN EPIC SERIES OF FAILURES

CHRIS RYLANDER

PUFFIN BOOKS

PUFFIN BOOKS
An imprint of Penguin Random House LLC, New York

Copyright © 2020 by Temple Hill Publishing

Published by Puffin Books, an imprint of Penguin Random House LLC, 2020

Visit us online at penguinrandomhouse.com

Library of Congress Cataloging-in-Publication Data
Names: Rylander, Chris, author.
Title: The rise of Greg / Chris Rylander.
Description: New York: Puffin Books, [2020] | Series: An epic series of failures; book 3 |
Summary: Greg and his Dwarven friends seek a powerful amulet in the hope of averting a war with the Elves for the fate of magic on earth.
Identifiers: LCCN 2019045621 | ISBN 9781524739805 (trade paperback) | ISBN 9781524739799
Subjects: CYAC: Dwarfs (Folklore)—Fiction. | Magic—Fiction. | Elves—Fiction. | Adventure and adventurers—Fiction. | Fantasy.
Classification: LCC PZ7.R98147 Ri 2020 | DDC [Fic]—dc23
LC record available at https://lccn.loc.gov/2019045621

Printed in the United States of America
ISBN 9781524739805
1   3   5   7   9   10   8   6   4   2

Design by Eileen Savage | Text set in Apolline Std

For anyone who makes a difference and even those who don't

CHAPTER 1

Captain Smeltfeet's Left Hand Squawks Like a Parrot

By this point, I hope you'd assume the day I got eaten by a Kraken was a Thursday.

But here's the thing: this time you'd be wrong.

It actually happened on a Friday (formerly my favorite day of the week). To be precise, it was the fifth Friday after my friends and I finally convinced the Council to take action and send us on a mission to find the long-lost Faranlegt Amulet of Sahar. Which is said to possess the power to control magic (i.e., banish it from existence once again, or harness it for good, or use it for evil, depending on your intentions). And nobody knew where it was, except my current pal, Stoney the Rock Troll, and also my former best friend, Edwin Aldaron.

"Are we almost there?" Ari asked me as we stood on the top deck of our massive ship that Friday morning. "I smell like used gym shorts boiling in spoiled vinegar. I need a *real* bath on dry land."

"Hopefully by this evening," I said, my eyes searching the endless blue horizon for any sign of land. "At least that's what Captain Smeltfeet told me yesterday."

We'd been out at sea on this huge boat for nearly four weeks. Which is how long it takes to traverse the Pacific when there're no functioning machines left in the world. Ever since magic had returned, cars, phones, computers, blenders, and literally *anything* with a moving mechanical part was now dead and useless. Including boat engines.

The SVRB *Powerham** used to be a passenger ferry that transported people and cars at thirty knots, powered by a couple of engines that generated well over ten thousand horsepower at full speed. But now the boat was propelled by a complex network of Dwarven-engineered sails and a team of four Bugganes** rowing with huge custom-built oars belowdecks. Of course, the trip would have taken twice as long if not for the added help of Dwarven magic keeping the sails full of wind and the ocean currents favorable.

"And you trust that Captain Smeltfeet knows what she's doing?" Ari asked.

"Well, I mean, yeah . . ." I said, not knowing how else to respond. "Besides, it's a little late to question that now."

"No, you're right," Ari said quickly. "There's just . . . you know, a lot on the line."

She was right to be worried: we had put a lot of trust in a Dwarf who had some *peculiarities*, to say the least. For instance,

---

* Sailing Vessel Row Boat *Powerham*

** Before you get all up in arms, let me assure you these Bugganes were being well paid for their service. Bugganes are hulking creatures with powerful upper bodies and an extreme loathing for idle laziness—there's truly nothing they prefer more than productive manual labor.

Captain Smeltfeet had only one working eye, and so when she spoke to you, she tilted her head to the side like she was trying to get water out of her ear. She also had a talking "pet parrot" named Finnegan, which wasn't a parrot at all, but rather just her left hand, which she flapped around like a beak whenever her "parrot" was "talking." But if Dunmor trusted her enough to put her in charge of a ship embarking on the most important mission in the history of modern Dwarves, then I had to as well.

"Important cargo," a voice behind us said, startling me so badly, I nearly fell overboard. "Important cargo in thee ship's holds, aye, there be."

It was Captain Smeltfeet.

How long had she been standing there? What had she heard? She directed her one good eye at each of us in turn, head tilted, a wry grin on her haggardly unnerving face.

"Important cargo?" Ari asked helplessly.

"Aye, important cargo," the captain said, her fluffy eyebrows moving around so much it looked like they were break-dancing. "So says I. Har-har."

"Important cargo, the captain says!" she then said, using her "parrot voice" for Finnegan, while she flapped her left hand open and closed. "Squawk! Important cargo!"

Oh, yeah, I forgot to mention that whenever Finnegan squawks like a parrot, Captain Smeltfeet merely says "squawk" instead of actually mimicking the bird noise itself.

Ari and I glanced at each other. We had no idea what Captain Smeltfeet was talking about. There was no cargo on board as far as either of us knew.

"Umm . . ." I said.

"I know the preciousness of what be in thee holds," the captain continued. "And delivered safely it will be, aye, so says I.

Har-har! Magic comes, magic goes, but the stars, aye, the stars they remain. Dead and gone they may be, but their ghostly visages will remain, forever unchanged."

"Forever unchanged!" Finnegan added. *"Squawk!"*

I assumed the captain was referencing how she'd been navigating solely by the stars and sun. GPS was a thing of the past. Most (if not all) of the thousands of satellites orbiting the earth were now either cold space junk stuck in an endless orbit or had come crashing down over the past few months, scraping across the night skies in flaming balls of disintegrating parts. The return of Galdervatn had apparently stretched even beyond the reaches of our inner atmosphere.

"Well," I started, having no idea what to say to someone who might be certifiably insane, yet was also in charge of this vital part of the mission. "Thanks for getting us here."

"We're *not there* yet, lad," Captain Smeltfeet said briskly, her one eye now scanning the ocean ahead. "But we will be soon. Har-har, says I. You, and I, and the rest of the important cargo."

"Squawk!" Finnegan added.

Then she spun around and headed back inside the ferry's top-deck cabin.

"You think she means us?" Ari whispered.

"The important cargo?" I said. "Maybe . . ."

Perhaps the captain had a point. The ship *was* filled with important cargo, if you thought about it a certain way. Not Ari or me, specifically, but all of us, as a whole.

This time the Council had actually taken us seriously. This time they were not entrusting our entire future to a ragtag bunch of Dwarven kids still in training. In fact, the only reason any kids were on this mission at all was Stoney. He had refused to go unless we were allowed to join him. So we were only here as "Rock Troll liaisons" and pretty much nothing more. Dunmor had made that very clear.

The actual completing of the mission (i.e., recovering the long-lost Faranlegt Amulet of Sahar) would be left to the professionals. Along with Ari, Lake, Glam, Froggy, Tiki Woodjaw (one of our new friends from New Orleans), Stoney, and me,[*] the ship was also transporting twenty-five of the best and most highly trained Dwarven warriors alive today: two squads of Sentry Elite Guard special forces warriors, and the most feared and respected military officer in modern Dwarven history, Lieutenant Commander Dorak Thunderflower.

Commander Thunderflower was a lot like our old trainer, Buck Noblebeard. They both hated smiling, loved scowling, and possessed an extensive knowledge of Dwarven combat techniques. But Commander Thunderflower was taller, stronger, fitter, less lazy, and somehow even angrier and meaner than Buck.

I, for one, would never want to get into a fight with the commander.

To be perfectly honest, his presence (along with that of his twenty-four elite supersoldiers) was immensely comforting. For once *I* wouldn't have to lead the charge. I wouldn't have to stumble and bumble my way through a mission that would be successful only because of pure dumb luck. In fact, I sort of pitied whatever obstacles we would face while searching for the amulet. I had no doubt these Sentry commandos were

---

[*] Eagan had to stay behind. His new position on the Dwarven Council kept him too busy to embark on any more missions with us, no matter how important.

more than up for any challenge. For probably the first time ever, I was embarking on a mission fully confident it would succeed . . . because I wasn't the person leading it.

This time our mission, and the whole future of the Dwarves, wouldn't hinge on my clumsy mistakes.

Until, that is, I *did* haplessly sabotage it anyway.

CHAPTER 2

◆ →⊱✦⊰← ◆

I Somehow Catch Three Fish at the Same Time (Without Using My Fist!)

It was later that afternoon that I single-handedly sabotaged the whole mission before it even got started.

"What are you doing down here, buttercup?" Glam asked as she hopped down the steps onto the back deck of the boat, Tiki and Lake right behind her.

This section of the ferry was particularly low, almost to the water's surface, since it had been used for docking smaller vessels back before the world had changed. I was sitting on a small folding chair, near the edge, watching my fishing line descend into the depths as water flowed past underneath the boat.

"What does it look like?" I asked.

"'Tis appeareth thine chum hath clutch ye pike o'er ye high seas sooth purposes unbeknownst," Lake joked.

"Not for unknown purposes," I said, adjusting my grip on a huge fishing rod. "I'm trying to catch a fish."

"Yer doing it wrong," Tiki said. "Back in the south, we just used our plorping fists."

"Oooh," Glam said. "Fishing with fists? I like the sound of that!"

"Well, we didn't bash 'em or nothing," Tiki said. "We used our hands as bait to catch catfish. It's called noodlin'."

"Hah! Such prepost'rous notion be'est thee?" Lake exclaimed, laughing at the thought. "Thine singular clenched fist be'est ye bait!"

"Well, since we're on a moving boat in the ocean, I had to resort to a good old fishing pole," I said.

"Caught anything yet?" Glam asked.

"Well, no," I admitted. "But I'm enjoying the peaceful view."

I never expected to actually catch anything. Truthfully, I had no idea what I was doing. But four weeks on a slow-moving boat is a long time, and so we'd had plenty to spare. On the fifth or sixth day of the voyage, I'd found a storage hold in the lower decks containing a few old fishing rods and some tackle. My dad and I had fished on Lake Michigan at Montrose Harbor a few times when I was younger. I'd always enjoyed being outside, even though we rarely caught anything besides a few small gulpies.

Since I'd found the gear, I'd fished for at least an hour nearly every day on the voyage. I even hooked a fish once, but it got away before I could reel it in. Like I said, I didn't really know what I was doing. I'd just tied on a huge plastic lure with three sets of treble hooks and then let out the line, towing it behind the boat. It probably wasn't getting deep enough to target whatever it was designed to catch. But I really did enjoy the relative peace back here and the endless seas (first the Pacific Ocean, then later the Sea of Okhotsk) that sprawled out behind us.

Mostly, I'd been spending all this time fishing thinking about the antidote to my dad's condition.* When I was imprisoned on Alcatraz, Dr. Yelwarin told me that I'd never be able to make the antidote to her poison, since three of the ingredients went extinct thousands and thousands of years ago, during Separate Earth times.

But the prospect of searching for the Amulet of Sahar within a long-lost magical realm that had been cut off from the world since Separate Earth had given me some hope that I might be able to locate those supposedly extinct ingredients:

1. Three finger-lengths of *tafroogmash* root
2. A single wing from an Asrai Fairy
3. Seven petals from a toxic flower called *nidiocory*

But I wouldn't make the same mistakes I had before. This time I wasn't going to let my own selfish desire to help my dad interfere with the larger mission. I would search for the ingredients when I could, but never at the expense of the real goal: finding the amulet.

"Well, just so you know," Glam said, crouching down next to me on the boat's back deck. "Captain Smeltfeet spotted land up ahead. She said we'll be ashore in a few hours. So you may want to finish catching us dinner and get your stuff ready."

Tiki and Lake giggled.

"Okay, okay, I'll reel it in soon," I said with a grin.

They headed back up the stairs toward the middeck. I didn't

---

* In case you forgot, an Elven poison called *Shawara Marar Yarda* had resulted in my dad basically going insane, and the only cure, according to the Elven doctor who had brewed the poison, was yet another Separate Earth potion.

follow right away, wanting at least another fifteen minutes of peace and quiet before the real mission began. After twenty-six days on a small boat with the same thirty-two Dwarves, four Buggane rowers, and one Rock Troll, you learned to savor the quieter moments.

Especially now that we were finally almost to our destination: the remote northeastern coast of Russia.

Stoney didn't know the location of the amulet in the same way you or I might know where our hometown is on a map. But he knew how to get there in his head. Or, more specifically, he'd said, "STONEY NAVIGATIONAL FORERUNNER TO LOCALITY OF ROCK ONE WITH RELATIVE PRECISION. PRECONDITION: EXCURSION ORIGINATE MUNICIPALITY DESIGNATED CHUMIKAN."

After hours of research using old maps and a set of huge books called encyclopedias, we finally found what he was referencing: a tiny coastal village called Chumikan, located in the Khabarovsk Krai of far eastern Russia. It was a heavily wooded, sparsely populated area that fit the vague descriptions of the magical realm said, in the old Fairy fable, to contain the amulet. A place most Dwarves had since started calling, simply, the Hidden Forest.

Captain Smeltfeet had been pretty confident she could navigate us to landfall within a few miles of Chumikan using only an old Soviet-era wall map, the sun, the stars, and the horizon as guides.

I dearly hoped she was right as I reeled in my lure so I could collect my things from my stateroom and join the others on the top deck. I'd never been outside America before and I was pretty excited to get my first glimpse of a foreign land.

Suddenly the tip of my fishing pole jerked down toward the ocean. At first I figured the lure had gotten caught up in a current, or perhaps the boat's speed had changed, affecting the drag. But then the tip danced a few more times, and I knew for sure something *alive* was tugging at the other end.

I frantically began reeling, surprised at how excited I was.

My catch wasn't putting up much of a fight, so I just kept cranking on the reel. There was an occasional jerk, but it mostly felt like a deadweight. After several minutes of reeling, a small green fish came into view about ten feet beneath the surface of the sea. It was hooked through the lip and barely bigger than the lure itself.

"Fresh meat tonight!" I said aloud, practicing what I'd announce to my shipmates when I walked out onto the top deck holding up the fish. They'd be thrilled. All these weeks we'd been at sea, we'd been eating mostly cured and prepackaged meats like jerky, bacon, Spam, and Vienna sausages.

But just as the fish got to within a few feet of the boat, a huge shadow appeared suddenly from the depths beneath it. It zoomed up from the deep, faster than my brain could process.

I was still holding the rod in shock when a massive shark appeared. It opened its jaws and swallowed my fish whole in a single, toothy bite. One of the shark's glassy black eyes glinted in the sun for a second, before the huge animal spun around and retreated toward the depths.

The line on my rod began zooming out of the reel as I realized the huge shark had just swallowed my lure along with the fish. I held on for dear life as the rod bent in a half circle, the line unspooling so fast I thought I saw smoke.

But then, just as quickly, the spool slowed as the shark reached an apparently acceptable depth.

Standing on the back ledge of the boat, I leaned over and stared into the clear patch of deep blue seawater visible in the boat's wake. The line went almost straight down, as if the shark was directly below the ferry.

Then the line suddenly went slack and began floating up in spiraling tendrils.

I gave a few quick reels and the line kept coming up.

At first I figured the shark must have either spit out the lure or snapped the line. But if that was the case, I should have felt a sudden release of tension. This was more gradual, almost as if . . .

. . . *the shark was swimming back toward the surface.*

The realization hit me just as I saw the pointed nose and the wide grin lined with triangular teeth appear below me, rocketing up at an impossible speed.

The two-ton shark breached as I took a step back, falling onto my butt on the deck. Its razor-sharp, serrated white teeth snapped together as it fell toward me.

Only a Dwarf could manage to get eaten by a shark while on a boat.

But just before the huge shark's head landed on my legs, the ocean under its tail exploded. The shark was suddenly soaring even higher into the air, clutched in the jaws of a monstrous sea creature that I didn't recognize.

We had done a unit on water-based species in Monsterology class, but this beast didn't seem to fit the description of any that we'd studied.

It had two heads. They fought over the seventeen-foot shark, easily ripping it in half. As more of the massive sea creature's whale-size body came into view, I realized with terror that it was large enough to capsize our boat.

As if on cue, I was abruptly propelled into the air.

The world became a spinning blur of dark water, blue sky, clouds, and glimpses of our ship flipping end over end like a huge propeller.

Then my face collided with the surface of the cold sea. My vision blurred as salt water stung my eyes and poured down my throat with briny bitterness. I had been caught midbreath, so my lungs were already on fire as freezing water gushed in and seemed to swallow me whole.

With my clothes soaked, my natural buoyancy was gone and I began sinking into the depths of the Sea of Okhotsk, too shocked by the freezing temperature to struggle to stay afloat.

The light above faded.

Dark clouds seeped into the corners of my field of vision.

I'd die the same way as my ax, the Bloodletter: in a watery grave at the bottom of a sea. Fitting, I supposed, since I was the one who put him there. At least it wasn't my own best friend who'd thrown me overboard.

So, in that way, my death was a lot better than his had been.

And it was probably more than I deserved.

CHAPTER 3

Here Sinks Greggdroule Stormbelly: A Pretty Lousy Fisherman, but a Pretty Epic Failure

Essentially, my only job on this mission had been to keep a Rock Troll company.

And yet I'd still found a way to ruin the whole thing before it even got started. The boat had capsized, I was about to die a pretty unremarkable death at the bottom of a Russian sea nobody has heard of, and my friends were likely being devoured by a Dwarf-craving sea monster at that very moment.

Someday there'd be a buoy placed above me, bobbing on the surface of the dark sea. My floating tombstone* would read: *Here sinks Greggdroule Stormbelly, a pretty lousy fisherman, but a pretty epic failure.*

Or something like that.

Greggdroule.

---

* Though technically Dwarves don't believe in grave sites. Traditional Dwarven death rituals included scattering ashes in nature, or simply letting lost loved ones decompose back into the earth right where they fell, so we could once again become one with the elements.

The familiar voice cut right through my drowning brain like a magical blade.

Bloodletter? I thought back. *Carl?*

But how could that be? Distance affected our magical telepathic link, and he was currently sitting at the bottom of the San Francisco Bay. I was literally halfway around the world.

I chalked it up to near-death-induced delirium.

You're not delirious, but you are definitely about to be dead if you don't DO SOMETHING, you smidgy kunk! the voice said.

It was definitely the Bloodletter's voice. Or, well, as much as an ax can have a "voice," that is.

I can't believe the Dwarf I selected to be my owner, the Chosen One, is going to die in a simple fishing accident, Carl continued. *If I'd known what a spineless Gwint you were, I'd have picked someone else. Maybe even that one kid in your Metallurgy class who accidentally encased his hand in solid steel last year. At least he had the wherewithal to get his hand into nose-picking formation before it became permanently fixed.*

But what am I supposed to do? I thought back weakly, seconds from unconsciousness. *I'm drowning—too far down to possibly make it back to the surface.*

My magical ax somehow actually sighed in my head.

Use magic, dummy, he said.

Oh, yeah. Magic.

I'd almost forgotten I could perform magic anytime I wanted now. Since its full return, those of us with the Ability could cast spells at will. We no longer needed to directly ingest the swirling fog we called Galdervatn. It was *everywhere* now, it had fully seeped into the atmosphere, the elements, and the cells of every living creature.

Turning to stone probably won't help much at this point, though, I thought.

I sure hope this bout of idiocy and weakness is from the lack of oxygen to your brain, Greggdroule, the Bloodletter said. *And not just that you've gotten that much dumber.*

What do you mean?

I felt myself slipping away, surrounded by darkness.

Dwarven magic is limited only by the natural elements around you! the Bloodletter screamed, so fiercely it zapped a few more seconds of life into me. *You went to Human school for at least a little bit, didn't you?*

Yeah, so?

So what did you learn in chemistry? What is water made of?

Hydrogen and oxygen, of course.

Of course!

The Bloodletter was right: I was being a bloggurgin idiot.

With my last ounce of energy, I put all my focus and magical will into the oxygen atoms that I knew were in the water all around me. With seawater, there's also sodium and other odds and ends, but Dwarven magic is about genuine intent and need. It's not about the precise nature of chemistry at all. I didn't need to know the exact composition of my surroundings.

Suddenly I was forcefully vomiting out all the seawater I'd swallowed, spewing it back into the sea like some kind of super-charged sump pump. Once it was all out, instead of somehow taking a breath underwater, or growing magical gills, I realized I simply didn't need to breathe at all. Whatever Dwarven spell I had conjured was allowing the oxygen in the water to be absorbed directly into my bloodstream without the use of my lungs at all, as if through osmosis.

There you go, Greggdroule, the Bloodletter said. *Now what are you waiting for? Get back up there and help your friends!*

I kicked toward the surface. No longer drowning, I was able to swim like an Olympian, and I vaulted up toward the rays of sunlight filtering down through the water around me.

After what felt like mere seconds, I exploded up and out of the sea, taking a deep breath of real air with my lungs. As I bobbed on the water, it took only a moment to reorient myself and realize how far I'd drifted from our boat's wreckage.

The field of debris and floating Dwarves was almost fifty yards away.

But even from this distance, I could tell they were in trouble. For one thing, the huge two-headed beast that had destroyed the vessel was still present, its massive form thrashing in the water.

I swam toward the chaos.

As I neared, I got a better view of the creature. It looked like two bloated sea snakes, each one as thick as a semitruck, entwined and wrapped around each other like tangled shoelaces. As the slithering forms flailed and twirled on the surface I saw rows of fins lining the length of both, from huge dorsal fins at the tail end to smaller flappers up near their heads. It was hard to tell where one ended and the other began, or if they were even technically connected, or rather two separate creatures merely braided together.

Where the serpentine bodies separated, two long necks emerged, each topped with a separate head. They were similar, but not identical. Both looked sort of like an alligator with an extremely short snout. Dozens of long, uneven teeth stuck out like lances from their stubby jaws. One had a beard of slithering tentacles, and the other had bony spikes on the sides of its face.

The creature (or creatures?) slithered across the surface of the water toward a particularly large chunk of wreckage. Seven

Dwarves perched atop the platform of wood watched the sea monster approach. One of them was Glam.

She stood up and taunted the beast with a fist raised into the air.

"Just come and try, princess!" she shouted defiantly. "I'll untie and filet you with one hand, while using the other to prepare a marinade!"

The creature's heads screeched as it glided toward them.

Glam's fists turned into Glam-smash boulders, but I knew they would do little to stop this monster from devouring the lot of them in a couple of quick bites.

I swam desperately toward them, trying to summon a spell that would get me there faster. But unless Dwarven magic allowed instant teleportation (which was highly unlikely), I'd be too late. Both of the creature's heads were lunging at the survivors, and I was still over a hundred feet away.

But suddenly the beast was twirling up into the air.

At first I thought I might have unwittingly summoned a spell that had saved the day. But then I quickly realized it hadn't been a spell at all.

Instead, a second sea monster had collided with the beast from below, propelling it up and out of the water. The two-headed-snake thingy shrieked as it soared through the air, crashing back into the sea at least fifty feet away.

I turned my attention to the new arrival and immediately recognized it from the old drawings in our Monsterology textbooks.

A Kraken.

Human pop culture often portrayed Krakens as massive beasts with tentacles that resembled enormous octopuses or squids more than anything "mythological." But that's a modern take, inspired by tales of sailors seeing actual giant squids out at sea.

Real Krakens, the ones from Separate Earth, were much different. They had colossal bodies with huge horizontal tail fins, almost like a whale, but even fatter and larger. This Kraken, for instance, was nearly twice the size of an adult blue whale. It also had a gaping mouth. Krakens used a set of razor-sharp claws at the ends of two tentacles attached to their bellies to pluck prey from the ocean and toss it into their gullets whole. They also had four spindly legs, which folded up along their fat bodies when they swam. They were like giant crab legs, but more gnarly.

In short, Krakens sort of resembled an enormous whale-crab, but with more spiky parts, and they were a lot deadlier.

The Kraken and the two-headed-snake thing wrestled in the water, basically fighting over the spoils of the shipwreck (i.e., whoever won got to eat those of us helplessly bobbing on the surface of the water).

The fight was short-lived as the Kraken promptly snipped off one of the snake creature's heads with its huge claw. Bright blue blood sprayed everywhere, like an untended fire hose. The remaining head howled in anguish as it retreated beneath the surface of the ocean and back down into the depths.

The Kraken spun its massive body toward the wreckage, where Glam and several other blue-blood-soaked survivors stared in shock and horror. Two claws slithered out of the water on powerful, long tentacles, hovering above the Dwarves as if taunting them.

I had to act.

Thankfully, I had paid attention that day in Monsterology class. So I remembered that Krakens, although technically smarter than fish, were still easily distracted by flashy things that sparkled in the sun. They were not deepwater creatures, but instead stayed within a few hundred yards of the shore, where they would perch on the bottom of the ocean, using the sun's light to help them detect prey swimming past near the surface of the water.

I removed my dagger, Blackout, from my belt. It had the power to remove all light in its proximity for a short amount of time. Temporary total darkness would create the flashiest burst of light possible.

I held up the dagger, willing it to do its thing.

Screams, gasps, and the rumbling roar of an angry and confused Kraken marked the onset of total blackness. But the cold ocean was still there, and so were the sounds of my friends and the angry sea creature trying to eat them.

I kicked my legs in the darkness, treading water as I held Blackout straight into the air. I knew that at any moment, the flash of light returning would happen.

Even through closed eyelids, I saw a brilliant burst as Blackout released light back into the world. It was more intense than a camera flash in a dark room.

When I opened my eyes, I immediately noticed my plan had worked. The light reappearing had completely distracted the Kraken. It was no longer about to eat Glam and the other survivors floating on the debris. In fact, it wasn't even near them at all anymore.

Instead, it was now swimming right toward *me*.

CHAPTER 4

The Thanksgiving Day Parade Kraken

I wish I could say I acted heroically.

That I slayed the Kraken with just a small dagger and a little bit of Dwarven magic, saving everyone.

But you ought to know me better than that by now.

I was so frozen with panic and awe as the monstrous sea creature barreled toward me, creating a wake so violent it could have easily capsized the SVRB *Powerham* all over again were it not already in pieces, that I just kind of floated there, treading water, unable to look away.

Up close, the Kraken's eyes weren't like those of the shark that had tried to devour me. The shark's eyes had been empty pools of black where nothing resided but predatory instinct with an operating program for survival, as nature intended. But the Kraken's four eyes, two on the sides of its head and two on the front, almost seemed *Human*. I know that sounds crazy, especially since every single one of its eyeballs was bigger than a small car. They didn't even *look* Human. They had massive silver pupils surrounded by varying shades of bright yellow. Just the same, as I peered into the Kraken's eyes, even as its mouth opened up, displaying thousands of spiky "teeth" flexing out from its throat to grip me and shove me down its esophagus, I swore I saw a conscience. Emotions. Perhaps even regret.

But then all I saw was its stadium-size mouth.

And eventually, total darkness as it swallowed me whole like flotsam.

Were it not for two things, I'd already be dead, and you'd be done reading what would surely be the shortest part three of any story in history:

1. I was so small compared to the Kraken's usual prey that I managed to miss most of its front teeth as I was poured down its throat among thousands of gallons of seawater.

2. A tiny bit of instinct *did* finally kick in, and I felt myself turn to stone for part of my travels into the belly of the beast. If I hadn't, I'd surely be in pieces, since the Kraken's esophagus is lined with serrated bones the size of broadswords.

I was back to a full flesh-and-blood Dwarf by the time I landed in the soggy stew of thick goop and steaming, rotting fish parts that was the Kraken's main digestive chamber. It was pitch-black, and the air was so sour and humid that every breath felt like the last one I'd be able to squeeze out. So I did my best to hold each strained inhale as long as I could.

But before I worried too much about that problem, I needed to get a bearing on my surroundings and what had just happened.

You just got swallowed by a whale with crab legs is what just happened, the Bloodletter said.

Yeah, I know, I thought, as I tried to stand.

But there was nothing to *stand on.* My legs were entrenched in a bottomless pit of thick sea-animal paste being slowly dissolved by stomach acids—stomach acids that were already starting to make my exposed arms tingle and itch like I had a rash.

How are you even talking to me right now, anyway? I thought. *Are you close? Can you travel underwater?*

Ha! You wish. Just imagine if I WERE nearby. If you hadn't thrown me out like last week's trash. Then I could easily get you out of this. Heck, if you still had me, you wouldn't even be in this pickle to begin with.

I was about to come up with some sort of witty reply (no, really, I swear it would have been a really snappy retort), but I didn't get the chance. I was suddenly thrown sideways and completely submerged in Kraken stomach goo. This was followed by more jostling and pitching, as I worked to get my head back above the goo line, desperate to keep any more digestive juices and dissolving fish guts from getting into my mouth.

It was obvious the Kraken was moving rapidly, perhaps fighting someone or something.

I had to get out so I could help the others. Well, that and I also didn't want to die a slow, painful death being dissolved by stomach acid.

At least it's quicker than spending eternity at the bottom of the ocean near an overrated, overpriced, overly self-important city!

I wasn't sure if it was comforting to have the Bloodletter back (at least in my mind), or annoying, since he was just cracking lame jokes instead of actually trying to help me.

The Kraken lurched again, and my head finally broke free

from the stomach goo. I wiped as much of it away as I could and took a short, gagging breath inside the putridly muggy stomach.

The first thing I needed to make an escape was light. After all, I didn't know just how big this belly was. As far as I knew, I had yet to even touch the inner lining of the stomach wall. But how to create light where there was none?

You could try lighting a fart on fire? the Bloodletter suggested.

Ha-ha.

Just trying to help.

Blackout's handle was still firmly gripped in my fist. But could the dagger's magical powers have an effect that was the opposite of the usual? If I used it in a place with a total absence of light already, maybe it would *create* light instead of taking it away?

I thrust the blade into the air, willing it to do its thing.

Nothing happened.

The stomach stayed pitch-black.

I tried not to let myself panic, knowing that a panic attack would only use up more of what very little oxygen was left.

After all, there were other ways to create light. Ever since I had set my own pants on fire trying to fight a huge Gargoyle several months ago, I'd been working on fine-tuning that particular bit of magic: setting things on fire. And over the past few weeks on the ship, I'd gotten pretty good at it.[*]

I focused on Blackout's blade, not really knowing if the magic would work on metal. To my surprise and delight, the blade ignited with a bright yellow-and-white flame.

But then it promptly went out.

I gasped, becoming instantly light-headed. Which likely

---

[*]   Aside from one unfortunate mishap during which I almost incinerated Finnegan the parrot, i.e., the captain's left hand.

meant the last bits of oxygen inside the stomach were now gone.

Yeah, you just used up the rest of it setting your knife on fire, genius, the Bloodletter said.

Duh!

How could I have forgotten that fire burns through oxygen like a camel drinks water? At least, I assume camels drink a lot of water. Do camels drink a lot of water? Or was I already suffering the effects of asphyxiation?

Probably a little of both, the Bloodletter replied casually, as if he had no concern whatsoever for my life.

Help me! I thought back desperately.

There was no reply and so I started thrashing through the stomach goo in a vague swimming motion. The darkness was so disorienting, I could only hope I was traveling in a single direction and not "swimming" in circles in the rancid fish paste. But I had no way of knowing until I either passed out and died or found the stomach wall.

Seconds later, my hand brushed up against a slimy, hot slab of flesh. It had no beginning or end as my hand moved all along the slick surface. This had to be it: the inner lining of the Kraken's belly.

I hastily plunged Blackout into the wall of flesh, and visions of slicing my way to freedom flashed before my eyes.

The blade made a slash, then another. I kept cutting and slicing at that same spot, moving the knife up and down, struggling to keep my grip on the slimy handle. It felt like I was getting nowhere, and when I stopped to check my progress, I realized I *was* getting nowhere. The spot I'd been cutting was perhaps a foot long and a few inches deep, and already shifting and moving on me as the stomach churned its contents to aid digestion.

The Kraken's stomach wall was probably several feet thick at a minimum, perhaps even a lot more. It might take me hours to cut my way through it with a tiny dagger. And I didn't have hours—I had maybe twenty seconds before I passed out from a lack of oxygen, according to my burning lungs and pounding head.

Plus, even if you cut through the stomach lining, the Bloodletter added, *there's no way that knife could get through the massive layers of muscle surrounding it.*

So what then? Just die?

Greggdroule, I swear, sometimes talking to you is like conversing with a statue of a cow. Use Dwarven magic—use the plorping elements around you!

My ax was right. Why wasn't I using magic more? I guess having lived nearly my whole life without magic made it hard to adjust to a new reality in which, technically, the possibilities of what I could do were limited only by lack of necessity, my natural surroundings, and my lack of instinctual creativity.

I took a final desperate breath of stale, steamy, methane-filled air as I tried to sort out what was nearby that might actually help me. If I couldn't cut my way out, how else could I escape from a confined space?

A bomb would probably work, but . . .

Stop!

Rewind!

The answer had literally almost killed me a second ago when I breathed it in like a dolt: *methane.*

When organic materials were digested, one of the by-products was methane gas. Usually, animals are able to vent these gases by way of, well, farting and burping. But what would happen if I sped up digestion? If I used magic to help this thing digest its food faster than it could possibly vent?

You're going to escape by way of a massive fart?

I have to try something, I thought.

No, no. I like it. Really. Can't wait to see this.

I didn't bother trying to figure out if the Bloodletter was mocking me. Instead, I focused all my energy on biodegradation. I put all my magical will into the dissolving enzymes in the stomach acid breaking down organic materials. I wasn't sure if I needed to think so *specifically*, but it couldn't hurt. After all, I was desperate, which was one requirement of Dwarven spells.

Suddenly I was sinking. Not into the stomach goo, but *with* the stomach goo. The Kraken's stomach lining was expanding.

It was working!

Who knew a real science class in the Human world would someday help me escape a Kraken's stomach in a future where the old laws of science no longer fully applied all the time?

I could also tell that we were ascending within the ocean itself as the creature filled with gas. I was thrown violently around as the Kraken thrashed in the water with discomfort.

I held up Blackout and focused on the blade, using the latent bioelectrical energy around me to heat up the metal. Before long, the black steel was glowing red. It wasn't much light, but it was just enough to let me see that the stomach had expanded to the point where I was basically inside a huge digestive auditorium, filled with a lake of green goo, fish bones, wooden and metal chunks of boats, and half-dissolved shark carcasses.

The stomach walls kept expanding, up and out, into the shadows and out of view. From the outside, the Kraken probably looked like a huge sea-monster balloon. More like a ridiculous display in a Thanksgiving Day parade than an actual living Kraken. It probably looked like it was about to explode.

Then it *did* explode.

CHAPTER 5

I Turn Uda Bay into the World's Largest Jacuzzi

It took me a few seconds to figure out that the Kraken had literally exploded.

At first there was just a *whoosh* of air and a bright flash of sunlight that temporarily blinded me. Then I was cartwheeling across a blue sky, taking thankful gulps of fresh sea air along the way.

After a few dozen unintentional backflips, I slammed into the sea, never more grateful to be in freezing-cold salt water.

I swam to the surface and took a few more deep breaths. After cleaning the remaining goo from my eyes, I finally realized what had happened.

There were chunks of Kraken *everywhere*.

Bits of blubber and muscle bobbed on the surface of the water. Larger pieces, like two giant crab legs still attached to a hunk of torso, were sinking toward the seafloor beneath me. Blood and slime slicked across the surface of the water like an oil spill. Fish carcasses, boat debris, and other stomach contents were spread around me hundreds of feet in every direction.

But there was nothing else.

No sign of our ship, the wreckage, the two-headed sea serpent, or any other survivors. All I saw was Kraken stew and a comforting mass of green-and-gray land a few hundred yards away.

Had the Kraken really swum that far from where we'd capsized? It was either that or else one or both of the sea creatures had eaten the rest of our crew and all of the remaining pieces of the *Powerham*. But that seemed less likely, even as large as the two sea monsters were.

I tried to push those things from my mind as I began swimming toward the shoreline in the distance, doing my best to avoid the many chunks of partially digested Kraken meals all around me.

After just a few yards, I bumped into something metal. As I pushed it out of the way, I realized what it was: the chewed-up and bloody remains of Commander Thunderflower's distinct, ornately decorated, shiny combat armor. I'd never seen him without it on—ever. Not even bright and early during breakfast in the boat's makeshift dining room. There were rumors he even showered and slept in his armor.

Which meant the mission leader, and the supposed greatest living Dwarven military officer, had most likely been eaten by the Kraken.

I shoved the armor away, knocking it free from a hunk of blubber that had been keeping it afloat. The metal breastplate sank quickly.

I kicked harder against the cold ocean waves, desperate to get out of the sea before I came across the remains of any more shipmates.

The shore ahead of me was slate gray and rocky, with a solid, lush tree line rising above it on a shallow ridge. There were no people or buildings in sight.

The water was freezing cold, and I did my best to warm myself with a Dwarven spell. Nothing seemed to happen, but the effort alone distracted me from the biting salt water and the distance I still had to swim.

Bloodletter? I called out as I swam. *Carl?*

No reply.

Was he ignoring me? Or was whatever link we'd somehow had moments ago suddenly gone again?

I didn't know, so I just kept swimming.

A little closer to shore, the dark blue water became cloudy, brown, and murky. Which meant freshwater was emptying into the sea somewhere nearby. A good sign, since the huge map of Russia hanging in Captain Smeltfeet's quarters had depicted a large river named the Uda draining into the Sea of Okhotsk near the town of Chumikan. So I likely wasn't too far from our intended destination. Unless, of course, I was near the mouth of a totally different river altogether.

After what felt like hours of swimming, I pulled myself upright and looked over the rolling brown waves, toward the shore.

It seemed like I was even farther away somehow!

There must have been a nasty current. There was clearly no way I could swim against it, but perhaps I could propel myself with magic, like I had done in the past with wind. The same spell should, theoretically, also be possible with water. Which is, after all, another natural element of the earth.

Almost as soon as I attempted the spell, focusing on my desperate need to get to shore, I felt a surge from below on my backside. It was almost like a powerful, oversize Jacuzzi jet was suspended right behind me under the water. The magical current launched me forward so fast I actually created a wake. I struggled to keep my head above water as I skidded across the surface like a speedboat.

After just a few minutes, the rocky beach was approaching quickly. I did my best to cancel the spell as I neared the uninviting coast of what I hoped was eastern Russia. But I'd already built up too much speed.

Seconds later, I was rolling onto the shore, tumbling end over end on heaps of small gray rocks. After shaking off the minor cuts and bruises, I stood up gingerly, feeling solid land under my feet for the first time in a month.

The coast was a massive stretch of drab rocks as far as I could see in one direction. In the other, it came to a small point a hundred yards away, cutting off my view beyond it. About thirty feet from the water's edge was a gently sloped ridge, on top of which sat dense rows of tall *Picea obovata* spruce and *Abies nephrolepis* fir trees.

There were no buildings or any sign of Human activity, aside from hundreds of random pieces of garbage and plastic that had washed ashore from the sea. There weren't even any power lines or old fishing sheds in sight.

The plan had been to make landfall a few miles north of the small village of Chumikan, then begin our trek due west from there, into the dense, mountainous, and mostly uninhabited Siberian forest of Khabarovsk Krai. Stoney's brain was our only real map to the entrance of the Hidden Forest, where the Faranlegt Amulet of Sahar was rumored to be.

Without knowing where exactly I was, I had no clue which direction to go. But I at least knew Chumikan was near the mouth of the Uda River, so it stood to reason that if I headed inland and followed the shoreline toward the higher concentrations of murky freshwater, I would find the river (and thus the town) eventually.

It was at least a start.

I sighed and climbed up the rocky embankment toward the edge of the tree line. It was steeper than it had looked from the water, but using Blackout for leverage, I was able to get up to the forest floor, overlooking what I hoped was Uda Bay.

The muddy freshwater feeding into the sea stretched out in both directions. To my left, along the endless rocky shoreline, the brown water appeared to fade out somewhere along the horizon. Which meant I likely needed to head to my right, toward the point.

As I picked my way through the trees, I tried calling out again telepathically to the Bloodletter.

Carl? Say something.

Again, no reply.

The forest was unnaturally quiet. No birds, no animals, no voices, no nothing. The only noise was the whispering of a light ocean breeze and my own footsteps crackling across the dry forest floor.

Where was the Bloodletter? Had he really been talking to me back in the ocean? Or had it all been in my head?

After a surprisingly short hike through the woods, perhaps just several hundred yards from the water, I came to a break in the trees. A winding, light gray gravel-and-dirt road ran along the shore.

I knew from the old map that there were basically no marked roads in this region (if I was anywhere close to where I was supposed to be), and so I deduced that this path *must* lead to Chumikan.

I picked up my pace as I walked along the gravel road.

It stretched along the coast ahead of me, totally deserted aside from an old truck resting in the woods a few hundred feet away. This wasn't an uncommon sight anymore. There were now billions of cars stalled in the middle of millions of streets all across the world.

When Galdervatn made its full return about a week after I was liberated from Edwin's "prison" on Alcatraz, the world basically descended into chaos. Along with the resurgence of even more magical monsters and creatures, there came a total end to modern machines of all kinds. Not just computers and electricity, but also anything with an engine. Nobody knows how or why, but even refined fuels lost potency. You could throw a match into a barrel of commercial oil or gasoline and literally nothing would happen.

Modern society was barely functioning.

Humans, aside from the most stubbornly ignorant, were now fully aware that something otherworldly had taken place, and that things would never be the same. Most countries were under some form of martial law, with recommendations for people to remain in their homes as much as possible. It felt like the beginning of a very dark time. Or at least it would have, if I didn't still somehow believe in my dad's vision that we could find a way to turn this resurgence of magic into a time of lasting peace. That we could use magic to create a reality this planet has never seen before: one of harmony and natural coexistence.

I know it sounds ridiculous, but I had to believe it was possible.

The alternative was too terrible to imagine.

This particular roadside truck, however, was completely rusted out and very old. It had clearly been there, untouched, for several decades and was not a victim of Galdervatn. Just the same, it was at least a hint of civilization, and gave me hope I was close to where I needed to be. Chumikan was the only labeled settlement or town anywhere near the supposed location of the Hidden Forest.

Just beyond the dead truck was a lone road sign, roughly cut from driftwood and hand-painted with Russian letters. Unfortunately, I didn't know what any of the Cyrillic characters scrawled on the sign's weathered surface meant. But I took it as another indication I was probably heading in the right direction.

I shivered as I trekked on, the cold wind on my freezing, dripping-wet clothes making the walk nearly unbearable. It felt like my bones were rattling against themselves with each uncontrollable convulsion. The sun was getting low on the horizon, taking away any last traces of warmth.

Even if I found Chumikan at the end of this road, what then?

Were any of its thousand or so residents still there?

Would any of them speak English?

And if so, would they be willing to help an outsider who had swum in from the sea? Would they let me warm myself by their fires? Would they turn me away, or worse? Would they help me find my friends?

But most frightening of all: What if I had no friends left to find?

What if I was alone?

What if this already insane mission to save the world now rested squarely and solely on my shoulders?

CHAPTER 6

Грэг Воняет Как Конский Зад

Chumikan was larger than I expected.

I walked through the unpaved streets of the quiet, seemingly deserted seaside town, shocked at just how many buildings and houses it took to make a town of a thousand people. There was maybe even a small hotel, though it was difficult to tell for sure given my complete inability to read Russian. The surprising size of the town made the total absence of people, of any signs of life (including animals), even creepier and more unsettling.

The sunlight had almost completely faded now, casting the road ahead of me in a strange orange light. I walked through the dark streets shivering uncontrollably, my feet so cold they were numb. It was probably around fifty degrees, but as I had come directly from the cold sea, still soaking wet, it felt like *negative* fifty.

Carl, can't you help me? I thought a final time, as I walked through the streets alone, toward the northwestern edge of town.

I was convinced I had imagined my other interactions with him back in the ocean. Delusions caused by shock, the cold water, or adrenaline. Those had been, surprisingly, the first real moments of true danger I'd faced since I'd thrown my ax into the San Francisco Bay.

Ari had forged a new weapon for me, to replace the Bloodletter. Another ax, lighter and more agile than the enchanted relic of Dwarven legend. Also one with decidedly less personality, given that it didn't talk at all, telepathically or otherwise. Just the same, Ari was a master blacksmith for her age, and it had been a very fine ax that I'm sure would have served me well in battle. But I'd never know since it had surely sunk to the bottom of the Sea of Okhotsk, along with the rest of the SVRB *Powerham*'s remains.

But at least I still had my trusty dagger, Blackout.

I tucked the scabbard and handle into my pants and shirt so it wasn't visible as I continued past another block of darkened buildings. One was a market or a grocery store that clearly hadn't been open in weeks. The shelves, barely visible through the dirty front windows, were empty aside from a few layers of dust.

A sign reading Закрыто hung crookedly on the door.

It was so dark I could no longer make out the peaks of the mountains in the distance to the west. They simply blended with the gloomy clouds and sky. It was dead quiet, and I was still wet and freezing, but I suddenly sort of wished I were already in the forest itself. As if being alone in the woods at night would somehow be less unnerving than being alone in a small, deserted Russian village.

Though, of course, the truth was that both were equally terrifying.

I clutched at my wet arms, trying to stop shivering as I walked alongside the dark windows lining the road. A few houses, a few commercial buildings, another market, and what was definitely a restaurant—the tables inside were still set with plates and cups, as if it had been abandoned without warning. Several dirty cars dotted the gravel roads, parking lots, and driveways, having found comfortable places to die.

Near the end of town, with the sound of the Uda River close by, I turned around to search for any lights in the windows of the small houses beyond the road. For any sign of life. Of course, there was no electricity left in this world, but even candles or a fireplace would cast some noticeable light.

But from where I stood, there was nothing but increasing darkness.

Then I saw her.

A small girl stood near an alley behind a house, just a few blocks away. She had dark hair and wore a teal jacket. She was clearly watching me. We both stayed still as we stared at each other through the darkness, as if we were both afraid any sudden movements might scare off the other.

She looked to be seven or eight, but it was hard to tell from that distance.

I plastered the friendliest smile I owned on my face and waved.

"Hi!" I called out.

My voice echoed, surprisingly shrill and cracked, in the emptiness around us, as several more *Hi*'s faded into the forest.

The girl's eyes widened. Then she turned and ran.

Without considering how frightening it might be to have a pudgy stranger chasing you in the darkness, I instinctively ran after her. Only when she fled did I realize how comforting it had been to actually *see* another person.

Besides, at this point I *had* to chase her. She surely knew a place I could go to get warm or find some dry clothes. Without either of those, I doubted I would make it through what felt like would be a pretty cold night.

"Wait, I just want to talk!" I called out as I ran.

She didn't look back as she turned down one street, then another. The small village felt huge as I ran through the maze of dirt-and-gravel streets and alleys.

I was finally catching up to the small girl when she quickly darted to her right, through a gate, and up the walkway to a house. She opened the front door to a small cottage near the edge of town and disappeared inside before I could get another word out.

I stopped at the front gate and caught my breath for a second, before walking up to the front door. The distinct flickering glow of a fire or candles lit up the window behind a thin, faded yellow curtain.

The door was white and dirty, set against a rusted metal frame.

I knocked (rather politely, I thought) a few times.

There was no answer, and I heard soft whispering inside.

"Please?" I called out. "I need help! Just a place to warm up for a bit, and then I'll be on my way."

I punctuated this by knocking three more times in quick succession, anxious to get my cold hand back into my pocket.

"Please?" I tried again, trying not to whine, but also not really wanting to freeze to death in an alley somewhere in Russia.

I waited, debating whether to get more aggressive or to start bawling and pleading for mercy. I also could have just found a different house (one that looked vacant), and simply broken in.

But I didn't have to resort to any of those options, thankfully, as the door finally opened just enough for the shoulder and head of an older man to poke out into the cold night.

He was tall, at least six foot three, and had all-white hair and gnarly white eyebrows, a gaunt, tired face, and an expression of grim reluctance stretched across his lips.

Right away I suspected I might have just pounded on the door to an Elf's house. Which was surprising, since the Council had told us eastern Russia would be made up primarily of Humans, with some Dwarves, and very few Elves.

Just my luck.

"*Chevo ty khochesh`*, Gwint?" the man snarled.

Of course I didn't speak Russian, so I had no idea what he had said. But the last word solidified three things:

1. I had, indeed, of all the houses in all the villages in Russia, found one belonging to an Elf (an unfortunate happenstance wholly befitting a Dwarf's luck).
2. *Gwint* was pronounced the same in at least two languages.
3. He knew I was a Dwarf and was not pleased to see one.

But even if I had found a Dwarf instead of an Elf, I might not have fared any better. According to Commander Thunderflower, most Dwarves in Russia fully rejected their true origin. He claimed they didn't trust anybody who embraced anything besides being Human and he had warned us on the voyage across the Pacific that we should watch our backs in Russia. "Trust no one," he had said countless times. "Those in the Far East live in isolation for a reason! They've completely rejected their ties to Separate Earth. They chose long ago to live in the modern world and have no real allegiances to Dwarves."

So if Russian Dwarves felt that way about other Dwarves, I could only imagine what a Russian Elf would think of me.

"*Chto sluchilos`, Gwint?*" the man said, the words sounding hostile. "*Ty glukhoy, tupoy, ili i to, i to?*"

"I—I don't know," I stammered. "I don't understand. But I'm cold and wet. I just need a place to dry off for the night, and then I'll be on my way."

The man glared at me. I still had no idea if he understood English.

"*Ukhodi, takim kak ty tut ne mesto.*" He made a wild motion with his arms like he wanted me to look around. "*Vy zabrali u nas vsye!*"

"Please . . . at least tell me where I can go for help . . ." I tried.

The man shook his head, looking disgusted.

"*Ukhodi!*"

He started closing the door, but then the small girl appeared beside him and grabbed his hand. He looked startled at first, then annoyed.

"*Vosvrashchaysya vnutr`, eto tebya ne kasayetsya!*" he said to her.

"*My ne mozhem prosto ostavit` yego tam,*" she said back.

"*On Gwint!*" the man replied, motioning at me. "*On, veroyatno, opasen i kak minimum vonyuchiy.*"

"*On vonyayet kak konskiy zad,*" the girl said, glancing at me while holding a hand to her nose. "*No on kholodnyy i mokryy. On umret na ulitse segodnya vecherom. My dolzhny pomoch` yemu!*"

"*Net.*"

"*Da, Papa!*" the girl said, getting more animated and insistent. They were clearly close to an all-out argument over what to do with me. *"My vse yeshche khoroshiye lyudi. My ne mozhem otverg-nut' nuzhdayushchegosya. I ne vazhno, Gwint on, ili net!"*

The old man looked at her and finally sighed reluctantly. Very reluctantly. In fact, the sigh seemed like a theatrical display solely intended to show me just how displeased he was with what was about to happen.

"Khorosho!" the old man snapped, stepping aside. *"On mozhet sogret'sya i vysokhnut'. No potom on uydet!"*

The girl smiled and looked at me, then motioned for me to come inside.

Most Dwarves would have turned and run at this point (if they hadn't already). They'd rather take their chances out in the wilderness, freezing cold and dripping wet, than trust an Elf.

But I wasn't most Dwarves.

My former best friend was an Elf. The reigning Elf Lord, to be precise. Furthermore, when I was his prisoner for about a month, I'd gotten the chance to meet dozens of other Elves. And almost all of them were as kind as any Dwarf or Human I'd met in my life. That experience had shown me that, aside from some superficial differences, we were, in the end, more similar than not.

But the point is: in a position where most Dwarves would have run screaming into the forest to die cold and alone, I instead smiled gratefully at the small Elven girl and followed her into their warm home.

CHAPTER 7

Two Deaths Cannot Happen, but One Is Inevitable

The tension was unrelenting.

We sat at their small dining room table, the room lit only by the orange flames from the fireplace in the corner. I was draped in a huge bathrobe (one of the old man's, I assumed) and a massive blanket. My clothes were drying on a line strung up in front of the fire.

I could tell from the man's expression that he was going to promptly burn this bathrobe the moment I departed.

The bowl of beet soup with a deep red broth in front of me was half gone, and it had been a struggle to get down even that much. I mean, borscht with no meat? Who'd heard of such a thing! But I also didn't want to be rude, and so I forced down another few spoonfuls. It helped that I was hungry, which wasn't really different from any other time in my life.[*]

"Thank you again for your kindness," I said to the man.

---

[*] It has been said that Dwarves have only two states of fullness or hunger: 1. Starving or 2. Quite Hungry.

He glared at me, clearly aware of how much I was not enjoying his borscht.

"*On govorit spasibo,*" the girl said to him, translating for me.

"*On blagodarit menya, a sam korchit rozhi!*" the man scoffed back angrily.

"What did he say?" I asked the girl, who had told me her name was Roza.

Her English was surprisingly good for someone so young living in such an isolated rural area.

"He say, 'You are welcome,'" she said, though we both knew that was not at all what the man had said.

Despite the obvious tension, I knew I needed to try to get some information from these Elves. Too much was on the line.

The war between the Elves and the Dwarves hadn't technically resumed, but with Edwin attempting to seize control of all magic with the amulet, and the Verumque Genus Elves (led by my old school bully, Perry Sharpe) currently building an army of monsters to take over the world by force, it was only a matter of time before things got bleaker and more violent. It was essential to stay on track and finish the mission, even if I had to do it alone.

I had to locate the lost Amulet of Sahar before Edwin did.

"Ask him where I can find the Dzhana River," I said to Roza. "How far away is it?"

While I obviously didn't possess Stoney's mental map to the Hidden Forest, I at least knew the starting point was where the Dzhana and Uda rivers met. And on the old map in the ship, that spot hadn't looked too terribly far away from Chumikan.

Roza nodded and translated.

The man replied with something curt, which was true about everything he'd said so far.

"Why you want to know?" she translated. The man added something more. Roza nodded and faced me again. "Why you here?"

I nodded and looked directly at the old man's cold blue eyes. I'd learned, since realizing I was a Dwarf, that there's no better bridge to trust than honesty. So I would hold nothing back from these two. After all, they had already basically saved my life by welcoming me in to warm up and dry off.

"I am looking for a magical forest realm," I said, speaking slowly, pausing often so Roza could translate. "It is said to be somewhere in the Siberian forests of the Russian Far East. I have been told to begin my journey from the place where the Uda and Dzhana Rivers connect. I'm hoping to reunite with my companions there so we can resume our travels together."

Before the girl even finished translating, the old man was already shaking his head dismissively and saying something low and quick.

"What is this nonsense you are speaking?" Roza translated. "There are no magical forests around here."

I might have believed him if something in the girl's eyes hadn't told me he was lying.

"Well, that's fine," I said. "If there's no magical forest, then I will discover that in due time. And so surely there's no harm in me looking."

The room filled with silence as the man pondered what to say next. Roza watched him with an intensity I wouldn't have thought possible from someone so young. Finally the old man looked right at me and nodded, his icy-blue eyes almost hypnotic.

"*Ya znayu chto ty ishchesh` Amulet Sakhari,*" he said. Though I didn't fully understand him, I clearly recognized one word, and

I knew he wasn't just giving directions to the Dzhana River. *"No reka Dzhana ne pomozhet v poiskakh."*

I looked back at Roza.

She clarified something with the old man before facing me.

"He say, he know you seek the amulet," she said, and I dropped my spoon into my beet soup in surprise. "But Dzhana River will not help you find."

The man was speaking again, and the girl translated for him.

"The amulet does not exist," she said. "It is myth. If you go into magical forest, you will find nothing except . . ." She paused as the man spoke, his voice growing low and intense and dangerous. "Except darkness. And death. Creatures not existing for many times, and for good reason. He say even back in time of Fairies, this forest was forbidden to all who wish to be living long and happy life. It is filled with horrors. Pure-blood Forest Trolls!"

The man was standing now, waving his arms in a circle above his head, his expression of disdain replaced by one of fear of the things he was describing. The girl translated more:

"Danger you face there are unimaginable. *If* you survive, you still no find object you seek. Amulet is only rumor. Old tale told to child at night. Why you think no animals around here? Why you think people leave? Because they know. They know what is in forest you seek. When world change, the smart people see dangers here and leave. Even animals leave. Too dangerous."

Roza stopped as the old man sat back down.

"But you're here," I said, not wanting to imply that they weren't smart.

The girl translated, and the old man nodded thoughtfully. Then he said something low and full of regret.

"He say, we should have left with others," Roza admitted. "But his pride is . . . is . . ." She paused looking for the right English word. "*Nuisance.* He cannot leave his home. So we stay."

The three of us looked at one another, the tension gone. It was replaced with a sense of foreboding, and I got the distinct impression that the man believed he was sitting across from a pudgy, stupid Dwarf who would very soon become a pudgy, *dead* Dwarf.

But I had to continue. I had to *try*. Going back and doing nothing because of a cranky old Elf's warning would definitely not result in the world being saved. I needed to find out for myself if the amulet was real.

"*Ty ved` vse ravno poydesh`, da?*" the man said quietly, breaking the silence.

I looked at Roza.

"He knows you still going anyway."

I turned back to the man and nodded grimly, hoping he understood that it was because I *had to go* and not because I didn't believe him.

"*Dvum smertyam ne byvat`, odnoy ne minovat`,*" the old man said.

Roza hesitated, looking back at the old man again, as if not wanting to translate.

"What did he say?" I prodded.

"It is old Russian proverb," she finally said. "It mean, sort of: 'You cannot die twice, but one death is inevitable.'"

Roza must have noticed the look on my face, because she shook her head and held up her hands.

"You no understand," she said. "What he mean is: You are *right*, go find what you seek, if this what you determined to do. Because you will die someday anyway. We all do."

Then the old man started speaking again, sounding kinder than before, as if to confirm what Roza had just said.

She waited for him to finish and then translated again: "But you no need find Dzhana River. Better to go straight to place of magic. Or where rumor say it is. He was speaking truth before when he say nobody ever travel there. Not then, not now. Unlike Dwarves, he say, we listen to warnings of the past."

Then the old man added even more.

"Khot` ya i chuvstvuyu sebya soobshchnikom v ubiystve, ya skazhu tebe, kak tuda dobrat'sya. Tol'ko chtobi ty ushyel."

I waited for Roza to translate, but she only glared at the old man. He nodded at her to translate, but she shook her head. So he sighed and said something else entirely.

This time, the girl did translate.

And the old man proceeded to reluctantly give me directions to the magical forest that would, in his opinion, surely be the end of me.

CHAPTER 8

My Stomach Helps My Small Intestine Move Some Boxes

A few hours later, I trudged into the dense Siberian forest alone.

This was certainly not how I'd envisioned the mission when we'd "set sail" a month ago. I thought we'd all be together: me, my friends, and Stoney, escorted by two squads of the most highly trained Dwarven Sentry warriors on the planet.

Yet here I was, walking into an unknown forest in an unknown land, completely and utterly alone with no real idea where I was headed.

Sure, the old man had given me "directions." But calling them *directions* was a bit generous. It was more like he'd pointed me vaguely toward a general area roughly the size of Rhode Island. He'd been sure to clarify many times that since the Hidden Forest existed only with magic, and since magic had only recently come back, there was no way to be sure *exactly* where the magical realm began, or how to get there, or even how to get inside. But he'd also said there were areas within the vast Siberian forest that had always been rumored to be mystical places, even going back to the indigenous tribes that had lived on this land for tens of thousands of years. These mystical spots were said to have once been entry points into the Hidden Forest back in Separate Earth. Now that magic was back, perhaps they were entry points again.

"Inside magical forest realm," the old man had said (through Roza's translation, of course), "you are on your own. Nobody here believes amulet exists, which mean I am no help finding it within magical forest. If you are lucky enough—or *unlucky* enough—to find way in."

But I was still immensely grateful for his help. I wouldn't even be this far along without the generous assistance of the old man, whose name I was never told, and his granddaughter, Roza. In addition to letting me bathe and warm up, feeding me, washing and drying my clothes, and providing a lumpy but soft couch for me to sleep on, they'd also sent me on my way this morning with several tins of pickled herring, thick winter socks, and an old jacket that was a few sizes too big and hung down my stumpy legs nearly to my knees.

The whole interaction had been even more proof that this cold war—soon to become a hot war—between the Elves and the Dwarves was completely senseless.

But, alas, I trudged along, alone, into the thick forest.

I was heading vaguely northwest, inland, and deeper into the mountainous wilderness, where there were no towns, settlements, roads, or people for hundreds of miles. I would have felt a lot better if Stoney and my friends were with me. Not just because Stoney knew where to find the amulet, or even for companionship, but mostly because then I'd know they were okay and had survived the shipwreck.

Walking through uninhabited wilderness for hours on end with nobody to talk to was really *boring*. I deeply regretted, more than once, throwing away the Bloodletter. He may have been a savage, bloodthirsty weapon designed to kill, but at least with him I'd always had a companion.

In fact, the ax had almost never shut up. But his incessant urging of me to destroy things and endless string of macabre dad jokes would have been better than the lonely sounds of my feet crunching across dry foliage and rocks.

The relative silence did give me time to contemplate (read: second-guess) what I was doing out here in the most remote forest in the world in the first place. We were taking a chance going after the amulet, trying to reach it before Edwin did. Our mission either assumed that:

1. My dad was right about the nature of magic and its ability to bring lasting peace, or
2. The Separatist Dwarves were right that Elves were inherently bad and could not be trusted with the amulet.

Anything outside of those two potential truths meant we were wasting our time and energy. After all, even if we did get to the amulet before Edwin, then what? At least he had an actual plan for an object that powerful. The entire extent of the Dwarves' plan, as far as I knew, was to get the amulet first so Edwin couldn't have it.

But what would we actually *do* with it?

Maybe the amulet was the key to bringing about peace. The missing part of my dad's theory. It was, after all, supposedly the only object in existence with the ability to control and harness the essence of magic.

But all of that was assuming the amulet was even real to begin with, and this was far from certain, especially considering what the old Elf had just told me: that its existence was nothing but a myth.

By nightfall, I must have hiked at least a dozen miles deeper into the forest.

As I made a bed out of Yeddo spruce and silver-fir branches, I tried to figure out what to do about my food supply. The old man had estimated it'd take me at least three full days to hike to the region where one of the long-rumored "mystical spots" was said to be. A place where the Hidden Forest could theoretically be accessed. As a Dwarf, I was already hungry all the time, anyway. And now that I'd just hiked a full day on nothing but two small tins of pickled herring, I was so famished I felt like I wanted to burn down the whole forest in a hangry fit of rage.

My stomach grumbled so loudly, it almost sounded like it was talking to me as I huddled on my bed of branches next to the small campfire I'd started with magic.

Feed me, Greg! my stomach growled.

I can't, I thought back. *I have to preserve my last few tins of herring. I still have at least two days of hiking. And who knows how many more once I finally enter the Hidden Forest.*

You've always got excuses, haven't you? my stomach complained. *Well, guess what, buddy? I don't care. Just get some food and put it in me. Now!*

Get it yourself!

Well . . . maybe I will!

Good, do it, then.

Okay, watch me!

Fine, let's see it.

. . .

Well? I thought.

Shut up.

No, you shut up.

I was gonna go, I swear. But then your small intestine needed my help with something. So . . . I couldn't. Now I'm busy.

Yeah, whatever you say, stomach.

No, really! She needed me to, uh, help her move some boxes. And hang a picture on the wall.

So now there are boxes and photos of stuff inside my GI tract? Explain how that works.

Um, well . . . You know what? I don't need this! You wanna know what I think?

What's that?

You're gonna feed me.

No.

Yes. Yes, you will. Because if you don't, then I'll give you a whole night of THIS to look forward to.

Suddenly, my stomach twisted into a knot so painful I almost rolled into the fire. My toes curled and my fists clenched as my guts burned and ached like they were being stabbed with a hot blade.

Do you like that? Huh?

No, please stop!

I will . . . You just gotta give me some more of that herring!

I must have rolled and writhed and had a semi-delusional conversation with my stomach for nearly an hour before I finally gave in. I could figure out my food dilemma in the morning. But I knew if I didn't get some sleep, I'd never be able to make it the distance I needed to the next day.

So I dug inside the small nylon bag Roza had given me and removed my second-to-last can of pickled herring. I cracked the seal, rolled open the tin lid, and devoured the little fillets of oily fish one after the other like I was chowing on bottomless popcorn at a movie.

As I curled back up on my little bed of spruce and fir, my stomach practically purred with satisfaction.

See? Was that so hard?

I sighed and wondered if I might really be going crazy.

Now, why don't you go ahead and open that last can? Okay? Greg? Greg? Come on, Greg.

My stomach began gurgling again.

I was so frustrated and lonely, huddled there on those branches with an annoyingly Dwarven stomach, that I almost started crying. But the first Universal Dwarven Rule was: *Dwarves never cry.* The second was: *Dwarves don't lie.* Which, the more I thought about it, the more I realized that keeping rule one oftentimes meant breaking rule two.

The urge to cry is natural, a release of pent-up emotion. And forcing yourself to keep emotions in is essentially just lying to yourself, and to those around you. It's you betraying your own emotions.

I wondered, as my stomach finally gave up and let me drift off to sleep, if any other Dwarves had ever noticed that before. That the two foundational rules of our very being were at complete odds with each other.

If something so basic and simple as two straightforward rules to live by could be so flawed in their very design, then what other Dwarven beliefs might be incorrect?

In fact, the more I thought about everything Dwarves believed, the more I realized we might not actually be right about *anything*.

In which case, what was I doing in the Siberian wilderness all by myself, huddled up next to a campfire, arguing with my stomach?

Was I really on a mission to save the world?

Or was I about to do the only thing I'd observed to be a universal tendency of Dwarves: *Fail miserably and just make everything worse?*

CHAPTER 9

◆———►►◄◄———◆

The Way Sunlight Filters Through a Thin and Feathery Mustache Can Be So Beautiful

The smell of cooking meat is the easiest way to wake a Dwarf. Which is why I bolted upright less than a second after the luxurious odor of searing pork fat hit my nostrils. At first I figured I was still dreaming, or maybe it was my brain playing a cruel trick on me. Or perhaps I'd rolled onto the fire sometime during the night and was smelling myself being cooked alive.

But then a familiar voice told me I wasn't dreaming.

"Hey, buttercup," Glam said. "Want some bacon?"

She was hunched over the dying embers of my campfire, delicately balancing a cast-iron pan filled with bacon on the coals. She grinned at me, and when the morning sunlight filtering through the tops of the trees hit her face, I'd perhaps never been happier to see a glowing mustache.

"You're alive!" I blurted out.

"Of course I'm alive," she scoffed. "You think a two-headed snake or a Kraken could take me down? Ha!"

"Well, Greg did save you from the Kraken at first, remember?" another familiar voice said.

Ari was kneeling on the ground, reorganizing the contents of a huge backpack.

She grinned at me.

"Yeah, I guess," Glam admitted.

As I climbed to my feet to hug them, I realized there were others as well. Four Sentry Elite warriors—two men and two women—stood off to the side, having a serious-looking discussion.

"They've been arguing over who's in charge all morning," Ari whispered to me.

"Commander Thunderflower is dead," I said.

"Yeah, we know," Glam said. "And these four have been spending the whole time since we washed ashore arguing over who gets to be in charge now. Meanwhile, Ari and I have been discreetly ordering them around all along, and they haven't noticed."

"But it will be good to have their extra muscle once we're in the Hidden Forest," Ari said.

Glam nodded.

"Wait, is there no one else?" I asked, so panicked my belly was aching all over again. "No other survivors? Stoney? Lake? Froggy? Tiki?"

"We don't know where they are," Ari said. "But we think they're okay."

Glam held out the pan of sizzling bacon. I grabbed a slice and let it cool in the morning air for a second, watching the steam unfurl from the crispy edges. Then I stuffed the whole thing in my mouth. The salty, fatty, smoky flavor was so amazing I almost passed out.

"How do you know that?" I mumbled through the meat.

"Well, we only saw the Kraken eat you, the commander, and a few of the other Sentry," Ari said. "Which, by the way, Greg, we all thought you were dead. When we followed the smoke from your dying fire and found you sleeping here, I screamed so loud I'm shocked you didn't wake up—"

"Anyway," Glam interrupted. "We saw Stoney and the others swimming toward the shore while we battled with the Kraken. But in the chaos that followed, we lost sight of them."

"Stoney can swim?" I asked.

"With some help from like ten life jackets," Ari said.

"We figure if we all keep heading northwest, we'll run into them eventually," Glam continued, offering me another slice of bacon, which I happily accepted. "Since we're all going to the same place."

"We hope," I said. "Stoney is the only one who knows for sure."

"Not exactly," Ari said.

I gave her a confused look.

"While you were wasting so much time fishing," she explained with a grin, "I spent a lot of time with Stoney in his room, discussing the location of the Hidden Forest and the amulet. There's a lot I still don't understand—Rock Trolls interpret directions and spatial awareness a lot differently than we do—but I at least know the general area we need to find."

I nodded, relieved that I wasn't going to be walking in a vague direction anymore. And it definitely seemed like we were all heading to the same spot the old Elven man had told me to go to.

"Hey, kids, time to get going!" one of the four Sentry warriors barked at us. "We got a mission, in case you forgot."

"Don't talk to them that way," another said.

"I'm the ranking officer here," Sentry One responded. "I can do as I please."

"No, you're not. We've been over this!" a third chimed in, and then they were all speaking at once, their argument over rank resuming, clearly far from resolved.

I helped Ari and Glam repack their bags, which they said they'd found in an abandoned hunting cabin a few miles back.

They had salvaged more supplies from the boat than I would have guessed possible, including several packages of bacon and other cured meats, sleeping rolls, tents, cups, and a few cooking tools. They'd also collectively managed to save several weapons from the SVRB *Powerham*'s cargo hold before it sank. Two of the Sentry had battle-axes, one had a Dwarven broadsword, and the last had a huge mace with stout spikes on the end. Ari had her dagger and a battle-ax. Glam also had a battle-ax, but it wasn't her own.

"It's gone," she explained sadly when she saw me looking at her new weapon. "Lady Vegas is gone." *

"Okay, this way, ladies and gentlemen," Ari announced to the group once we were all packed up.

Glam and I followed close behind as Ari led us through the forest in a slightly different direction than I would have gone, were I still alone.

I wasn't sure the Sentry had heard her announcement over their squabble, but once they noticed we'd resumed the trek, they fell in line a few dozen yards back, somehow *still* arguing about rank. Which made Glam and me smirk when we locked

---

* Lady Vegas was her ax's name. Despite my repeated attempts to find out, she never revealed the origins or the meaning of the name.

eyes a few seconds later. Because we both already knew what those four clearly hadn't figured out yet: their rank didn't matter anymore. At the moment, there was clearly someone else already in charge: Ariyna Brightsmasher.

And we all followed her into the depths of the dense forest without a second thought.

CHAPTER 10

Giant Talking Spiders, Trolls in Loincloths, and Sarcastic Centaurs Are Every Bit as Scary as They Sound, Even as a Joke

By nightfall, after a full, exhausting day of hiking, our party of seven became twelve.

We found five more travelers at dusk, gathered around a cluster of boulders, which wasn't all that surprising, knowing my friend and his obsession.

"PRECAMBRIAN IGNEOUS ASSEMBLAGE!" Stoney bellowed, as he hunched over the boulders, pointing them out. "PRECAMBRIAN ORTHOGNEISS! GRANITE 40 PERCENT QUARTZ!"

"What's with this thing?" the Sentry warrior behind him complained. "Do we really have to stop at *every single* cluster of rocks?"

"Leaveth thy gent be'est," Lake said. "Hath scrupulous proclivities failingly procured in thyself?"

Froggy nodded an agreement for the Sentry to leave Stoney alone.

"Guys!" I shouted, running toward them.

When they turned and finally saw us, they looked even happier to have found us than we were to find them. The Sentry warrior with them quickly rushed over and bumped fists and single-arm bro-hugged our group of four Sentry. Ari practically tackled her twin brother, Lake, to the ground. Froggy, silent as usual, grinned and gave Glam and me a single, relieved nod. Tiki Woodjaw let loose an excited string of obscure Dwarven curse words as she hugged me and called me a "purbogging hanklebump."

"GREGGDROULE!" Stoney bellowed, the rocks forgotten. "STONEY ENVISAGE ORGANIC VESSEL CONVERT ASSIMILATED WASTE AMIDST KRAKEN GASTROINTESTINAL TRACT!"

He charged at me like a puppy left home alone for too long.

I tried to dodge him, but the massive Rock Troll scooped me up in one of his trademark near-fatal hugs.

"Stoney . . . I can't . . . breathe . . ." I sputtered, my vision blurring.

He gave me one last bone-cracking* squeeze and finally released me.

"Happy . . . to . . . see you . . . too," I said, catching my breath.

"Tis thine delight of ye night hath descended upon thine company yonder present occasion," Lake said, patting me on the back as I wheezed.

"ROCK ONE," Stoney said. "STONEY NAVIGATE."

"Are we close?" Glam asked.

---

* No, seriously, if Dwarven bones were as weak as Human bones, I'd have been jangling like a sack of M&M's.

Stoney considered this as we gathered around him, looking as if he knew exactly how far away we were but couldn't decide if it was technically "close" or not. Then finally he bared his stonelike teeth in a Rock Troll's unique version of a smile.

"CONVENTIONAL PROXIMITY PERSPECTIVE DIMEN-SIONS, BEARINGS NOT EQUIVALENT PURSUING ROCK ONE," he said. "SUFFICIENT RESPONSE PROBLEMATIC COHERENT ARTICULATION."

Though it was always hard to track exactly what Stoney was saying, the general message of his response was clear: Where we were going, concepts like "a mile away" or "we're getting close" did not apply. The Hidden Forest apparently did not abide by the modern world's rules of measurable proximal relationships.

And why would it?

That would only make things sort of easy for once. But we were Dwarves, and Dwarves and things being easy couldn't coexist.

We set up camp for the night in that very clearing, alongside the cluster of rocks and boulders Stoney had been admiring. The forest had been getting denser and denser as we'd trekked through a sloping valley at the base of two mountains. Which meant there was no telling when, or if, we'd come across another suitable campsite.

We made two fires.

The five Sentry set up their own at one end of the large clear-ing, where they sat around it yelling ceaselessly at one another. Their argument over who was the ranking officer had become even more vigorous with the addition of a fifth soldier to the group. They'd been standoffish all day, refusing to tell us their names and barely speaking to us at all outside of purely necessary questions related to the mission. Even back on the ship, during our voyage over here, the Sentry had made very little effort to interact with anyone but themselves, sometimes even going out of their way to avoid us. But actually, we were glad their evasive ways meant we could stay out of their incessant and petty power struggle.

We even jokingly started calling their separate campfire the "adult fire," and our own the "kid fire."

Stoney sat away from everyone, near the boulder pile. He seemed to be lost in his own thoughts as he ran his thick, craggy fingers across the various boulders, perhaps entranced by the knowledge that we were drawing ever closer to the fabled Rock One. Its technical name was *Corurak*, the rarest mineral in the universe. So rare, in fact, that the stone said to be at the center of the amulet was the only quantity of it in existence. At least in this known universe.

"So what was the deal with that deserted village?" Tiki asked, the firelight making her face glow with strange shadows. "Chumikan or whatever."

The six of us, Glam, Ari, Lake, Tiki, Froggy, and me were gathered around the kid fire in a circle, sitting in the dirt, trying to soak up its warmth.

"I have no idea," Ari said. "I've been wondering that all day."

"The residents probably cleared out when the world ended," I said, not mentioning that the Elven man in Chumikan had told me as much.

"The world didn't end," Glam corrected me. "Some would say it's only now just beginning."

"Yeah, but for most Humans, it probably felt like the world ended when Magic came back," Ari said. "I mean, suddenly there's no internet, no phones, no Instagram, or Netflix, or cars, or any of the things that made their lives worth living."

We nodded somberly in agreement.

There was no denying the struggle Humans faced in adapting to this new world. And I'd have been right there with them seven months ago, back when I still had no clue I was really a *Dwarf.*

"What do you guys think the Hidden Forest will be like?" Ari asked.

"Well, based on the last lame fantasy movie I saw, I'm expecting a bunch of clichés," I said, trying to make a joke instead of telling them what the old man in Chumikan had told me we'd find: *death.* "You know, like giant talking spiders and trolls in loincloths and sarcastic centaurs and talking trees and stuff like that."

But my friends didn't laugh.

Aside from a courtesy chuckle from Tiki, the joke actually seemed to make them more nervous than ever. Because even if those things were clichés, if they turned out to be true it wouldn't make them any less scary or dangerous in real life. And we all knew it.

"Thy own personage doth be'est enthusiastically pursuing discovery ye roots beholding thine heritage," Lake said, breaking the nervous silence. "Tis ye nearest semblance ye domain thyne peepers hath beset yonder proximity ye lyfe doth Separate Earth!"

"It *will* be cool to see a part of this earth wholly untouched by the modern world," Ari agreed.

"I personally don't care what we find," Glam declared. "As long as I get to smash stuff!"

Though she loved smashing things, Glam clearly meant this as a joke, and we all burst out laughing.

"Hey, quiet down over there!" one of the Sentry called out to us from the adult fire.

"Yeah," another added. "You trying to broadcast our presence to the world? Huh? To any Elves or monsters nearby, listening in?"

After scolding us, they went back to their deafening, expletive-laced arguments over who was technically in charge. I even heard one of them try to build her own case around the fact that her toe most closely resembled that of Borin Woodlogger, from the only known remains of a statue of him.

At the kid fire, we all rolled our eyes and smirked.

"Would your Sentry warriors tell you their names?" Tiki asked. "The one we washed ashore with wouldn't even purbogging introduce himself!"

"No," Glam said. "It's weird, right?"

"They won't ever reveal their names," Froggy said, speaking for the first time in hours. "Because they don't have names."

"What do you mean they don't have names?" Tiki demanded. "Everyone's got a klonking name!"

"Not the Sentry," Froggy said, as we all leaned in. Even Glam seemed unaware of this bit of Dwarven history and tradition. "They all *had* names. Once. But they gave them up as part of the oath they took when they joined the Sentry Elite Guard."

"Why would anyone bloggurgin want to do that?" Tiki asked.

"I think it sounds cool," Glam said. "A bunch of nameless warriors!"

"Where's the sense in it?" I asked. "Why would having a name matter?"

"Because a name implies individuality," Froggy explained, already having said more words in the past two minutes than he had in nearly the whole month on the boat. "Their belief is, in a war or a battle, there's no place for names. For individuals. Armies aren't made up of individuals, but of intertwined components that function as one mechanism. A name creates a person, an individual with their own thoughts and feelings, which in turn comes with baggage that distracts from objectives and such. The Sentry Elite are the most effective combat unit among Dwarves because each member pledges an oath devoting their whole life to the larger cause. They relinquish their individual existence to instead become a part of the Sentry Elite, which is devoted *only* to the protection of the ongoing Dwarven race and *nothing* else."

"How do you know all of this?" Glam asked.

"My dad told me," Froggy said, referring to our old mentor and combat instructor Thufir "Buck" Stonequarry Noblebeard. "He used to be in the Sentry Elite."

"Used to be?" Ari asked. "I thought you said it was a lifelong commitment?"

"It's supposed to be," Froggy confirmed. "But he was expelled when he met my mother. Getting married and having a kid is bad enough. It's already grounds for a dishonorable discharge. But the fact that she was an Elf, well . . . he's lucky he and Dunmor go way back or else he might have been expelled from the Dwarven sect entirely."

A long, loaded silence followed. The only sounds were the crackling of the fire and the ongoing argument over rank at the adult fire. So that was why Buck hadn't lived in the Underground when we first met him. And also partially why he always seemed so perpetually angry with the Dwarven political infrastructure and, well, pretty much everything else.

I finally cleared my throat and brought the conversation back on track.*

"Did you guys see any sign of Elves the past couple days?" I asked Froggy, Tiki, and Lake.

Lake shook his head.

"We've seen nothing but the bloggurgin wilderness," Tiki said. "Not even wildlife, which is plorping weird."

I nodded—she was right: that *was* weird.

Ever since magic started coming back, animals across the globe had, for some reason we still couldn't fully explain, been attacking Dwarves at random. In cities, in zoos, *everywhere*. And now we were deep inside a remote forest that should have been teeming with wildlife, and yet we hadn't seen a single squirrel, or even a bird, in days.

The old man in Chumikan had told me this was because the animals sensed the dangers within the nearby Hidden Forest, now that it was once again accessible from this world. They had fled, hoping to escape impending danger. But again I chose not to share this with the group, as I didn't see the point in scaring them even more.

We all fell silent, letting the sounds of the fire crackling and the Sentry arguing fill in the spaces.

Froggy's revelation about his dad's past made me wonder about my own parents. The truth was, I barely knew anything

---

* Because we did still have a mission, a very dire mission upon which rested the fate of, if not the whole world, then at the very least the lives of a great many people.

67

about my mom. She died before I could remember, and my dad almost never talked about her. I didn't used to question this very much, but as I learned more about my true heritage—being a Dwarf and everything—I couldn't help but wonder what she had actually been like and why my dad never talked about her.

Eagan once told me she was an Axebrew and came from a long line of weapon enhancers. But that's pretty much all I knew.

And it made me wonder if perhaps my true calling was to be a weapon enhancer, and not some legendary hero. Maybe that was why I was so bad at this: I was meant to be a simple weapon enhancer like my mom. (I mean, if Dwarves were supposedly so enlightened in treating women as equals, why did all the kids get the father's last name? And their father's predetermined skills and destinies?) Or what if I was neither of those things and was merely *Greg*: an epic failure at pretty much everything except somehow making things worse? Or what if I was just supposed to become a dentist or something?

But the more I'd thought about all this during the long nights aboard the *Powerham*, the more I'd realized how little sense traditional Dwarven family lines actually made.

As Dwarves, were we really all predestined for a specific career or hobby based solely on our family line? Was all we would become predetermined based on our last name and our ancestors' skills? Did any of that really matter? Didn't we still have a right to do whatever we wanted? Could we, *should* we, turn our backs on skills we were supposedly destined to be good at?

What my name was shouldn't have any bearing on what I am or would become or would do.

The only thing I really knew was that I almost certainly was not *supposed* to become *anything great*. I'd already pretty much rejected the idea of predetermined legacies. I'd made the decision to avoid that path back in San Francisco, when I told Ari to throw the Bloodletter overboard.

But that was part of what made this new mission so scary.

When the Bloodletter chose me as its next owner, I'd thought my "destiny" was to save our race, fulfill my namesake, and be a brave, courageous warrior. I was supposed to lead us all to triumph over the Elves and any other foes. But if I didn't believe that anymore, it meant that *anything* could happen.

That my failure was as likely as my success.

More likely, even, considering my propensity for failure.

Which meant there was a decent chance, even as we closed in on the supposed whereabouts of the Faranlegt Amulet of Sahar, that we were all doomed regardless of what we found.

CHAPTER 11

The Sentry Throw Their Weapons into a Lake

That's *it*?" Glam asked incredulously. "Really?"

"CONFIRMATORY," Stoney replied.

It was late afternoon the next day, and we all stood at the supposed threshold of the Hidden Forest, a magical realm of enchanted lands that had been cut off from the outside world for thousands of years. A realm supposedly containing a great many dangers, unspeakably terrible creatures, and an amulet so powerful it could either save or destroy the world, depending on the owner's whims and fancies.

But I sort of agreed with Glam: on the surface, it was pretty underwhelming.

That morning, we'd gone partially up the side of a small mountain, and then down into a valley between it and another peak. The valley was heavily wooded, and we had to pick through dense rows of spruce and fir trees until we finally reached a clearing at the edge of a small, clear lake fed by snow runoff from both mountains. We walked around the lake and reached a thick line of trees at the convergence of the twin peaks.

Don't get me wrong, the view itself was spectacularly pretty—unlike anything I'd ever seen, or could dream of seeing, in Chicago. But beyond that, we were on a rocky beach at the edge of a remote mountain lake, staring into a row of tall, spindly Ajan spruce trees. It was *pretty*, sure, but it certainly didn't look like the doorway to a long-lost enchanted realm.

"You're sure this is it?" Ari asked again.

"PRECISELY," Stoney bellowed, the delicate word sounding unnatural in his gravelly, loud voice. "PERMEATE YONDER FOLIAGE ADMITTANCE HIDDEN FOREST."

"That's it, then?" Sentry Five asked. "We just got to walk past those trees and we'll be inside the Hidden Forest? What are we waiting for?"

"AFOREMENTIONED UNDERTAKING PARADES SPU-RIOUSLY HUMBLE FACADE," Stoney warned.

"How so?" Glam demanded, taking a few steps forward. "It looks pretty simple from here. See trees, walk past trees. Easy as shaving a Buckletooth Felinity, as my grandpa used to say!"

We watched as Glam marched ahead toward the trees. It seemed for a second as if she'd prove herself right: that there was no trick needed for passing into the ancient magical forest, aside from simply *walking into it*.

But when Glam was ten feet from the nearest tree, she suddenly spun around and took a few bewildered steps back toward us.

She stopped, her eyes wide.

Glam turned around and tried again. Once more, she spun back toward us just as she neared the trees.

"What in Hagglewheat's beard is the meaning of this?" she shouted at the sky.

She kept trying, over and over. To us, it appeared as if Glam was just madly walking in a tight circle in front of the trees. It would have been hilarious if it weren't so confusing and bizarre. At one point, she got so frustrated that her fists turned into Glamsmash boulders, which she used to swipe at the air in front of her.

"Glam, stop," Ari eventually said.

Glam looked at us helplessly, red-faced and out of breath.

"I . . . I don't know what's going on," Glam admitted. "It's like . . . every time I walk toward the trees, suddenly I'm not. It's . . . well, hard to explain. It won't *let* me get any closer. Like I'm being forcefully spun around so quickly I don't realize it's happening until I'm already facing the other way!"

It wasn't long before all of us were walking in tight, desperate circles on the shore of the rocky beach in front of a row of spruce that jutted up from the ground like pointy teeth.

We must have looked insane: eleven Dwarves walking in random circles between a lake and a valley forest, while a huge Rock Troll stood nearby and calmly watched the futile madness.

But it was true: the forest simply *wouldn't let us* get close to it.

Every time I tried to walk into the trees, and was just about there, suddenly I found myself facing the other way. I didn't feel it, didn't see it; it just happened. Instantaneously. As if through magic.*

Froggy was the first to give up.

"I think it's the trees," he said quietly.

I stopped my own mad, endless circle walking and asked, "What do you mean?"

---

* And, of course, it *was magic!* It was, after all, the secret entrance to an enchanted forest.

"The trees are *making* us turn around."

"I don't follow," I said. "They look like normal Ajan spruce to me."

But Froggy just shrugged in defeat instead of explaining further.

Eventually, we all gave up.

We stood there, lined up along the shore of the small lake with our hands on our hips, shaking our heads in frustration. Why couldn't getting into this magical forest be simpler and more suited for a Dwarf? Like fighting past a three-headed dog, or solving a stupid puzzle? Instead, we were dealing with a seemingly invisible, wholly metaphysical barrier. There was nothing to stab or chop or slay or trick.

We quite simply *could not enter* the forest.

"Stoney, do you know how we can enter?" I asked. "You said it wouldn't be easy. How did you know that?"

"ROCK ONE ANECDOTES," Stoney said. "MOTHER ENCHANT SIBLINGS NOCTURNALLY FABLES APROPOS ROCK ONE. DOMAIN ADMITTANCE NECESSITATES TRAVELER DEMONSTRATE MERIT. *PICEA AJANENSIS* AUTHORIZATION REQUIRED. TREES COMMISSIONED SAFEGUARD TIMBERLAND PERSONAGES ILL-SUITED UNDERTAKE ACCOMPANYING PERILS."

"Huh?" Glam said, sounding as confused as we all felt.

"He said, basically, that the trees are the guardians of the realm," Ari explained. "They will only grant passage to those proven worthy to face the dangers within."

An involuntary groan escaped my throat, followed by an eye roll so pronounced that for a second I thought my eyes might not make it all the way around and would get stuck staring back into my brain forever.

"I knew it!" I whined. "I told you we'd find trees that came to life! I knew it!"

I said this even though, as of yet, the trees had technically done nothing but usual tree stuff: which is to sit there and rustle in the wind and not fall over. For all we knew, the tales Stoney's mother used to tell him were just that: stories to entertain troll children at night and nothing more.

"Stand aside!" Sentry One said. "Let the ranking warrior handle this!"

"You mean me?" Sentry Three said.

"Well, I was referring to *me*, but I suppose we can all at least agree that the five of us outrank the rest of this lot?"

The five Sentry warriors nodded their heads and pulled out their weapons—an array of axes, swords, and one mace.

"Now stand aside, children," Sentry One repeated. "We'll take care of these supposedly sentient trees in no time."

The small army approached the trees and stopped just short of where they would have spun back around involuntarily.

"Let us enter!" Sentry One announced to the forest. "Or you shall perish!"

"Yeah!" Sentry Four added pointlessly.

The trees did not respond.

"Very well, then . . ." Sentry One said. "Sentry, prepare to attack—"

"Hey, why do you get to issue the order?" Sentry Five whined. "I thought *I* was the ranking officer here?"

"You mean I am!" Sentry Four shouted.

This went on for some time as they argued over who technically should give the order to attack. The rest of us watched with morbid curiosity. Not so much to see who might win this pointless argument, but more to see what would happen if they ever got around to actually "attacking" the forest.

Eventually, they compromised and agreed to give the order to attack all at once. Ari rolled her eyes at me, and we smirked as the Sentry began their countdown.

"Three!" the five of them shouted.

"Two!"

"One!"

"Attack!"

All five Sentry warriors hurled their weapons forward at the closest tree. After traveling just a few feet, the axes, swords, and mace quickly flipped in midair and rocketed back toward the Dwarves who had thrown them. The Sentry dove for cover as their own weapons narrowly missed maiming the lot of them.

The weapons continued their journey backward as the rest of us dove out of their path. They flew out into the middle the of the cold mountain lake and landed with an icy splash.

The five Sentry walked back to the group, looking equal parts confused, embarrassed, and distraught.

One of them threw her shoulders into the air. "Well, that's all we got," she announced. "We're warriors after all. We've been trained to fight Elves and monsters, not find a way to sneak past a bunch of stupid trees."

"How do we get our weapons back?" Sentry Two asked.

"I don't know; you tell us!" Sentry Three countered. "*You're* the ranking officer here."

"No, I'm not!" Sentry Two shot back. "She is!"

"No, no, no!" Sentry One said, taking a step back. "We all agreed that *he* was in charge, and as the ranking warrior, he must now find a way to retrieve our weapons! All I do is follow orders!"

"I am *not* in charge!" Sentry Five cried out. "That's been well established . . ."

The rest of us ignored their argument and turned back to the trees, facing the real problem at hand. As frustrating as the Sentry were, I tended to agree with them: fighting something you couldn't see and didn't understand was perhaps even worse than knowing you were outnumbered. At least then you got the comfort of a foreseeable resolution. Even if it was defeat.

But here, now, we faced a problem with no discernible, solvable mechanism.

We didn't even know how to begin to find an answer, because we still didn't know exactly what the question was.

It was then, while we all silently brainstormed (and the Sentry continued their argument over who was or wasn't the ranking warrior), that I realized the others weren't brainstorming at all.

Instead, everyone else was looking at *me*.

As if they all thought I might know what to do next.

I sighed loudly and approached the trees, not knowing what else to do.

Trying *something* would be better than just standing there on the shore of a clear, green glacial lake, waiting around to die, listening to the only adults present argue about how to retrieve their weapons from the bottom of said lake.

"Trees of the forest . . ." I called out to the woods, feeling every bit as stupid as you'd expect to while talking to a bunch of trees. "Oh, uh, *wondrous*, uh, Ajan spruce in all your, um, glory and majesty and stuff. *Please* grant us entry to the Hidden Forest yonder which you guard."

I thought I heard someone snicker behind me, but I ignored it.

"Um, please?" I added again after a few seconds of silence.

I stood there, arms outstretched, waiting for . . . well, waiting for what? A reply? I didn't know. An answer from a bunch of trees did seem like a pretty stupid thing to be waiting for. Maybe I'd try another angle.

"Nay," I called out. "We *demand* entry! Now!"

I gave it a few seconds and then marched forward. After just a few steps, I was instantly and forcefully turned around by the weird magic. As I unwillingly faced my companions, they looked away uncomfortably.

Rage built up inside me as I spun back around to address the trees again.

Magic surged through me and the ground shook under my feet as I tried to literally uproot the trees with a Dwarven spell. But then everything went still, and the old trees remained intact and upright as my spell was easily diffused.

"Let us in!" I yelled. "Dumb trees . . ."

This was answered with more silence and a gentle breeze.

I was just about to give up when I finally heard it in the wind blowing across my ears: amazingly, the trees spoke back.

"Hey, we're not dumb. You are!"

CHAPTER 12

The Shadowy Forest of Endless Death and Destruction

Billiam?" a faint voice whispered in my ear. "*You hear that? This sod just called us dumb! Him, the boy begging and pleading at our roots like a prat!*"

"*I ain't even heard a bloody fing . . .*" another voice answered.

I couldn't believe it. Were the trees really talking? Not just talking, but speaking in British accents. Or was it all in my head, like when I thought I'd heard the Bloodletter speaking to me back in the ocean?

"I hear you!" I said. "Is that you . . . uh, trees?"

"*Of course it's the trees, you dolt,*" the first voice responded. "*Don't be an arborist! Just because I sound like English pine don't mean I is one! Ya prejudiced little mug . . .*"

"No, I'm sorry," I said quickly. "I've never heard a pine or a spruce talk before, so I didn't assume anything. No offense meant."

"*Come on, Reginald,*" the second voice, the one called Billiam, said. "*Why you wasting your time talking to this Gwint?*"

"Hah!" I shouted. "Now who's the racist one?"

I spun around and grinned at my companions, sure they'd be relieved I was finally getting somewhere. But their faces were filled with shock, confusion, amusement, and a lot of concern.

"You guys *are* hearing this, right?" I asked them. "The trees are talking!"

They all shook their heads slowly in unison.

"He's lost his mind," Sentry One whispered loudly, holding a dripping ax, having apparently figured out a way to retrieve it from the lake.

"Maybe," Glam agreed. "But let's just see where this goes. Greggdroule's been known to pull a trick or two out of his hat before."

"He doesn't have a hat," Sentry Three said.

"For the love of Godwin the Proud, it's an expression," Glam snapped back.

"Maybe this has something to do with his love of trees?" Froggy suggested.

This did seem like a plausible explanation.

"Could be," Ari agreed. But she still looked more concerned than confident. "Go on, Greg. Um, keep talking to the, uh, trees, then . . ."

I nodded and turned back toward the forest.

"Which two trees are you?" I asked. "I'd like to, uh, you know, look at who I'm speaking to. Face-to-um-face . . ."

The trees laughed.*

"Hear that, Billiam?" Reginald said. *"The boy thinks we got faces!"*

"Ha-ha, yeah," Billiam added, sounding less amused. *"Like he's never seen a bloody tree before."*

---

* Yes, I'm fully aware of how insane that sounds.

"Look, it don't rightly matter which one of us you is speaking to, right?" Reginald said. "'Cause all of us trees, we all stand together, yeah? In unity and such! We are all one and one is all."

I thought I detected a hint of playful sarcasm in his voice, and this was confirmed seconds later when Billiam and a few other trees exploded into fits of laughter.

"Okay, okay, fine," I said, trying to get the trees back on track. "But what I want to know is: Can we enter the Hidden Forest?"

"Hidden Forest?" Billiam asked. "What the devil are you talking about?"

"He means the Shadowy Forest of Endless Death and Destruction," Reginald said. "Them blokes out there must just call it the Hidden Forest, yeah?"

"The Shadowy Forest of Endless Death and Destruction?" I said, my throat suddenly so dry I was barely able to swallow. "Really?"

There was a long pause and then they both erupted into more guffawing. These trees were really starting to get on my nerves.

"Nah, bruv," Billiam finally said. "We just call it a forest. Why does every bloody forest or river or pond got to have a proper name? Who gives a toss what it's called?"

"That's a right good point, mate," Reginald agreed.

I shook my head, trying not to get too frustrated. After all, the whole mission now hinged on me befriending these trees.

"Well, whatever you want to call it," I said. "Why can't we enter? Why can't we get past you?"

"Because, bruv, you ain't the . . . the, uh . . . Chosen One!" Billiam said.

"Yeah, yeah, that's right, innit?" Reginald said, sounding suspiciously as if he was making this up as he went along. "Only the one foretold by the, uh, Prophecy of, uh, Zandbroz Zingy Zulzannah may enter these forbidden and holy lands! So it was said many moons ago by the Great and Wondrous Wizard and Prophet, um, Lord Sorcerer Pricklebinkadink, yeah?"

The rest of the trees were barely holding it together, and stifled chuckling whistled past my ears in the wind.

"Another lame prophecy, of course," I muttered under my breath—even if this one had just been made up on the spot by a couple of trees.

But that was fine; if they were going to play this game, then so could I.

"Well, for your information," I announced, "I *am* the Chosen One. I am Greggdroule Stormbelly! Famous among Dwarves everywhere for fearless courage in battle! Selected by the holy relic Bloodletter to one day rise up and restore our people to glory!"

I waited for some sort of oohing or aahing from the trees, but a brief silence was followed only by quiet snickering.

"Oh, is that right, bruv?" Billiam asked. "Well, I ain't ever heard of no bloke called Thundergut or whateva."

"Plus, if you is right about the Bloodletter choosing you, mate," Reginald added, "well, then, where is it? I don't see it with you, yeah?"

"Thank the gods, too," Billiam added. "I hate that guy! Always running off his mouth like he's got nuffin betta to do."

"You know Carl?" I asked, surprised they knew my old ax.

"Is that what he goes by now, then? Carl?" Reginald asked. "He used to call himself Hank. Yeah, we know him. A mug of a fellow, really."

I supposed it made sense that they wouldn't like an ax. Most axes were originally designed to chop down trees, after all . . .

"Hey, bruv," Billiam said. "You remember the Norwood Massacre of Piney Ridge?"

"*Oh, yeah, right mess that was,*" Reginald said. "*Your old pal Carl or Hank or Bloodletter or whateva slaughtered a whole family of Norwegian pine just for jollies!*"

"Oh, well, that's horrible," I said, not wanting to come across as rude by reminding them that technically whoever wielded the ax was more responsible than the ax itself. "I mean, *I* would never ask Carl to do something like that . . ."

"*Maybe so, maybe not, mate,*" Reginald said. "*But since you ain't got the ax with you either way, we can't even be sure you're telling us the truth now, yeah?*"

I sighed because he had a point.

For probably the tenth time, I found myself regretting throwing my ax into the San Francisco Bay.

"*Right, well, see here, bruv,*" Billiam said. "*We ain't gonna let you enter regardless, seein' as this old curmudgeon to me left decided a long time ago to not ever let anyone past us again. Not after what them Fairies did all that time ago. I mean, if it was solely up to me, bruv, you'd already be on your merry way frough them woods behind us!*"

"*Hey now,*" Reginald interjected. "*Don't you go puttin' all this on me, mate!* You *were the one who convinced* me *to stop admittin' folks, yeah?*"

"*Maybe so, but I've since changed my mind,*" Billiam shot back. "*And now I'm sayin' we let this chap and his companions pass frough.*"

"*Well, I still say no, mate,*" Reginald said curtly.

"*Sorry, bruv, you heard him,*" Billiam said to me. "*I'm afraid we can't let anyone pass unless the vote is unanimous.*"

What he'd said about the Fairies renewed my hope. It seemed to indicate that at least some part (or maybe all) of the rumors of the Fairies hiding the amulet within the Hidden Forest were true. So I had to keep trying.

"Billiam," I said, "what eventually made you change your mind to think of starting to allow people to enter?"

"*Boredom, bruv, simple as that.*"

"*Which is dangerous!*" Reginald added.

"*Oh, come on now!*" Billiam argued. "*Dangerous how? What are these travelers going to do, pee on all of us?*"

"*They could set us on fire . . .*"

"*Oh, well, yeah,*" Billiam agreed. "*That is certainly possible. We be hearing stories about you fools out there settin' your own forests on fire and doing all sorts of other horrible fings to your natural environment. I suppose we wouldn't want that in our forest now, would we? In fact, you've convinced me, Reginald. I'm voting no as well now.*"

Doh!

Typical for a Dwarf, me trying to use Billiam to convince Reginald to change his vote had just completely backfired. Now I was twice as far from getting us admittance as I had been before I'd tried anything at all.

"*Now, now, don't be so quick to change your mind, Billiam,*" Reginald said. "*We've talked about this: Be resolute in your convictions, yeah? Besides, it's like you been telling me before: It is pretty boring not to let anyone in, yeah? In fact, I'm convinced: I'm changing my vote to yes!*"

"Great!" I said, barely able to believe what had just happened. "So we can go in?"

"*Well, not exactly, lad,*" Billiam said. "*The vote is still a one-to-one tie. I'm still saying no, in spite of Reginald changing his mind.*"

"But you just voted yes a few minutes before," I pleaded.

"*Is a tree not allowed to change his mind, then, bruv?*" Billiam snapped. "*Is that it? Is that a right reserved only for you special Dwarves with workin' arms and legs and such? Huh?*"

"No, no, I didn't mean that," I said. "No offense was intended."

"Well, it never is," Billiam said. "But that still don't take the sting out of them words now, do it?"

I shook my head, feeling helpless and alone as my friends watched me argue with the wind (from their perspective).

"So the vote is still one to one, but now just switched?" I asked.

"That's right, mate," Reginald said. "Sorry about that. If it were up to me, we'd let you in, yeah? But Billiam over here . . ."

"Hey now," Billiam said. "Don't be puttin' this all on me, bruv! After all, I'm the one who convinced you to let that tall fellow and his friends pass just a day ago, remember?"

"Oh, right, I almost forgot about that chap!" Reginald said. "A polite little mug, that one!"

"What?" I asked, panic rising in my throat. "You mean, you let someone into the Hidden Forest just yesterday?"

"Yeah, mate, a tall boy," Reginald said. "Very handsome."

"And quite polite!" Billiam added. "For an Elf."

I knew immediately it was Edwin. It had to be. What other tall, handsome Elf might be in the middle of a Siberian forest? Which meant he was already at least a day ahead of us.

I had to do *something* to get past these trees, and quickly.

But *what*?

The trees were so fickle, I was afraid if I even sneezed, they might suddenly both be voting no again. I turned around and faced my traveling companions, who looked even more distressed and confused than before, having watched me engage in a bizarre, lengthy argument with seemingly *nobody*.

"I don't know what to do," I told them. "I just found out that Edwin is already inside the Hidden Forest. Ahead of us by at least a day."

"I told you this would happen if you didn't put me in charge!" Sentry Two yelled at the others, which immediately set off another round of arguing.

"I wish we could hear the trees as well," Ari said, ignoring them. "Then maybe we could help somehow . . ."

"Maybe that's it," Froggy said.

We looked at him, waiting for an explanation. When he saw we weren't following, he sighed and took a deep breath.

"Why can *only Greg* hear the trees?" he asked.

"Tis surely be'est thy disposition for ye trees," Lake said.

"Right, but that's not what I'm getting at," Froggy said. "The *why* doesn't matter; it's the point of my theory itself that matters: *Greg likes trees.*"

It was clear we still weren't getting it. Froggy sighed and took another deep breath, as if talking this much was like asking him to sprint a mile.

"Have you used any of that knowledge yet?" Froggy asked me. "What kind of trees are they?"

"*Picea ajanensis,*" I replied, finally starting to see what he was saying. "More commonly referred to as the Ajan spruce, also commonly classified as the Jezo spruce. But either way, I've never come across a talking spruce at all, Ajan or otherwise!"

"Talking or not, they're still *trees* in the end, right?" Froggy asked. "What sets this type of spruce apart?"

I nodded, seeing now what he wanted me to do. I still wasn't sure how knowing that Ajan spruce trees can grow up to 150 feet tall or that a musical instrument named the *tonkori* is made from its wood, could possibly make a difference in convincing them to let us into the Hidden Forest. But at this point, literally anything was worth a try.

"Okay, I'll give it a whirl," I said, turning back around.

As I took a few steps toward the forest, I heard the trees whispering.

"Shh, ssshhhh, he's coming back," one of them said.

"Won't take no for an answer, then, bruv?" Billiam asked.

"No, I'm just curious," I started, taking a deep breath. "How does it feel to have light brown cones with flexible scales, rather than orange-brown cones with rigid scales like your close relatives to the south?"

The trees seemed stunned into a momentary silence.

"Well, what do you know?" Reginald finally said. *"We got ourselves a right little tree expert here, yeah?"*

"Thinks he knows everything about trees, he does," Billiam added.

"He does seem to know a lot, mate."

"I know he does," Billiam agreed. *"I wasn't being sarcastic, bruv."*

They seemed so impressed that they didn't even bother answering my question. I had their attention now and so I ran with it.

"I mean," I said, "I bet there are all kinds of trees in the forest behind you that I've never seen before. That nobody who loves trees as much as I do has seen in thousands of years."

"Aye, I suppose so," Reginald agreed.

"I suppose you'd like to go see for yourself, then?" Billiam asked.

"It would be pretty amazing," I said. "I'm curious if there are more firs or spruce. How much pine? Any hints of a Daurian broad-leaved forest?"

"Oh, now I'm curious meself!" Reginald said. *"I been wondering that for eons, I have!"*

"'Course we can't never go look for ourselves, seein' as we ain't got feet that move and such," Billiam added.

"I can go look and then come back and tell you," I suggested.

A pretty long silence followed as they considered this.

"You promise you'll come back and tell us what you find, tree-wise and the like?" Reginald asked. "You won't be skipping out on us now, yeah?"

"I promise," I said. "Unless I die in the forest, I'll be back eventually."

"Well, bruv," Billiam said, "it's pretty bloody likely you will die, seein' as nobody we let in has ever come back out in one piece. But I'm willing to take that chance. So I vote yes. Reginald?"

"Indeed, he and his friends will likely perish," Reginald said. "But I'd also be curious to hear the ratios of birchwood to dark conifers within our realm. So yeah, mate, I agree."

"Okay, Greggdroule Stormbelly," Billiam announced. "You and your chums may enter!"

I spun around and motioned at my companions to follow me.

"Come on, we can enter!" I said to them excitedly. "Hurry up before they change their minds."

Glam, Lake, Ari, Froggy, Stoney, Tiki, and the five Sentry quickly collected their things and joined me at the edge of the forest.

The Hidden Forest.

"Well, what you waitin' for, bruv?" Billiam cried impatiently. "A welcoming committee?"

"A marching band perhaps?" Reginald added.

I shook my head and took several steps forward. Nothing stopped me or turned me around or interfered in any way. My companions followed, and we walked right past the first line of trees and into the enchanted realm of the Hidden Forest.

And hopefully that much closer to the amulet.

CHAPTER 13

A Pack of Squirrels Eat a Reindeer

The Hidden Forest was a little underwhelming.

I mean, of course there was an initial moment of wonder and shock when we all realized the mountains that had loomed in the distance on either side of the forest were suddenly gone, as was the glacial lake behind us. Suddenly everything had been replaced by a seemingly endless, dense world of trees.

But beyond that, it simply felt like we were standing in any old normal forest. The trees looked like trees. The ground still appeared to be made of soil littered with leaves and branches and rocks. Regular sunlight still shone through the foliage above, streaking in rays like flashlight beams.

Everything looked mostly, well, *normal*.

Of course this would all change when we encountered the Rocnar, a massive beast so savage and bloodthirsty that I wouldn't wish a meeting with one on even my worst enemy.

But I'll get back to that in a bit.

Because the first matter of business, now that we'd finally entered the Hidden Forest, was to get our bearings straight. Edwin and his party had entered the day before, which meant we had a lot of ground to make up.

"Okay, Stoney," I said, once we'd all come to grips with being in a forest untouched by the modern world—a place that for all intents and purposes was a slice of the past, an actual living remnant of Separate Earth. "Where to now?"

Stoney looked around, spinning 720 degrees. For a second, I thought he had no clue and was now just as lost as the rest of us. There were no directional markers here, no way to know which direction we were facing or which way we needed to go, just endless rows of trees.

But as Dwarves tended to do historically, I once again completely underestimated the Rock Troll.

"PROGRESS," he said confidently, pointing in a direction (east, west, north—did any of those even exist here?) with an obscenely huge finger. "ROCK ONE."

"Okay, let's go!" I announced. "We have no time to waste."

Surprisingly everyone listened. Moments later we were carefully picking our way forward through the trees. Unlike the forest back in Russia, which had been bizarrely quiet and seemingly devoid of animal life, this forest was teeming with noises: birds cawing, bugs buzzing annoyingly in our ears, and then, of course, there were the giant squirrels.

I mean, probably they weren't squirrels at all, but that's the easiest way to describe them. We noticed their presence right away, seeing several scurry past as they darted up into the trees.

The animals resembled squirrels in that they had brown-and-gray furry bodies, scampered around on four little limbs, had bushy tails, and could climb trees as easily as they ran on the ground. But did I also mention they were giant? At least, by squirrel standards. Most were roughly the size of a small dog, perhaps a pug or a corgi. But others were nearly as large as a Saint Bernard.

The tree trunks here were thicker than those in the Russian forest (and were of a species I couldn't quite place). When the Giant Squirrels climbed the trees, the large trunks masked the creatures' size. But the squirrels also seemed relatively harmless. More wary of our presence than threatened by it. In fact, we noticed rather quickly that unlike animals back in the real world, these Giant Squirrels seemed to have no desire to savagely attack Dwarves without rhyme or reason. They mostly ignored us, only occasionally glancing over cautiously as we passed.

After about two hours of uneventful hiking through this new forest, we came upon a clearing. A huge animal carcass sat in the middle. It appeared to be some sort of furry deer. Like a reindeer, but even larger and without antlers. Surrounding the carcass were roughly two dozen Giant Squirrels savagely tearing into the flesh of the fallen beast. They had razor-sharp teeth, and their eyes glowed red as they stopped feasting long enough to determine if we were there to encroach on their dinner.

We carefully backed away and went around the clearing instead of through it.

In conclusion: Giant Squirrels were definitely *not* squirrels.

Conversation was pretty limited the first few hours of our journey into the Hidden Forest. Which was fine by me, since I was too distracted searching the forest floor for any sign of the three ingredients I needed for the serum that could cure my dad's ailment. Now that I was actually inside the Hidden Forest, seeing creatures and plants that nobody had laid eyes on for eons, my hope that I might be able to someday cure him was at an all-time high.

The problem was, I still didn't quite know exactly what *tafroogmash* root and *nidiocory* flowers (two of the three ingredients) looked like. I mean, I had seen drawings from old texts, but ancient ink drawings were a far cry from an actual color photograph. Especially when dealing with things like flowers and roots, which can look similar to one another even *with* color. That's not even mentioning how I was supposed to get a wing from an Asrai Fairy (the third ingredient), given that Fairies were the one creature not expected to ever come back, even now, after the return of magic.

So despite carefully keeping an eye out for all three items, I didn't spot anything that resembled the drawings I had studied over the past few weeks on board the *Powerham*. But I would keep trying anyway. I owed it to my dad to never give up.

That first evening of hiking was surprisingly uneventful— aside from seeing a pack of Giant Squirrels with glowing eyes and razor-sharp teeth eating a reindeer carcass, that is. We eventually set up camp in a small cluster of clearings, large enough to hold all three of our tents. The decision was made not to start a campfire that night. We were still unfamiliar with the Hidden Forest and any dangers that might lurk there. So it was better not to draw any unnecessary attention.

It ended up being a peaceful night.

After a quiet dinner, we were all so exhausted from the trek that Froggy, Glam, Ari, Lake, Tiki, and I retired to our two tents and promptly passed out. Stoney slept curled up near a pile of rocks at the edge of the clearing, and the five Sentry slept in their tent three at a time, with the other two on rotating guard duty.

As far as I knew, we peacefully dreamed of flowers and sunshine.

But then, early the next morning, the Rocnar struck.

Remember the Rocnar? The one I mentioned earlier?

Yeah, well, any fanciful hopes of the mission getting easier inside the Hidden Forest were violently dashed with the blood-chilling, deafening roar of the Rocnar, and the sight of the horrible, lumpy beast easily bashing a Sentry warrior onto some nearby rocks like it was spiking a football.

One Rocnar would have been bad enough.

But the roar of a second, as it charged through the forest behind me and into the morning light of our clearing, immediately doubled the trouble and tripled my panic.

Did I forget to say that earlier?

That there were actually *two* Rocnars?

Well, silly me.

CHAPTER 14

Glam-Smash Boulders Undergo Some Modifications

Rocnars are about as ugly as a pile of horse dung.

They're massive lizardy beasts with scaly brown skin covered in huge warts and oozing pustules. They stand on two legs like a T. rex, but they don't have a tail and their arms are much longer. They have huge hands that could crush a pickup truck like a paper cup, and big, knobby knees. Their heads are stout and grotesque, with four cavernous nostrils and a gaping mouth full of gore-stained teeth. They roar a lot, have extremely bad breath, and also breathe jets of white-hot fire when they get really angry.

So even though it was technically two against twelve, we were, in reality, severely outmatched.

As I scrambled from my tent, I realized that the Sentry tent was already completely engulfed in flames. I didn't know if any of the three warriors inside had escaped, but I didn't have time to stop and look.

The second Rocnar bounded toward me, a massive, knuckly, clawed hand already reaching to snatch me up.

I quickly pulled Blackout from its scabbard and held it up.

All light suddenly disappeared, casting the whole clearing in total darkness.

Both Rocnars roared savagely, their ferocious bellows sounding even scarier in the dark. Someone screamed. The sound of a Rocnar's feet slamming onto the ground continued thudding toward me.

I rolled out of the way just as a burst of white flame erupted from the pitch-black darkness in front of me. It was so hot I could feel my arm hairs basically evaporate. In that momentary flash of light, as the Rocnar rained down hot fire, I saw the following:

1. The Rocnar's uneven teeth and huge nostrils
2. The feet of several of my companions nearby, some scampering away, others running toward me
3. The other Rocnar literally eating one of the Sentry in two quick bites

My stomach lurched as the flames went out and we returned to total darkness. The Rocnar roared again as someone hauled me back to my feet by my armpits.

"Come on, Greg, run!" Ari said into my ear.

"Which way?"

She grabbed my hand and pulled me away from where the Rocnar stood. I didn't know how she could see in the dark, but I trusted her and willed my feet to move in unison with the sound of her running.

To our right and farther away, the other Rocnar, having finished its Sentry meal, let loose another barrage of white flames. Several forms dove out of the way into the shadows as two entire trees caught fire.

Ari finally stopped, and we both crouched near the edge of the clearing.

"We need a plan," Ari said. "We can't end this way."

Before I got a chance to respond, Blackout stopped suppressing light and the natural morning sunlight returned. Ari and I were now fully privy to the chaos at hand and were both rendered momentarily speechless.

The campsite was in ruins.

One tent was completely torched, and the other two were crushed flat. Weapons, sleeping rolls, and supplies were strewn about, as were the scrambling forms of several of our friends. Lake and Tiki were pulling an obviously injured Froggy out of the clearing and into the brush.

Two separate battles had developed.

Glam and Stoney were side by side, fighting one Rocnar. Stoney was large—over seven feet tall and several thousand pounds—but the enormous Rocnar dwarfed him as he furiously fended off blows from the monster's massive hand. Glam pummeled the Rocnar in the knees with her magic boulder fists, but the creature barely seemed to notice.

The other battle was between the three remaining Sentry and the second Rocnar. This was technically the first time I'd really seen Sentry Elite warriors in action. And, true to their reputation, they were fearsome warriors. The three Sentry danced and weaved around the Rocnar, quicker than my eye could follow, dodging its blows and fire attacks with ease, then darting back in to take quick hacks at its soft underbelly. The creature already had several nasty wounds and looked to be losing steam. The Sentry, though they never stopped moving, looked like they could keep fighting ferociously for hours without needing a break. They definitely seemed to have that Rocnar under control.

Ari and I ran across the clearing toward Glam, Stoney, and the other Rocnar.

That battle had taken a turn for the worse. Stoney lay on the ground as the Rocnar repeatedly stomped on him with its knobby, ugly foot. The Rock Troll desperately tried to block the blows with his powerful arms, but the weight of the Rocnar was simply too much.

Glam had given up pummeling the Rocnar's knees with her Glam-smash boulders and now had her eyes closed as she worked on another spell. Seconds later, her granite-boulder fists turned black like obsidian and sprouted razor-sharp spikes made from shiny black igneous rock.

She swung both fists like she was swinging a baseball bat, and the spikes dug into the Rocnar's right calf.

It roared in pain.

Stoney used the distraction to roll away from the beast as it turned its attention to Glam. But one of her spiky boulder fists was lodged in the creature's leg, completely stuck.

She couldn't get away.

The Rocnar opened its mouth, white flames already igniting somewhere deep inside its throat. Glam's eyes went wide with fear as she struggled to pull her spiky boulder fist free from the beast's leg.

She was a sitting duck.

Ari and I were still too far away to help.

I debated summoning a wind spell to knock the beast over, but with Glam still attached to it, that might only make things worse.

But it was too late either way.

As Glam finally pulled herself free and stumbled backward, the blue-and-white flames were already streaming down toward her.

The last thing I heard was a horrible scream before the flames engulfed her.

CHAPTER 15

My First Hole in One

I stumbled and then nearly fell from the horror and shock of seeing my friend consumed by white fire.

But Ari grabbed my arm and pulled me along, forcing me to keep going.

"Greg, look!" she yelled. "She's okay!"

Stoney had thrust himself between Glam and the Rocnar's flames at the very last second. His massive form huddled over Glam, shielding her from the fire as it spewed and rolled across his craggy back.

A rumble of pain escaped his mouth.

Glam recovered from her fall and scrambled away, rolling in the dirt to put out her flaming clothes.

The Rocnar finally ran out of energy and the fire ceased, but Stoney was on his knees, holding his face as smoke drifted between his fingers and up into the soft blue morning sky visible between the tall trees.

Then Ari and I were upon the Rocnar, slashing and hacking at the beast wherever we could. But my small dagger, Blackout, as sharp as it was, could not penetrate the Rocnar's tough, wart-ridden hide. Even Ari's battle-ax bounced off its skin like it was made of plastic.

"The belly!" I shouted, remembering the Sentry warriors' strategy for battling the other Rocnar. "Go for the belly!"

Ari nodded and lunged with her ax. But the Rocnar, aware of its own soft spot, quickly deflected the blow with its elbow. Then it backhanded Ari, and she went sprawling in a backward somersault across the forest floor.

The Rocnar turned its beady, emotionless black eyes toward me and roared.

The inside of its mouth was covered in gore and rotting flesh from an untold number of unfortunate prey. But it was also red and soft and not at all like the rough terrain of its exterior skin.

I rolled away as the beast attempted to grab me.

Ari and Glam were both back, lunging for the monster's belly with their weapons. But they weren't fast enough. It was easily able to dodge or deflect all of the blows.

The Rocnar was massive but didn't stand up straight. It almost had a hunched back as it sat on its haunches, as if in a perpetual squat. Though a funny posture, it provided a lot of natural cover for its obviously vulnerable soft belly.

I glanced across the clearing at the Sentry warriors battling the other Rocnar.

They were still engaged, dancing and twirling and making little nicks and slashes here and there at the creature's soft spot. They were going to win, but it would take a while to actually fell the beast. It was more a war of attrition than brute strength. It seemed like a solid strategy against a Rocnar. The problem was that Glam, Ari, and I weren't skilled enough, or fast enough, to pull it off the way the Sentry Elite special forces soldiers could.

We needed a different plan of attack.

As Ari and Glam dove out of the way of yet another burst of flame from the Rocnar, I rolled to my left and behind the beast as it spewed fire in a curvy path trying to catch Glam as she scrambled away.

I got a good look at the monster's lumpy, ugly head, surprised to see it had many of the same features as a Human head. Despite some obvious differences, it still had nostrils (four gaping nostrils are still nostrils), a mouth (large and filled with teeth), and two ears (which were nothing more than two holes in the sides of its head).

Inspiration struck.

"Ari and Glam!" I yelled, as the beast stopped breathing fire to reset. "Stay back, stay in front of it, and be ready!"

"For what?" they shouted in unison.

"You'll know," I said, and then ran toward the monster before it had a chance to turn around.

I got to its rear right flank and leaped into the air. With a little assist from my Dwarven wind spell, I landed squarely on its right shoulder blade area. The Rocnar's warts and slimy pustules, as disgusting as they were, actually made for pretty stable hand- and footholds.

I scrambled up the side of the monster as it flung its arm back, trying to swat me off.

Once I got onto its right shoulder, I reached an arm toward the side of its head to get a good grip, then pulled Blackout free from my belt with my other hand. I quickly focused on another spell I had done a few days before inside the belly of a Kraken.

Blackout's shiny blade began to glow red-hot.

I turned my attention to the Rocnar's exposed earhole and lunged at it with the blade.

But just before I got there, its hand finally found me, and easily ripped me from its shoulder. As it pulled me toward its face, presumably to eat me, I knew I only had one last chance before I'd be Rocnar chow.

I reared back and threw the dagger toward the earhole, which was no more than seven inches across, and also a moving target. I tried to use magic to guide the blade, and I have no idea if that's what did it, or if it really had just been an impossibly accurate throw. But either way, my knife hit its intended target.

The searing-hot blade plunged into the Rocnar's right earhole.

The beast howled in pain as it dropped me.

"Now!" I screamed as I fell.

It all happened so fast that I had no idea if Ari had heard me or simply knew what to do by instinct when the moment arrived. I watched from the ground as she hurled her battle-ax up toward the creature's face as it roared in pain.

The ax flew into the Rocnar's mouth, and the beast flinched, convulsing suddenly as it gagged. A squeal escaped from the creature's throat as it teetered backward.

The massive Rocnar fell over, landing with a heavy THUMP. A loud, thick gurgle of blood erupted from its mouth as it convulsed a final time and died.

I sat up, breathing hard, unable to fully believe what had just happened.

I looked over, expecting to see Glam and Ari high-fiving in celebration or rushing over to high-five me. Or maybe we'd all high-five one another awkwardly. But there was no high-fiving or celebration of any kind.

Instead, they were hunched over Stoney, who was still kneeling and holding a hand to his face.

I rushed over as he finally got back to his feet, his skin singed.

He turned to look at me, but his eyes were gone. Instead there were two crusted and blackened spaces. Two tendrils of gray smoke drifted up from his face, toward the sky like evaporating tears.

"GREGGDROULE?" he said. "OBLIVION."

"Greg, I think he's been blinded," Ari said.

CHAPTER 16

❖

Rock Troll Jokes Are About as Unfunny as a Punch to the Eye

S toney was indeed blind.

And it wasn't one of those temporary things where his eyesight would return after a few hours or days or weeks. No, his eyeballs had basically been incinerated, and his eyelids fused shut by the heat. Stoney would be blind forever.

Dwarven magic was powerful, but as far as anybody knew or had ever heard or read about in the texts, there was no spell that could re-create lost eyes or resurrect the dead, etc. Dwarven magic was still rooted in nature, and fixing such severe injuries was, well, *unnatural*.

But Stoney was actually taking it pretty well. He didn't even seem distraught and was already making jokes about it. Like when he held up one of the Rocnar's long, severed fingers by the knuckle and tapped it on the ground in front of him a few times and said, "AMBULATORY ASSISTANCE CANE?"

"Gross, Stoney," Ari said, gagging, even as Lake and Tiki howled with laughter behind her. "You can't use that thing's finger as a walking stick!"

Glam was definitely taking Stoney's injury the hardest. She had apologized to him (and thanked him) so many times in the hour after the battle that we'd basically had to restrain her to keep her from going near him. We all knew he'd do it the same way all over again if he had to.

Sadly, though, Stoney wasn't the only casualty of the battle.

Sentry Two and Sentry Three had both died during the initial Rocnar ambush. But it was weird; the other Sentry didn't seem to care. They didn't express sadness or regret for being unable to save them, and in fact didn't even mourn their fallen comrades at all. They just got to work butchering the two Rocnar carcasses for meat and salvaging what was left of our tents and supplies.

"Don't you even care?" Ari asked at one point. "They were your teammates, your fellow warriors, your—your . . . *friends!*"

"Incorrect," Sentry One replied, emotionless. "None of us are friends. The Sentry don't have friends."

"At least take some time to mourn the loss of your squad members," I suggested.

"Negative," Sentry Five scoffed. "Death is a part of our job. We do not mourn our losses. That only wastes time and distracts from objectives. Once you join the Sentry, you cease to be an individual whose death can be mourned. We are all small parts of a larger whole and shall be treated as nothing more."

"It's part of the Sentry code," Sentry One added. "'We serve, we fight, we protect, we uphold our mission, and die for it willingly if the gods make it so.' There is nothing to do now but reassess how best to proceed in an efficient manner, having lost 40 percent of our forces."

Ari and I exchanged a look and finally gave up.

After all, they did make a valid point: the fate of the world possibly rested on the success of our mission, and so it was largely irresponsible to waste time mourning the loss of two, when our failure would mean the loss of millions, or perhaps even billions.

Thankfully the only other casualty (aside from minor bumps and bruises) was Froggy, who had suffered a badly sprained ankle. But Tiki was already busy working on a spell to reduce the swelling and pain in his leg.

Tiki Woodjaw had always had the Ability. But she never received any training until she moved with us to the Chicago Underground. Once there, she began magic training with Fenmir Mystmossman while I was a prisoner in Edwin's base at Alcatraz. And it turned out that Tiki had two talents:

1. Vulgar and creative cursing
2. Learning and casting healing spells

While her spells couldn't always instantly fix an injury, they did go a long way to reducing the pain and speeding up the recovery process.

All in all, we considered ourselves very lucky as a group, which was a very un-Dwarf-like feeling.

A few hours after the Battle of Rocnar Clearing, we'd salvaged what we could of the tents, butchered and packaged as much of the Rocnar meat as we could carry,* and carved Stoney a walking stick.

We gathered up our things, ready to embark again on our quest.

---

* None of the old texts really addressed whether Rocnar meat was edible, but our food supplies were desperately low, and so it was a chance we'd have to take. Besides, it was part of the old Dwarven code that if you killed a living creature, you had to find a way to use its remains in a practical manner. No death should ever be wasteful and senseless.

"Okay, which way from here, Stoney?" I asked.

Then we all went still. One by one, our heads turned slowly toward the Rock Troll. We stared at the charred remains of his eyes in silent realization.

"STONEY'S CURRENT BEARING?" he asked. "STONEY DISORIENTED."

"Um . . ." I said.

"We're really kunked now," Tiki said. "Our navigator can't even plorping see where he's going!"

The Sentry gasped at Tiki's infamously obscure and obscenely vulgar Separate Earth curse words. But she was right: What were we going to do now? Stoney was our only guide to the amulet.

"Regular compasses don't work in this forest, Stoney," Ari said quietly. "None of us can tell you what direction we're facing."

Then Stoney began making a gravelly, lurching noise, almost like he was about to barf. But I recognized what it really was right away: Rock Troll laughter. Stoney was giggling, almost in stitches.

"HOAX," he said. "STONEY UTILIZE PAGEANT WITTICISM. COMEDIC SUBTERFUGE. MACHINATE PSEUDO-APPREHENSION. CONSTRUCT JOVIAL SCENARIO. STONEY DISCERN APPROPRIATE BEARING. ADVANCE FORTHWITH."

The huge Rock Troll pointed a finger and then began walking in that direction, tapping his massive walking stick on the ground in front of him to help detect obstacles.

Nobody laughed at Stoney's practical joke as we followed.

But I was pretty sure I heard the sound of nine collective sighs of relief as we trekked deeper into the Hidden Forest.

CHAPTER 17

※◆※

The Long-Lost Estoc of Galdadroona from the Legend of Sir Darormir Beardsbane

If our battle with the Rocnars taught me anything, it was that I needed a new weapon.

More and more, throwing away the Bloodletter (which was rumored to be the most powerful Dwarven weapon ever created) was proving to have been a colossal mistake. If he were here, he'd definitely agree: *Of course it was a mistake, Greggdroule! It's that moment in every story when the reader is slapping their palm to their forehead, completely beside themselves at the apparent idiocy of the hero.*

But that was the thing: I was *not* a hero.

And the ax had been turning me into something I wasn't. Someone I liked less and less the more I was around it. Violent. Selfish. Brash.

Just the same, I couldn't continue this clearly dangerous journey without a weapon larger and more intimidating than a small dagger.

Which was why it was incredibly fortuitous (and a little suspicious) that we came across a sword in a stone the following morning.

Yes, a real sword in a stone. (I know, I'm rolling my eyes, too.)

We found it probably around ten miles from the campsite the Rocnars had attacked the day before.

Glam was the first to spot the hilt sticking up from a large boulder.

Aside from being lodged in a solid rock, the sword didn't look particularly special. The hilt bore no artisanal flourishes or inlaid gemstones. It wasn't made of gold or adorned with intricate carvings. It was just a steel hilt with a straight cross guard, and a spherical pommel roughly the size of a golf ball. Any leather, wire, or wood that might have once been wrapped around the hilt to protect the wielder's hand had long since been eaten away by the elements. The blade, too, appeared rather ordinary, aside from the fact that the seven or eight exposed inches were shiny and polished as if the sword had been lodged there for just a few hours, rather than the far more likely decades, centuries, or even millennia.

"A sword in a stone?" I finally said. "*Really?* I mean, *come on . . .*"

It was no secret that I didn't like fantasy movies or books, even before I'd found out I was a Dwarf and that many of them were actually based on real historical events. None of my friends liked fantasy movies or books either, but for them it had more to do with how many things these works of "fiction," like *The Hobbit*, got wrong, rather than a distaste for the tropes. You know, stuff like enchanted weapons with names, special amulets with magical powers, prophecies, wizards, and bizarre creatures like talking trees and Rocnars.

And now here was a literal sword in a stone, perhaps one of the most famous fantasy tropes of all time.

"I think it's cool," Glam said. "It probably has, like, sick powers and stuff."

"Lest couldst be'est ye mislaid Estoc of Galdadroona," Lake said excitedly. "Per ye Legend of Sir Darormir Beardsbane."

Ari and the three Sentry nodded thoughtfully. This was clearly another story they'd all grown up hearing time and again as children in Dwarven culture.

"Okay, fine." I sighed. "I'll bite: What's the legend of Drama-mine What's-His-Beard, then?"

"Sir Darormir Beardsbane was a Knight of the Cerulean Tooth from Galdadroona"—Ari began what was sure to be a long and ridiculous story—"a region in the Southeast Shire of Sepa-rate Earth, known for producing the best swords in the world. Anyway, he got drunk one night at a tavern in Malconia called the Foamy Dessert Pub and lost his prized possession: his sword. It was rumored that a rival knight from the Order of the Gray Finger found it and lodged it in a stone nearby as a joke. Darormir spent the rest of his life searching for his sword, but to no avail."

I waited for more, but Ari simply shrugged.

"That's it?" I asked.

"Yeah, what were you expecting?"

"I don't know," I said. "Some long yarn about betrayal and revenge that ends with a wizard embedding an enchanted sword in a magical stone until some prophesied, special Chosen One can come free it and save the world from a Dark Ice Lord named Zamboni?"

"Heh," Glam snickered. "That sounds more like the Tale of the Treacherous Quest of Progtail Orcheart! You've heard that one, then?"

"No!" I said. "No, not at all, I just . . . I mean, *how many* old tales *are there* that involve swords stuck in rocks?"

"Well, that depends. Are we only counting broadswords, longswords, estocs, and shortswords?" Glam asked. "Or are we also including rapiers, katanas, and Ulfberhts?"

"Also, what's your definition of a rock?" Ari asked. "Because in at least a few of them, it's a bridge or a castle wall . . ."

"You know what?" I said, giving up on fantasy tales altogether. "Never mind. I don't even want to know, and it doesn't matter. But anyway . . . if this *is* Darormir's long-lost sword, how would we know? If there are that many tales, why would you assume this sword in the stone is that one, and not one of the apparently four hundred others?"

"Swords from Galadadroona were exceptionally rare," Ari said. "The whole region only had two armory blacksmiths. Only one hundred and fifty swords were ever made using Galdadroona steel. Thus, just two of the sword-in-the-stone tales involve Galdadroona steel. This appears to be one of them, if the legends about Galadadroona steel never rusting are true . . ."

The blade *should* have been rusty; I'd give them that. Even after just a few months out in the elements, most steel showed at least some wear.

"Is there any way to be sure the sword is from Galdrooney or wherever?" I asked.

"Galadadroona swords are said to have a stamp halfway to the tip," Ari said.

"Ye emblem ye skilled artisan," Lake added.

"Okay, then," I said sarcastically. "Welp, should we try to pull it free, to see if this is it? A legendary powerful sword just sitting here conveniently for us to find?"

"Geez, Greg, try to be a little more positive," Glam said.

"Or thankful," Ari agreed, but they were both grinning.

Most important, nobody said *not* to try to pull the sword free. And so I put a hand around the exposed hilt. It felt cold and rough, and not at all like anything more than just a normal sword lodged in a stone.

I gave a pull, but the sword didn't budge.

"Come on, put some muscle into it, buttercup!" Glam taunted.

I laughed and wrapped my other hand around the hilt and put a foot on the boulder to try to get more leverage. I tensed all my muscles and pulled as hard as I could, using my leg to help. The thing wasn't budging. My hands slipped off the hilt, and I went sprawling backward into the dirt.

"Well," I said, as my friends tried their best to stifle their laughter, "I guess I'm *not* the Chosen One of this sword's prophecy or legend or whatever."

Lake helped me to my feet as Glam scoffed and stepped up to the boulder, cracking her knuckles loudly. After tugging at the sword and swearing for the better part of five minutes, she finally gave up as well.

"Maybe it's in there for a reason," Ari suggested. "And not meant to be freed."

"Or you could just have that *thing* pull it free," one of the Sentry said, pointing at Stoney.

It had been obvious, throughout this entire journey, that the Sentry didn't like or trust Stoney. And if it weren't for the fact that his knowledge was vital to the mission, they would surely have tossed him overboard that very first night at sea.

"Want to give it a try, Stoney?" I asked.

He nodded.

We guided him over to the stone. He ran his hands along the surface of the boulder and along the hilt of the sword. At one point, he even bent down to sniff the rock.

"ESTOC INFILTRATE BONINITE BASALT IMPECCABLE VENEER," he said. "OBLITERATE FUNDAMENTAL LUSTER. ABERRANT FEATURE."

Stoney pinched the tiny (to him) hilt between his thumb and forefinger. Then, as easily as if he were plucking a toothpick from a jar, he pulled the blade free from the stone.

He held it out.

It was a pretty standard two-handed estoc sword, though perhaps shorter and thicker than most. It had been relatively well preserved by the rock surrounding it, but otherwise it appeared to be nothing more than a finely crafted, but unexciting, run-of-the-mill sword. There were no markings on the blade, so it was not Sir Darormir's sword from the legend, or apparently from Galdadroona at all.

But it would still serve me pretty well as a new weapon, assuming Ari could restore the hilt with leather or wood.

"Who farted?" Glam blurted out as I examined the sword.

I hadn't noticed the smell at first, but now that she'd said something, I had to admit it did suddenly reek near the boulder. Everyone covered their faces with their shirts, jackets, and tunics. Even Stoney was gagging, which sounded like a bucket of rocks being shaken up.

"Seriously, who *did* that?" Ari asked, shooting her twin brother an accusatory glance.

But nobody owned up to it.

That was when I noticed the goop oozing up from the hole in the boulder left by the sword. The thick brown-and-green paste bubbling up out of the stone was clearly the source of the unbearable stench. It spilled to the side and slithered down the boulder. It pooled at the base in a steaming pile of slime so thick you could have molded it like clay.

"Ugh!" Ari shouted, taking a step back. "What *is* that stuff?"

"It can't be poo, can it?" Glam asked as we all took several steps back.

"Stoney?" I asked, since he was somewhat of an expert on minerals.

He gagged again and shook his huge, craggy head, clearly as baffled as the rest of us. Likely even more so, since he couldn't actually see.

The goo continued oozing from the sword hole and glopping down the side of the boulder. We watched in horror as the pile on the ground grew to nearly the size of a large beanbag chair, four feet high and four feet across.

And then, just as suddenly as the strange substance had started oozing out, it stopped.

The last bits of brownish-green pus gushed from the hole, ran down the side of the boulder, and plopped onto the massive mound of gloop. It didn't leave behind a single drop, nor any residue on the rock. I didn't need to be a geologist to know that wasn't natural.

Whatever this was, it was purely of Separate Earth's world and not our own.

Then the blob began moving on its own.

We all took two steps back, and the Sentry drew their weapons as the smelly pile of goo rolled and folded itself, forming a rough sphere at the base of the boulder. The shades of brown and green morphed and separated as the surface of the blob rippled like it was taking in its surroundings.

What had we just unwittingly unleashed?

"It's . . . it's alive . . ." Ari said weakly.

Nobody responded.

At least none of *us* responded.

Because, after a short silence, the blob spoke.

And it spoke perfect English (go figure).

CHAPTER 18

Blob Blog Globbenblog

Ahhhhhh!" the blob cried out in a relieved, masculine voice. "That feels soooo nice! Do you know how long I've been trapped in there?"

Nobody replied. We all just gaped at the pulsating mound of disgusting goo, which, by the way, didn't smell any better now that it had been out in the fresh forest air for several minutes.

"No, I mean, do you *actually know* how long?" the blob asked, rolling toward us a couple of feet. We all instinctively took a few more steps back. "After the first few hours, it became hard to judge the passing of time!"

More awkward silence followed, and the blob rippled, seeming to deflate a little bit.

"Umm, hi?" I finally said.

"Oh!" it said. "So you *can* understand me? I wasn't sure if I was saying it right. I haven't spoken the Plain Tongue in a while. Thought maybe I was a bit rusty!"

"You . . . you speak more languages?" Ari asked.

"Of course!" the blob answered. "Only selfish, insular dolts don't bother to expand past their one native language, no?"

We all kind of shuffled our feet uncomfortably. Aside from Stoney, none of us spoke anything but English,[*] or, in Lake's case, the English version of Ancient Dwarven, which in reality was a lot more like regular English than like real, actual Ancient Dwarven.

"Oh . . . oh, I see," the blob said. "Well, I'm sorry. I sort of pegged you lot as a bit more enlightened. But that's fine. That's okay. No reason we can't still be pals! Right?"

As it spoke, it rolled toward us again. The festering stench was nearly overwhelming. Several of us stepped back, but I did my best to stay in place, not wanting to offend this thing . . . whatever it was.

"Right," I finally answered weakly. "Pals. My name is Greggdroule Stormbelly. This is Ari, Glam, Lake, Froggy, Stoney, Tiki, and these three with the weapons drawn are the Sentry. But they mean you no harm. They're our security detail, so they have to be extra cautious, you see."

"Ah, indeed!" the blob replied, rather cheerily for a creature with an ax, a sword, and a mace pointed at it. "Caution is the cousin to survival, after all. My name is *blaaaarcctt*." The noise it emitted sounded like a kid stomping in the mud with big rain boots on. "Though, no doubt your unsophisticated and primitive tongues cannot pronounce that, so you can just call me Blob Blog Globbenblog. Or just Blob for short, if you wish, as my old master used to."

"Master?" Ari asked. "You were . . . *owned* by someone?"

---

[*] Apparently also known as the Plain Tongue back in Separate Earth

"Well, technically, yes," Blob replied. "But I like to consider us more symbiotic friends, rather than associates of a proprietorial sort of relationship."

"What happened to your old master—er, uh, friend?" I asked.

Blob deflated slightly, then rolled to the right and back again, as if nervously shuffling its "feet."

"I don't know," he finally said. "He was quite displeased with me at the time we parted. In fact, he was *always* unhappy with me. Rightly so, too, for I am nothing but a worthless pile of feces. Not literally, of course. But this is what he always told me. I am not a good servant. I am not a good companion. I tried and tried to please him, to serve him well, but alas, I always failed . . . failed rather spectacularly, if I might add . . ."

Blob's voice had become strained, and his gooey mass was dripping a yellow liquid all over the ground in what I can only imagine (or hope) was his version of crying. Either way, it only amplified his stench in ways I couldn't possibly describe without offending nearly everyone reading this story.

"I'm *so* sorry," Ari said. "Your old master sounds so mean . . ."

"Oh, no, no!" Blob said suddenly, lunging forward so quickly that Ari almost fell over trying to get away. "No, no, no, no. Don't ever speak poorly of Master. He was a great man. Wise and noble. The wisest and noblest creature who ever lived! I would have died for him! Still would, if he were here . . . though I'm sure I'd fail at that task, too, somehow . . ."

"Oh," Ari said. "Sorry . . ."

"We're wasting time," Sentry One interjected. "Let's dispatch of this thing and move on, shall we?"

While I didn't agree with her sentiment exactly, I did have to admit that we were wasting a lot of valuable time. We needed to press on. We couldn't forget that Edwin had a pretty significant head start.

"Blob, we definitely mean you no harm," I said, shooting Sentry One an annoyed glance. "But we must indeed continue our journey now. It was nice to meet you, though."

"Wait! Can I not come along on your adventures?" Blob asked, rolling toward me, the stink almost making me choke. "I am a wonderful companion. And can provide many helpful services . . . or, well, I will at least try my best."

I took a subtle step back and glanced at my companions. I could see in their expressions and shaking heads that nobody wanted this smelly, sort-of-annoying, poo-booger-blob to come with us on the journey.

"Um, well, see, it's a pretty dangerous mission," I said. "And I wouldn't want you to get hurt or anything . . ."

"It's the smell, isn't it?" Blob asked. He rolled in a tight circle and shrank back against the boulder. "I've heard people speaking about my aroma before."

"No, no, I mean, that's not it . . ." I said. "What, what smell?"

"You don't have to lie," Blob said. "I'm not stupid. But I can't help it. That's just the by-product of how I consume the energy within the materials around me. I either smell this way or die. What am I supposed to do? Would you rather I die? Because if so, I will certainly acquiesce here and now . . ."

I felt horrible.

Were we really going to make an outcast out of this thing just because it had a smell that didn't fit with what we'd always considered pleasant? I mean, his musk *was* nearly suffocating (like a combination of rotten eggs, the Souper Bowl, old diapers, spoiled milk, and vinegar), but it still didn't seem fair to leave him behind because of something totally outside his control.

"Okay," I said. "You may join us."

"Greg, no!" Sentry Five whined.

"Blob *is* joining us!" I said louder. "But I want you to know, Blob, that this *is* a dangerous mission. You may—*we all* may—perish. You accept that risk?"

"Of course!" Blob said, clearly excited. "Yes. Yes, I will do what I can to help. You know, my old master once said that I was about as helpful as paraplegic mule, and though I don't know what a mule is, or what *paraplegic* means, I can only assume it is something of great assistance in times of danger!"

Ari and Lake shot me a look. I could feel everyone's eyes on me, wondering what on earth I had just done. But I was going to stand by the decision. We did not have the right to discriminate against this creature based on his smell or appearance or general annoyance levels. At least Stoney seemed to be on my side.

"WELCOME!" he bellowed down in the general direction of the blob of pus and goo. "AGREEABLE CONVOKING ACQUAINTANCE!"

"Likewise!" Blob said. "I've never met a stack of talking rocks before! I mean, hah, now I've seen everything! No, I mean, literally *everything*. I bet there's nothing left in this world I have not witnessed, aside from a mule, now that I have met a talking mound of stones."

"Okay, then, yes," I said, interrupting his babble. "Onward, Stoney?"

Stoney nodded and continued walking in the direction we'd been heading all day. As I strapped my new sword to my belt, I wondered if finally getting a suitable replacement weapon would be worth the addition of the slimeball it had unwittingly unleashed.

But, as with most things of such an unusual nature, only time would tell.

CHAPTER 19

The Time Sir Wylymot the Agile Got Flattened Like a Bug

Unfortunately, it didn't take very long to discover that Blob never shut up.

In fact, as we walked, I began to speculate about all the totally valid reasons he might have been sealed inside that stone for who knew how many years. But to be fair, even as he regaled us with long and often pointless tales about things like all the many uses for a bucket, or the surprising variety of moods pill bugs experience, he did seem generally harmless and eager to please.

Not that it completely made up for the constant chatter. Or the stench that, for some reason, we never got accustomed to. Each time a whiff of his distinctly ripe stink hit your nose it was like you were smelling it for the first time all over again.

But Froggy eventually took one for the team and fell back alongside Blob, encouraging his stories with an endless series of interested nods. It was just the sort of quietly noble thing

Froggy was becoming known for. He even slowed his pace so they were the last two in line. It mostly kept Blob's stench away from the rest of us, barring a shift in the wind.

At the front of the pack, Ari, Glam, and I walked side by side, a few paces behind Stoney, who was in the lead with his walking stick slapping the ground in front of him.

"So I've been meaning to ask, now that we're getting closer," Ari said, "what happens when we find the amulet? *If* we find it . . ."

I was about to tell her: *Well, to beat Edwin to it of course!* But I realized that didn't really answer her question.

"Yeah, I've been wondering that, too," Glam said. "I mean, we all know the goal is to get the amulet before Edwin does, so we can stop him from banishing magic and all that. But . . . *then* what? If we get the amulet first, what will we actually *do* with something so powerful?"

"I mean, it will be the Council's ultimate decision," Ari said. "But what do you guys think we should do with it?"

"I—well—" I stammered. "Ummm . . ."

The truth was—and this was so obvious by now I didn't even need to say it aloud—I had no clue what would come next. I still didn't even quite understand what the amulet *was*, let alone the limits of its powers. Nobody did. Our understanding was that it could harness and control the very essence of all magic. But what exactly did that mean?

I didn't think there was a way to know until we found it.

"I guess," I said slowly, "I hope we find a way to use it to prevent the war with the Elves from fully resuming. After we use it to stop the Verumque Genus Elves from unleashing total destruction on the world, of course. But I think we should ultimately find a way to use it to bring about peace. Then again, I still have no idea how exactly to do those things, even with a special, all-powerful amulet."

"So basically, we're on a dangerous mission to do who-knows-what, with something superpowerful in a way nobody gets, and we don't know how or what or why?" Ari summarized.

There was a long pause, and then the three of us laughed, because there was really nothing else to do but laugh. Something about the way she'd so succinctly and casually pointed out the billions of flaws in our world-saving mission just felt so utterly . . . well, *Dwarven*.

"You want to hear something really scary?" I asked, after our laughter died down.

"Not really!" they both said in almost perfect unison.

"Okay, then, never mind . . ."

"Fine, tell us," Ari said. "It's not like things are safe as they stand now!"

I finally told them about the old Elven man who had welcomed me into his house in Chumikan that first night, after I'd washed ashore all alone.

"What's so scary about a cranky old Elf?" Glam asked.

"It's not him, but what he said," I clarified. "I mean, what happens if we find the supposed hiding place of the amulet, but then discover that there *is* no amulet?"

"What makes you say that?" Ari asked.

I told them about how certain the old man was that the amulet was a myth. About how he'd said all the locals considered the story total hogwash.

"He was *sure* the amulet isn't here," I said.

"And we're just supposed to trust the word of some Elf?"

Glam said dismissively. "Elves lie. Even when they're not trying to!"

Ari considered everything further before responding, not instantly assuming the old man's claims to be false. But even after her long, thoughtful pause, she seemed unconcerned.

"We always knew that was a possibility," she said finally. "I mean, nearly half the Dwarven Council still thinks this mission is a total waste of time and resources. The vote to send us here was pretty narrowly passed. I mean, to be totally honest, *I'm* not even convinced we're going to find the amulet. Just like the old Elf in Chumikan, a lot of Dwarven historians think the story *is* a myth. It might even be a story purposely concocted by the Fairies to throw everyone off the real trail of the amulet. If it exists at all."

"If you don't think it exists either, then what are we even doing out here?" Glam asked. "This is a dangerous mission. Why bother if it's all for nothing?"

"We have to try, in case it *is* real," Ari said. "Besides, I didn't say I don't believe it's real, just that I have my doubts. The main reason I still have hope is *him*."

She pointed at Stoney, who was several paces in front of us, leading the way confidently, as if he knew precisely where we were going, eyesight or no eyesight.

"I trust Stoney," Ari continued. "If he says the rock at the heart of the amulet is real, then I have to believe it until he's proven wrong."

Glam and I both nodded.

Ari was right: Stoney was the main reason we had all risked so much to be here. Well, that, and also my former best friend, Edwin. He was among the smartest people I'd ever met, and if he thought the amulet was real, then so would I. Plus, like Ari said, we had to at least try. Because if it *was* real, we couldn't just sit back and let Edwin find it first.

The rest of the hike that day was relatively uneventful.

I would have said peaceful, were it not for Blob's never-ending stories about stuff like:

1. The things he ate for breakfast once, thousands of years ago (he mostly ate plants, twigs, and dirt, which made most of my Dwarven traveling companions hate him even more)
2. The one time he helped his old master play a joke on someone by convincing them his master's poop could talk (I'll let your imagination figure out how they achieved that one)
3. The time he thought the sun was a god named Bright Shiny Hot Round Shape, and spent the better part of three decades worshipping it, until finally his master set him straight and told him the sun was really a giant firefly that got stuck up in the sky when it flew too high

But all in all, I'd take Blob's inane stories over more skirmishes with Rocnars or other such monsters any day.

That evening, we set up camp near a stream that ran through a narrow ravine winding around a rocky slope. I wish I could tell you if the slope eventually became a mountain, but I can't. Starting around late afternoon, a heavy fog settled on the tops of the trees above us, blocking our view of anything beyond the immediate forest and branches overhead.

As we worked to set up camp, I saw Blob rolling away down a narrow path between a few bushes that looked like Siberian cypress, but definitely were not (due to the slightly glowing leaves).*

"I better go see what he's up to," I said to Lake and Froggy as we were setting up the tent.

They both nodded, and I hopped to my feet and followed Blob into the forest. He was already a good way ahead of me. That rolling mass of goo could move pretty fast when he wanted to. But it wasn't difficult to stay on his trail due to the awful stench left in his wake.

It wasn't long before I heard his loud voice speaking to someone.

"Yeah, we're on a mission!" he said loudly. "Hunting for some rare mineral, as best I can gather . . ."

Instantly I had visions of him being a spy for the Elves, or worse. And if this had been a trap all along, it was my fault we were in it since I had allowed him to join us against the protests of the others. I supposed I should've expected no better from myself by that point.

I didn't want to ruin my chance to see who Blob might be working for, so I crouched down among some bushes, and then slowly crept forward with the softest steps I could manage.

"They're all pretty determined, as I was saying," Blob continued. "And I got a good feeling they're going to find it. There's this one—Froggy is his name—he reminds me of Master in a lot of ways, but a lot quieter. Which is saying something! Anyway, the party is led by an especially short and stout one named Greggdroule. He's pretty nice, I guess . . ."

---

* Since we were now in an ancient, magical forest, teeming with talking blobs and bloodthirsty Giant Squirrels, I couldn't be sure of what anything actually was anymore, including the trees and bushes.

I slowly peeked around a massive tree trunk until Blob finally came into view.

And then I breathed out a long sigh of relief.

Blob was lumped up near another tree, speaking to one of the Giant Squirrels. The large animal cocked its head at the smelly blob, trying to figure out whether it was a threat or food or neither. It definitely didn't look like it had any clue what Blob was actually saying.

"There you are," I said, stepping into the clearing. "I thought you'd run off on us!"

The Giant Squirrel looked startled when it saw me and darted off into the forest.

"Ah, Greg!" Blob cried out. "It seems as if you've chased off my new friend. I didn't even catch his name . . . quiet one, that fellow!"

"You know, Blob, you should be more careful telling strangers about our mission," I said.

"Ah, is it a secret mission, then?" Blob asked, rippling with excitement, which unfortunately only made him more pungent. "I never was privy to many of Master's secrets. He always said I was terrible at keeping them. But how would he know if he never let me try!" Blob was in full-on rambling mode now as he began rolling slowly forward, continuing along the creek, away from the campsite. "I mean, of course there was that one time he told me about his secret Fairy mission, and I accidentally gave it away to this innkeeper. . . . Oh, yeah! *And then* there was the time he entrusted me with a special coin that glows when it gets near a vampire, and I lost it at the Westordom Market . . ."

"Blob, hang on!" I said, trotting after him, struggling to keep up. "Wait just a second! Where are you going in such a hurry?"

Blob finally rolled to a stop and, well, he didn't exactly

turn to face me since, you know, he was a Blob with no front or back or eyes or face, but he shimmered as if he was indeed now *looking at me*.

"When you started setting up your tents, I realized I'd been here before," Blob said. "And I seem to remember that there's a Forest Troll den around here somewhere."

"A Forest Troll den!?"

"Yes, it's pretty close if memory serves me right," Blob said casually as if he were talking about trying to find a mediocre restaurant he ate at once. "I even met one of the Trolls that lived there. A fellow named Zunabar. Real cranky guy, too, let me tell you. Ha-ha! He smashed me with his fist once! Good thing I've got no bones or organs, or I would have surely perished the way that poor knight, Sir Wylymot the Agile, did when the Troll smashed him. Ugh, an awful *mess* that made . . ."

"What?" I asked, my voice almost squeaking. "Why . . . I mean, why on earth would you want to find this violent Troll?"

But I had to admit I was curious myself now. I mean, we *should know* if we were setting up camp near a Forest Troll den, right? It might save us from a surprise attack in the night.

"Hmm," Blob said, as if he'd never even considered why he'd set off to find this Troll on a whim. "Guess I just wanted to see a familiar face. Is that weird? That's weird, isn't it? Master always said I was strange. Should we not go? We don't have to keep going . . ."

Of course I should have agreed right then and there and said: "Yeah, that's weird, let's not go."

But my curiosity was like an uncontrollable demon now. And my brain even rationalized it by telling me: *Greg, you NEED to know if there's a den of monsters nearby. It'd be irresponsible to let this potential threat go uninvestigated.*

Yeah, but we could go back and get a proper search party, I reasoned with my own curiosity.

No, it would take too long, my curiosity argued. *It will be dark soon. You shouldn't be wandering around these woods alone at night. Let's just go check it out real fast while we can still see by the foggy daylight. We'll go, we'll see, disturb nothing, then hurry back to camp to report what we saw. Harmless.*

Yeah, good point, I foolishly agreed.

"How much farther is it?" I asked Blob.

"Oh, not far now," he said. "Shall we continue?"

"Yeah, let's go!" I said.

Now I will admit this: I'd made a lot of mistakes in my life up to that point. The time I drank my dad's tea, setting off all the terrible things that came after, the time I set my own pants on fire trying to battle a Gargoyle, and the time I capsized our boat because I went fishing, all came to mind just off the top of my head. Which means you can only imagine how bad things were about to go for me, since I now must admit that this ended up being one of the worst decisions I ever made in my whole life.

As in, this one colossal mistake (or series of mistakes, really) was about to get more people killed.

CHAPTER 20

Never Wake a Sleeping Troll

The entrance to the cave wouldn't have been visible without two things:

1. Blob knowing it was there
2. The unmistakable flickering orange glow of a fire

And the cave *was* close to where my friends were setting up our camp. Blob and I had trekked maybe just half a mile along the creek when we finally spotted the sliver of an opening in the rocky slope on the other side.

"How do we get up there?" I asked.

"I can just slide up the mountainside," Blob said. "You can't?"

We both knew I couldn't, and it was sort of annoying that he was playing dumb like a passive-aggressive pile of boogers.

I gave him a look.

"Oh, *right*." Blob pretended to just figure it out. "Arms and legs and such. Well, luckily there's a path over there behind that row of trees."

Of course he had no fingers, so I couldn't see where he was "pointing." But there were only a few trees along the opposite bank of the small stream. We splashed across and began a steep hike up the rocky trail. As we neared the mouth of the cave, a thought struck me (one that probably should have struck me well before this point): *What on earth was I doing?*

Was I really about to approach a possible Forest Troll den with only a smelly ball of goo for backup?

Yes. Yes, I was. Like a Dwarf.

The cave's entrance was a fang-shaped opening in the side of the mountain, twenty feet across at the base, with the point reaching up about forty feet above my head. It had looked a lot smaller from the other side of the creek.

The area around the cave was littered with gore-covered bones and skulls from a variety of animals. Some looked familiar, but others looked like they could have been alien. Heaps of bloodied armor and rusted weapons lay strewn about in the bushes, littering the side of the mountain like urban garbage dotting a highway ditch.

Whatever lived in this cave was clearly violent and savage.

"Come on, let's go check it out," I whispered to Blob.

"Yeah, I'm hoping Zunabar still lives here," he said. "I sort of liked it when his knobby fist splattered me all over the place. Ha-ha, took me three hours to collect all my parts back up! In fact, some of me might still be stuck to the walls of the cave. I mean, it was pretty—"

"SSSHHHHHH!" I hushed him.

Blob fell silent and rolled alongside me toward the cave. I knew this was a terrible idea. But I'd already come this far.

Going back to camp without any real knowledge of what was up here would defeat the whole purpose.

We slowly crept toward the entrance of the cave.

There were no sounds but the crackling of a fire inside. We neared the wall, and I had to step over a pile of bleached skulls that were unmistakably from several of the Giant Squirrels that plagued the forest below.

I carefully poked my head around the corner.

An elongated chunk of Blob, like a periscope, stretched around the corner below me, near my knees.

From there, we couldn't see anything but more bones and armor and the intense orange flickering of firelight on the dripping cave walls. We would have to actually enter the cave to see what was inside.

I drew my new sword from my belt. It was heavy and uncomfortable in my hand. My temporary fix for the hilt had been to wrap some thin shreds of cloth around the metal handle.

"Come on," I whispered as I tiptoed into the cave.

Blob rolled after me.

We rounded a slight bend near the entrance and finally entered the main cavern.

It didn't take long to spot the mammoth shapes of four Forest Trolls sleeping around a smoldering fire. Chunks of bones and flesh from some unfortunate animals were scattered about the cavern, as if the trolls had just finished a feast, then passed out where they sat with their bellies full of meat.

Two of them were, in fact, slumped over in a sitting position, snoring loudly. The other two were curled up like cats on the stone floor. Except, cats with heads bigger than a car. Forest Trolls were by far the ugliest and nastiest-looking type of Troll I'd seen yet.

The Forest Trolls were larger than Stoney, but smaller than the Mountain Trolls who had attacked the Underground. And unlike Mountain Trolls, who almost looked like giant Humans with a skin condition, Forest Trolls barely had any Human features aside from the whole two legs, two arms, and one head thing. Their skin was craggy and lined with small spikes and horns. Their faces were elongated. Massive fangs on their lower jaws jutted up and over dry, blood-caked lips, all the way up past their nostrils. Speaking of noses, the Forest Troll schnoz was more like a heaping, misshapen mound of green warts than anything recognizably used for smelling. A gold hoop hung from at least one of the Trolls' noses. They had stout, muscular arms and legs, and hunched bodies, and wore only rough, rotting loincloths for clothes, all of which appeared to have been stitched together from a variety of different animal hides.

All in all, they looked like savage monsters.

And their odor was so unbearably wretched, they made Blob smell like freshly baked cookies.

"Welp!" Blob suddenly said loudly. "Zunabar doesn't seem to live here anymore. I don't recognize any of this lot. Which I suppose makes sense, being that I was trapped in that stone for probably many generations of Forest Troll. But either way, I guess we can probably go, then, huh?"

All I could do was glare at him, stunned by the loud outburst that was surely about to get us both killed.

"What?" Blob asked. "Did I fart or something?"

I pressed a finger to my lips and quickly glanced back at the sleeping Trolls. Amazingly, aside from one of them flipping onto his back, none stirred.

"Oh, right," Blob said, a little quieter. "Better to not wake the Trolls, huh?"

"Come on, let's just get out of here," I whispered.

I can only assume Blob did his blobby version of a nod, because he followed me as I quickly scooted back toward the cave's exit. But I was so panicked to get out of there, by now realizing what a huge mistake coming this far had been, that I didn't see the top half of a skeleton lying in my path. The skull's jaw gaped open still in the screaming-in-terror position it had been in when the poor soul had perished.

My foot got tangled in the skeleton's rib cage, and I was suddenly sprawling as I crashed face-first into an even larger pile of bones. Heaps of femurs and spines and other odds and ends skittered loudly across the cave floor.

As I lay there trying to figure out if I'd accidentally impaled myself on a loose bone, I couldn't help but rationalize how much it likely didn't matter either way. Because surely the sleeping Trolls would be awake now, and that'd be all she wrote for a clumsy Dwarf named Greggdroule and his pal the stinky blob, Blob.

"Are you okay?" Blob asked as I climbed to my feet, wondering why I still wasn't hearing the noises of startled Trolls grunting as they woke.

But shockingly, all four Trolls were still fast asleep by the fire. It seemed as though Forest Trolls were pretty heavy sleepers (in addition to being insatiable carnivores).

"Whew—that was close!" I said to Blob, as I spun back toward the entrance. "I thought for sure we were as good as Troll meat. Come on, let's get out of—"

But the rest of my words got stuck in my suddenly very dry throat as I faced the cave's only entrance (and thus only known exit).

Blocking the entire mouth of the cave stood a fifth, very much awake, and very much angry Forest Troll.

CHAPTER 21

GRangAHN og CHOngO GlurponDERIN IH aH ggg GrongOb!

U h, wrong cave?" I tried weakly. "Um, sorry about that, if you could just step aside, we'll be on our way . . ."

The Troll growled a thick, phlegmy, guttural roar of pure violence so dreadful and menacing that I would have collapsed and died right there on the spot if I hadn't been too afraid to move at all.

Then he yelled out, gargle-y and incoherent, "GRangAHN og CHOngO GlurponDERIN IH aH ggg GrongOb!"

It immediately roused his four housemates from their seemingly unbreakable slumber. The other Trolls stood quickly, saw Blob and me, and joined the chorus of guttural growling.

"Hey, have any of you seen Zunabar?" Blob asked as if he was making small talk with a harmless mailman. "About your height, maybe a tad taller, used to live around here?"

The Trolls only responded with more gurgling, menacing growls. Or maybe they were hungry growls?

Time would tell.

"Zunabar was an old acquaintance of mine, you see," Blob continued, seemingly unaware of the immediate danger we faced. "*None* of you have seen him?"

The five Trolls slowly surrounded us.

"I don't think they speak the Plain Tongue, Greg!" Blob said to me. "Perhaps I'll try some Orcish. Supposedly, Forest Trollian and Orcish come from the same phylogenetic tree."

Blob began making strange noises that didn't sound like any language I'd ever heard. The Trolls seemed unfazed as their massive, rough hands clenched and unclenched.

Then the first Troll struck, swinging his hand down onto me like a mallet.

I turned to stone a moment before the impact, reanimated, and quickly rolled to my left to dodge another blow. But then a third Troll caught me with his foot, and I flew back into the cave like a deflated soccer ball.

I slammed into the rock wall, which was covered in thousands of years of accumulated Troll slime, with a swampy THWANGCK!

My new sword clattered to the ground nearby.

The impact knocked the wind out of me. I wheezed silently as I struggled to get back to my feet. Near the entrance of the cave, the Trolls were taking wild swats at Blob with their feet and fists. He weaved in and out of their clunky legs with surprising agility, dodging their blows with ease.

"Hey, now!" Blob cried out. "This is a rather rude way to tell me that you and Zunabar have had a falling-out!"

I stood and picked up my sword, still struggling to breathe.

Then I charged at the Forest Trolls.

They were too preoccupied with Blob to notice me, and I walked right up behind one of the Trolls and took a massive swing at his Achilles tendon with my new weapon. But the blade bounced harmlessly off his calf, as if his skin and muscle were made of rubber. Ari had warned me that the sword might be pretty dull after spending so many years lodged in a rock.

The Troll spun around and actually roared like a lion. Its rotten breath nearly knocked me unconscious as I collapsed to the ground.

"Greggdroule, run!" Blob shouted.

I looked up just in time to see a pile of goo soaring into the air and splitting into five separate pieces midflight. Each section of mini-Blob splattered onto a different Troll's face. They cringed and cried out as they bashed their own faces with their fists.

Blob had just created a diversion so I could get away!

I didn't want to waste his valiant effort, so I sprang to my feet and weaved my way through the staggering Trolls on my way out of the cave.

I knew Blob didn't have organs or bones, and was seemingly impervious to Forest Troll attacks, otherwise I would have stayed back to make sure he was okay. But the animated pile of boogers was older than me by at least several thousand years, maybe more, so I figured he knew what he was doing.

I sprinted down the mountain path, keeping my eyes on the ground in front of me to avoid tripping on the larger rocks and pits.

When I got to the bottom, I stopped and glanced back. For some reason, I had envisioned I'd see nothing, the five Trolls still tied up in chunks of my good friend Blob. But that was clearly the sort of hopelessly optimistic thinking that Dwarves were not supposed to engage in.

Instead, I saw Blob, back in one piece, hurtling down the hillside after me, equal parts rolling like a getaway snowball and slithering like a liquefied snake.

Behind him, the five angry Forest Trolls were in close pursuit, holding an array of primitive but deadly-looking club-type weapons.

The Trolls may have had stumpy legs, but they could book it when they were mad enough.

"Keep running, Greggdroule!" Blob shouted as he neared.

It was the first time I'd ever heard fear in his voice, and the sound of his panic absolutely terrified me. I didn't need any additional encouragement, and so I turned around and resumed running.

We reached the stream a few moments later. I realized it was a crossroads, with three potential options (and only a few seconds to decide):

1. I could run back toward our camp, where I had a small army of reinforcements waiting. Or, well, not exactly waiting . . . In fact, they'd be caught pretty off guard and therefore be not at all ready to defend themselves from the Forest Troll ambush I'd bring with me.

2. I could lead the Trolls as far away from the camp as I could, pretty much ensuring that I would be dissolving inside a Troll's belly by morning, but also keeping my friends safe for at least one more night.

3. I could turn around and make a stand here and now, using Dwarven magic and my new sword (and a smelly blob named Blob) to fend off five pretty large and intimidating Forest Trolls.

As far as options went, they were all pretty lousy.

But it was what I had to work with, so there was no point whining about it or hoping that some other person from my past was going to swoop in out of nowhere at just the right moment to save me.

And so I quickly made my decision.

Yet another in a long series of mistakes that would prove disastrous.

Legend always said Dwarves were doomed to failure. But I'd found at least one thing I was supremely good at: failing with style.

CHAPTER 22

Blob: The Steak Sauce

The Battle of the Forest Trolls started off better than expected. It turned out I had been gone a lot longer than my companions had anticipated. And so rather than sitting around a campfire casually cooking up dinner and telling funny Dwarf stories, the group was already on high alert, fully armed, and ready to send out a search party looking for me and Blob.

Which means they met the five Trolls charging behind me through the woods with a thunderous clang of weapons and spells.

First, someone (either Ari, Glam, Tiki, or Sentry Five, being that they were the only ones in our group besides me with the Ability) cast a spell that lit up a huge wall of fire across the path behind me, theoretically cutting off or slowing the Trolls' pursuit. Unfortunately, the wall of fire did basically nothing, and the Trolls charged right through it like they were fireproof.

Next, Glam came flying in from above (apparently she had been perched up in a tree the whole time). Her fists transformed into boulders as she landed on one of the Forest Troll's shoulders. She pummeled the Troll in the head and face repeatedly.

Stoney was probably our best asset, in terms of translations (he spoke fifteen languages, including Forest Troll), navigational skills, mission knowledge, generosity, geological aptitude, and, most of all, combat. And he wasn't going to sit this one out, blind or not.

He charged toward the thundering rumble of the Trolls' massive footsteps. Even though he was at least seven feet shorter and weighed probably three or four hundred pounds less, he still collided with one of the Forest Trolls with enough force to send them both sprawling into the trunk of a massive spruce nearby. The tree split in half and crashed down into the forest behind them, taking several smaller trees with it.

At that very moment, I actually thought we were going to win.

Foolish me, I'd never learn.

Because a short time later, we realized how *tough* these things really were. Literally nothing fazed them; nothing seemed to injure them, not even magic.

I did seem to remember something from Monsterology class about the Forest Troll's legendary *resiliency*. Which is a word that sounded harmless on paper (and thus was easy to forget), until you actually saw it in action.

For instance:

- No matter how many times Glam battered the Troll in the face and head, her Glam-smash boulders merely bounced right off the thing as if they were made of foam. Even the blows that did appear to inflict a wound, or split its head open, didn't slow it down or seem to cause any real pain. A few moments after she'd landed on its shoulder, the Troll simply flicked her off like she was a bug.

- The Trolls broke through magical vines like they were made of brittle straw, were completely unfazed by magically summoned winds and fires, and didn't seem to care at all when a magical lightning bolt was fired from the sky and hit one in the arm, singeing its biceps black with a smoking sizzle.

- Even Stoney couldn't seem to hurt these things as he battered them with rock-like blows, twisted their limbs, and fought with all the fury of a fellow Troll. Through all his brutal assaults, they swatted him easily away, laughing as if he were a gnat and not a two-ton Rock Troll with unimaginable strength.

- Our weapons mostly bounced off their tough skin without leaving so much as a mark. Froggy somehow managed to stab one of them in the left eyeball, surely partially blinding it. But the beast didn't even flinch as it plucked Froggy from its shoulder and then pinned him to the ground under one of its knobby, stinking, bunion-covered bare feet. The Troll grinned triumphantly, purple blood oozing down its cheek from its eye socket as Froggy futilely squirmed under his foot.

To put it bluntly: we were completely outmatched.

We stood no chance against these things. Just ten minutes after the battle had started, it was over, and we had lost.

The remaining Sentry guards (unwilling to stop fighting and surrender like the rest of us had, once we realized we couldn't win) were all dead. Stoney (our one chance to negotiate with these beasts) was nowhere in sight and presumed missing in action, or worse. Glam, Froggy, Ari, Tiki, Lake and I were all lumped on top of Blob near our campfire, in a heaping, injured pile of broken Dwarves.

The five Trolls loomed over us, ensuring we wouldn't try to escape. But the truth was, we were all too sore and tired and defeated to do anything but tend to our wounds and wonder what horrible fate awaited us.

It didn't take long to find out.

The Trolls quickly engaged in some sort of heated conversation. Their native tongue sounded like just a bunch of primal grunts, growls, and raspy wails.

"I think they're having an argument," Ari said, wincing as Tiki wrapped her badly wounded arm in a loose piece of cloth while also attempting a healing spell.

"What do you think it's about?" Glam asked.

The rest of us shrugged, as Blob slowly oozed out from where we sat and gathered himself back into one slab of slime next to us.

"Whether to eat us raw like tartare," Blob answered, "or butcher us and grill our steaks over a fire."

We all turned to look at him in horror and shock.

"I totally forgot back in the cave that I *can* actually speak Forest Troll," he said. "Ha-ha, silly me. I'm always forgetting which languages I can or cannot speak. Rather amusing, no?"

Nobody else found it funny at all. Instead, we swallowed back our urge to vomit everywhere, knowing we were about to become Troll food.

"They're . . . they're really going to eat us right here and now?" Ari asked, her face pale—whether from blood loss or fear, I wasn't sure (but probably both).

"Indeed, it seems they intend to eat us," Blob confirmed as the Trolls continued their argument.

"How can we get out of this?" I asked.

Nobody responded. We all knew there was no escape. We were no match for these things, even with magic. Magic suddenly didn't seem so, well, *magic* anymore. Or perhaps we simply didn't know how to use it to the fullest extent of its power. We still hadn't technically completed our training yet.

The Trolls finally stopped arguing, and one of them produced a massive knife with a curved blade longer than two of us put together. Another stalked off into the woods. A third lifted his huge shield and spit a glob of Troll saliva onto the concave side in what I can only assume was a futile attempt to clean it.

"Oh, it seems they've made their decision!" Blob said as if this was good news. "Apparently, they're going to butcher you and go with the seared-Dwarf-steak option! And they're going to use *me* as the steak sauce!"

CHAPTER 23

A Tasty Sack of Dwarf Brand Pretzels™

I've never been a sauce before!" Blob said. "I'm totally flattered, but still, I don't really *want* to get digested. That *might* actually kill me! But of course I always *did say* I'd probably taste good, proving that . . ."

"Blob, please!" Ari said, close to tears. "We're all going to die unless we find a way out of this!"

"On the count of three," I said in a low voice, "everyone run in a different direction. They can't catch us all, can they? Then maybe at least one or two of us will get away."

"I don't *want* to be the one who gets away," Glam said. "I'm not leaving anyone behind."

"'Tis nary ye superlative strategy," Lake said somberly. "Notwithstanding doth be'est ye dismally ideal per thy foreseeable liberation."

But we didn't get a chance to debate it any further. We were scooped up by the Trolls and thrown into a huge sack made from finely netted rope. The holes were large enough for some of our arms and legs to poke out, but too small for any hope of slipping out entirely. Unless, of course, there was a Dwarven spell that could somehow temporarily liquefy us.

Speaking of liquefied people, Blob obviously couldn't be contained by a mesh rope bag, and so he clumsily rolled along on the ground as the Troll carried us to a nearby tree.

"Blob, run!" I yelled down to him. "Make your escape now while you can!"

"And abandon my new friends?" he cried out from ten feet below. "No way! Unless this is a trick? Are you trying to get rid of me? You are, aren't you? I knew it! I knew my smell was more than you could take. I mean, I always suspected it, even back when . . ."

I sighed in frustration and tried to tune out the insecure ramblings of the slimy, smelly, yet undeniably loyal blob of goo trailing behind us.

The Troll strung up the rope sack from a high tree branch. Another Troll was setting up a pile of wood nearby for a fire. The shield (likely a makeshift frying pan) lay next to it. The Troll with the knife was sharpening the curved blade on an oddly shaped rock.

It grinned at us hungrily as yellow saliva ran down his chin and dripped onto the forest floor in a steaming pile.

"There's got to be a spell that can get us out of this . . ." Ari said.

"Indeed!" Lake said. "Ye Ability-laden companions commence spell casting forthwith!"

Ari, Glam, Tiki, and I all began attempting some sort of spell that could break us free from this rope sack. I thought of a fire igniting the rope threads, and plants with razor-sharp edges that would sprout down below to cut us free. I even tried to simply will the rope itself to dissolve or break or weaken.

But nothing happened.

"Are you guys trying?" Froggy asked after several minutes.

"Yes!" all four of us responded at once.

"Oh, are you trying to cast a spell?" Blob asked below us. "Because it won't work. Ha-ha. I mean, good luck with that . . ."

"What do you mean it won't work?" I asked, a little annoyed that he was still being so casual about all of this.

"Well, that net is made from *Phem* fiber strands, sourced from a local plant called *Scibanna*," Blob said.

"So what?" Glam shot back rather rudely.

"*So what?*" Blob mocked her. "Heh, well, *Phem* fibers dull the effects of most types of magic. *Duh.* Everyone knows that."

"Well, not *everyone*, apparently . . ." I muttered.

"Great!" Glam said. "So now what?"

"We're purbogging kunked!" Tiki cried. "*That's* what!"

"Doesn't anyone have any hidden weapons on them?" Froggy asked.

I would have slapped my palm to my forehead just then if both my arms weren't awkwardly folded underneath me, pinned between Glam's back and Tiki's leg (we'd been crammed inside the rope bag like a bunch of Dwarf Brand Pretzels™).

"I'm pretty sure Blackout is still in my belt," I said.

"*Now* you tell us!" Glam said.

"Arguing isn't helping," Ari interjected. "Can anybody reach it?"

"I definitely can't," I said, my arms going numb from being so tightly pinned to my back.

The rope sack spun with a series of grunts and *oofs* as everyone inside strained and jiggled and reached, trying to get to the dagger attached to my belt near my left hip. Eventually, I felt someone tugging at the handle.

"I got it!" Froggy said.

Before I knew it, we all tumbled from the sliced-open net, falling a substantial distance to the forest floor. Had we been

Human, we wouldn't have dreamed of just cutting ourselves free at that height. But as Dwarves, we knew our strong bones could withstand the fall.

That's not to say it didn't hurt. It did. A lot.

But we didn't have time to writhe in pain. As soon as we landed in a tangled heap, we immediately helped one another to our feet so we could make a getaway.

"You're free!" Blob said. "Well done, friends, well done!"

But before we could even think about running, we were suddenly sprawling and rolling across the ground as something massive swept us along the forest floor like a broom sweeping up shards of glass. I smashed into Blob, and some of his goo got into my mouth just as someone's foot hit me squarely in the jaw. I gagged as we tumbled across the rough forest floor. It wasn't until we stopped, probably fifty feet later, that I realized what had happened.

One of the Trolls had come out of nowhere, using a huge tree branch like a broom to sweep us all toward the Troll with the butcher knife. We sat up, dazed, still hurting, and fully realizing that these creatures were simply too big and powerful for us to make an escape.

The Troll with the knife finally dropped the strange rock it had been using to sharpen its knife. That's when I realized what it was. It was no rock. It was Stoney's severed arm.

I cringed at the sight of it, my stomach melting right out from under me. I was so stunned, so shocked and horrified and defeated that I didn't even fight back when the Troll plucked me up from the ground and laid me on top of a tree stump. A sort of impromptu Troll cutting board, if you will.

I was about to get filleted alive, like a fish, and there was nothing I could do to stop it.

Not even Stoney would be able rush in and save me this time.

CHAPTER 24

⟡

A Couple of Well-Done, Rare Steak Puns Spoken at Medium Volume

I heard the panicked screams of my friends down below.

But I chose instead to focus on the Troll's face. Perhaps there was one last spell I could conjure up to distract or maim it. Based on what I'd seen so far, I knew it was hopeless to try, but at this point, what did I have to lose? I'd literally be chopped liver in about five seconds.

I looked up at the Troll's greedy, knobby, wart-covered face and summoned all the hate and bad feelings I could possibly muster.

Then the Troll's face promptly exploded in a ball of red light and gooey purple Troll blood.

As the Troll's lifeless, headless body teetered over backward and out of view, I knew immediately I had not been responsible. For one, Dwarven magic didn't work that way. It wasn't about creating energy, but rather using the earth's natural energy and elements that already existed. But also, you can't spend over a month in an Elven prison and not immediately recognize Elven magic when you see it.

I leaped to my feet on the tree stump, looking for the source of the Elven spell that had just saved me from getting butchered.

Several lithe bodies flew down from the tall trees above.

The Elves fired arrows from bows and cast more spells as they soared through the air. Their arrows actually pierced the skin of the remaining four Forest Trolls in ways our arrows had not. They each did little real damage individually, but the cumulative effect was clearly hurting the Trolls more than any of our attacks had. Perhaps the tips of the Elven arrows were poisoned. But even more effective were the Elven spells. Our elements-based magic had been mostly useless against the *resilient* Forest Trolls, but the Elves' energy magic easily laid waste to the monstrous goons.

Two balls of green-and-yellow energy fired across the forest and collided with the Troll who had been working on the fire. The dual pulses of energy hit it on either side and basically vaporized the Troll right where it had stood. Literally all that was left was a pair of smoking, wart-covered green feet.

I stood on the stump and watched in awe as more Elves descended from the trees. My first thought was: *Why are they helping us?* But then I recognized one of the Elves running across the clearing.

"Get down!" Lixi yelled at my friends as she drew another arrow and fired it at a Troll bounding toward us holding a huge rock over its head.

She was the Elf who had taken me out for "recesses" during my time on Alcatraz. And she was someone I now considered a friend, despite being my supposed enemy.

The arrow Lixi fired hit the Troll in the wrist.

It must have pierced a tendon, because the Troll dropped the rock, having lost all use of its right hand. The boulder landed on its own head with a dull *thump*. The Troll stood there, dazed, unsure why it couldn't feel its own fingers anymore.

Then two pulses of Elven magic zoomed in and finished it off for good.

I was stunned by the destructive power of Elven magic. How did my dad think something that could instantly vaporize a massive Forest Troll could also bring about universal peace for the first time in history?

Another Elf landed softly next to me on the tree stump as his companions easily finished off the last two Forest Trolls.

"Man, one second later and you'd have been a nice *filet Gregnon*," Edwin said with a grin.

I couldn't help but laugh at my former best friend's lame pun.

"Yeah, the *steaks* couldn't have been higher," I said back.

"Steak puns, hah," Edwin added. "A medium where anything well done is rare."

And then, in spite of us technically competing to reach the amulet first, and in spite of the supposed consequences of him beating us to it, and in spite of the fact that we were supposed to be enemies, and in spite of him having held me prisoner on Alcatraz, and in spite of us never before having done what happened next, I lunged at Edwin and embraced him.

He hugged me back.

I was grateful to be alive.

But surprisingly even more grateful to see his stupid smiling face again.

CHAPTER 25

Bigfoot Is Not Only Real but a Total Kleptomaniac

W hy did you save us?" I asked.

Everyone was gathered around the base of the massive cutting-board tree stump. Ari, Lake, Glam, Froggy, Tiki and I stood on one side. Across from us were Edwin and four other Elves, including Lixi, Foxflame Farro (the skateboarding hippie religious cleric I'd met on Alcatraz), Wrecking Ball (the janitor from Alcatraz), and an older Elf I did not recognize.

The tension between the two groups was obvious.

The Elves still had their weapons drawn and had not offered to let us retrieve our own, which were scattered all over our campsite clearing, the banks of the stream, and the edges of the forest.

"That's difficult to answer simply," Edwin said. "And it also depends on how you'd feel about teaming up with us."

"Teaming up?" I repeated back dumbly. "With you?"

"Yeah, you know, joining forces," Edwin said. "Combining armies, a partnership, Elves and Dwarves working together like we always thought was possible back when the world was still the world and we were playing chess in Chicago just for fun."

"Never!" Glam shouted. "We can't team up with them; they're the enemy!"

Several of the Elves glared at the imposing Dwarf with the immaculate mustache. Ari and Lake did their best to hold Glam back and calm her down.

"Don't forget we just saved your lives," Edwin reminded her. But his tone was graceful and not smug.

"You did," I confirmed. "And for that we definitely owe you. But teaming up? I mean, no offense, but beating you to the amulet is, um, well, sort of the whole reason we're here."

"It will be a rather complicated arrangement, no doubt about that," Edwin admitted. "However, circumstances have changed. We have a common enemy, one who must be stopped before we—or you—do anything else at all."

"The Verumque Genus?" I said.

Edwin nodded.

"My spies have sent word that they are gathering their armies outside St. Louis now, as we speak," Edwin revealed. "They plan to march toward Chicago soon, leaving a trail of death and destruction in their wake. They will take Chicago first, wiping out the Dwarven Council, then move on to the rest of the country. Eventually the world. Pretty much the only way to stop them is the amulet. With it, we could take away their ability to use magic, their control over their army of monsters. *Without* the amulet, well . . . the battle will be devastating, win or lose. But probably lose."

I nodded slowly.

Even Glam said nothing, seeming to understand the dire importance of making sure at least *someone* found the amulet and stopped the VG Elves.

"And you think we can find it faster working together?" I asked.

"Yes, well, these woods have proven far more dangerous than expected," Edwin said. "And I think we each have something to offer one another. And, well . . ." He stopped for a second, his eyes wide in revulsion and shock. "What in the world *is that*?!?!"

I spun around to see where he was pointing.

A huge ball of brackish brown-green goo rolled slowly into the clearing from the forest.

"Oh, that's just our friend Blob," I said.

"Hello," Blob said. "It's been a long time since I've seen Pointers."

The Elves flinched at Blob's use of a derogatory word.

"I mean, the last time I saw one was back in Houndwich, before I got trapped inside that boulder," Blob said. "Master and I were out on a contract job, raiding a supposed Elven fence to recover Lord Gifferoy's stolen scepter, when—"

"Not now, Blob," I interrupted. "We've got critical things to discuss here."

Amazingly, he stopped and rolled back a few feet, seeming to pick up on the gravity of our situation.

"He's cool," I said, turning to Edwin. "Sorry about the Pointer thing . . . He's, you know . . . a blob."

"He smells like a Troll's loincloth," the older Elf said.

"Hey . . ." Blob said, sounding hurt. "Well, *you* smell like a— like a—a . . . well, a very stinky thing, let me assure you!"

"He's sensitive," I explained to the Elf. "Anyway, Edwin, you were saying we could help each other?"

"Yeah," he said, still eyeing Blob curiously. "You see, we entered this forest with a squad of twelve of my most skilled and trusted Elven warriors. This is all that's left. The problem is we don't know exactly where to find the amulet. And so we've been wandering aimlessly for days, encountering more dangers, and losing more of our crew. I mean, first there was the Basilisk. It killed two of us. Then there was the Elemental and the pack of Nymphs. And then of course there was the Bigfoot thing—"

"*Bigfoot?*" I said.

"Yeah, I guess he's real," Edwin said with a shrug. "At least he used to be, back in Separate Earth. Anyway, he didn't actually harm us, but he did sneak into our camp and steal most of our provisions."

"Weird."

"Tell me about it," Edwin said. "Anyway, that's why I'm proposing we team up. You know where to find the amulet, I suspect. We've been tracking you, and you're definitely moving with purpose. And we can offer you greater protection from the dangers that await. You know you need it. And, to perfectly honest, we also could use yours. We *need* each other to survive this mission."

Edwin spread his arms out to remind me of the mess they'd just gotten us out of.

It was a solid point.

"Greg, you can't do this!" Glam pleaded. "They're lying! We can't trust them!"

I ignored her and stared into Edwin's intense sky-blue eyes.

"Stopping the Verumque Genus should be everyone's number one priority," I said, turning back to face my group. "And so I think he's right. We need to get the amulet as soon as possible, so we can get it to the States and help end the VG Elves' campaign of destruction before it gets started."

"But what happens when we find the amulet?" Ari asked. "Who gets it? As we all know, after stopping the Verumque Genus, both of our groups will have very different plans for it."

"That is certainly a conundrum," Edwin agreed. "But I figure we can cross that bridge when we get there."

"We'll play chess for it or something," I said, mostly kidding. "You know, the old let's-put-the-whole-fate-of-the-world-on-a-game bit? A classic."

Edwin knew I was kidding, but he still nodded.

"Maybe," he said with a grin.

"Okay, well, since Dwarves do not run an autocracy like Elves do, with Lords and rulers and all that," I said as Edwin rolled his eyes dramatically, "I will need to consult with my associates."

"Okay, do what you must," he said.

Ari, Lake, Glam, Froggy, Tiki, Blob and I huddled up about twenty feet away from the Elves.

"I think we have to accept," I said softly. "They did already save our lives once. Plus, if it comes to blows here and now, we're already hurt and tired and wouldn't stand a chance."

"Don't tell me I can't beat up a couple lousy Elves!" Glam said, her fists transforming into boulders at her sides.

"Greg has a point," Ari said, trying to calm her. "I mean, we stand a much better chance of finding the amulet in time to defeat the Verumque Genus if we work together. And they *did* already save us, like Greg said. What better show of good faith could they possibly make?"

"I agree," Froggy said, and left his argument at that.

"I suppose we really got no smidgen choice, then," Tiki agreed reluctantly.

We turned to look at Lake. His wild tangles of blond hair were even more frazzled than usual, with bits of leaves and dirt dotting the matted kinks like forest sprinkles. He frowned and finally nodded.

"Tis pursuant ye collective benefit," he finally said. "Thyne company alliance ye Elves, temporarily, in pursuit ye whereabouts of ye amulet."

"Plus," Blob added, even though nobody had asked him, "I really like the one called Edwin. Seems like a right good fellow, that one. I met an Elf like him once. Except it wasn't a *he*, and it wasn't an Elf. But it reminds me of this just the same. It was at a fair, I believe, St. Siggins Fair of Ulinore. Which is held every tenth month of the tenth equinox . . . or is it the seventh month of the seventh solstice . . . ?"

We all groaned and rolled our eyes and did our best to tune out the rambling blob.

"Okay, so we will accept?" I said. "The vote stands at five to one. Glam, will you be able to abide by the decision of the group?"

Her mustache, which had grown in substantially over the past few months, twitched as her fists returned to normal.

She scoffed and nodded.

"Of course I can," she said. "I'm not some kind of uncontrollable, violent monster. Geez, guys."

We grinned and walked back over to where the Elves were waiting.

"We're in," I said to Edwin.

"Great!" He grinned and slapped my arm. "Edwin and Greg: together again!"

I wanted to smile back, but a devastating reality wiped any trace of humor off my face.

"There's just one problem with all of this," I said somberly.

"What's that?" Edwin asked, frowning.

"I'm pretty sure our friend Stoney," I said, pointing at his severed arm on the ground nearby, "the only one of us who knew exactly where to find the amulet, is dead."

CHAPTER 26

———◆—————◆◆◆—————◆———

John the Riddler with Tiny Feet

Y our Rock Troll?" Edwin asked.

"No, he's not *my* anything," I said. "He's not . . . *wasn't* a pet."

"I didn't mean it that way . . ."

I sighed, fighting back tears. Though I'd only known Stoney for a short time, we'd gotten pretty close. It's funny how being the only person someone trusts—at least for a while—can have that effect.

"Just because he lost an arm doesn't mean he's dead," Lixi suggested.

"Let's look for the rest of this beast before we write him off," the older Elf suggested.

"He's not a beast!" Glam shouted, stomping toward him as Lake and Ari held her back.

"Watch what you say about my friends!" I snapped at the guy.

"Yeah, cool it, Rhistel," Edwin said, then turned and whispered to me: "Sorry, he's a holdover adviser from my dad's reign. Still a little rough around the edges."

"He's right, though, Greg," Ari said. "We shouldn't just write him off. I mean . . . he *could* still be alive."

But even as she said this, Ari eyed the severed arm warily.

"But where is he?" I demanded, not meaning to come across so harshly. "He would never abandon us like this. If he was alive, he would have been here fighting alongside us until the end!"

"Aye!" Lake agreed.

"He may be incapacitated," Froggy said. "Also, he *is* blind now . . ."

"Wait, wait, wait," Edwin said. "Your supposed navigator is *blind*?"

"Yeah, well . . ." I started, but then I realized I didn't really know how to explain how Stoney still knew where he'd been going, because I didn't really get that part myself. "It just works somehow," I finally finished with a shrug.

"Okay, well, either way, let's start looking for him!" Edwin commanded with natural authority. "We're wasting time—something we don't exactly have ample quantities of to waste."

Even though by now it was completely dark, we all agreed to team up to begin searching the area in spiraling concentric circles for any sign of Stoney. We tried to keep the Dwarves and the Elves separated, with the groupings as follows: Ari and Froggy; Lake, Glam, and Tiki; Edwin and Rhistel; Foxflame and Wrecking Ball; and finally me and Lixi. Everyone agreed we'd be the combination of Elf and Dwarf least likely to start fighting.

Blob's role was to patrol the perimeter and watch out for any signs of more Forest Trolls or other possible dangers while the group was split up.*

---

* Mainly just to give him something to do so he wouldn't follow us and distract us constantly with inane stories.

The plan was to search for one hour, then meet back up at the "butcher block" tree stump to check in (and hopefully report news of finding Stoney). We knew we'd need to get some sleep before morning, but at the moment finding our navigator superseded that concern.

As Lixi and I worked our way toward the creek and the mountain beyond, the sky eerily lit with blue moonlight, I kept my eyes on the ground, looking for any sign of my lost Rock Troll friend: other body parts, his thick gray blood, *anything*.

Almost immediately, once we'd departed from the group, Lixi looped her arm casually through mine. I was so surprised by the gesture, I almost flinched. But I managed to catch myself before making it awkward.

"It's so good to see you again," she said. "I never got to thank you for . . . well, for saving my life back on Alcatraz."

I nodded and waved my hand as if it were nothing.*

"You'd have done the same for me," I said. "Right? I mean . . . *right?*"

Lixi laughed her musical laugh—and until I heard it again, I hadn't realized just how much I'd missed it. For over a month in Edwin's prison, I'd heard that laugh several times a day.

"Of course," she said.

We walked in a comfortable silence for a few minutes. She didn't take her arm from mine, and I didn't mind.

"Do you think we'll eventually find the amulet?" I asked.

"I don't know," she said. "I hope so."

"An old Elven man back in Chumikan told me it didn't exist."

"Just because he said it doesn't mean it's true," she said, but I could hear doubt in her voice.

---

* Though in reality the decision to save her life almost cost the life of my other friend Eagan. But I'd do it the same way all over again if I had to.

"He was so *sure*."

Lixi didn't seem to know how to respond, and so she merely shrugged, finally pulling her arm away from mine. Then she suddenly and quickly unstrung her bow and armed it with an arrow.

I shot her a questioning look.

She nodded up ahead at the side of the mountain.

At first, in the darkness, it was hard to spot the small opening at the base of the rocky slope. I nodded back at her, and then realized I only had my dagger Blackout for a weapon. I'd lost my new sword in the battle and had no clue where it might be. But a magical dagger was certainly better than nothing.

I drew the blade, and we both crept forward toward the cave's entrance.

As we neared, I immediately noticed two small backpacks that had been torn open. Some of the contents were strewn about nearby: a few shirts, what looked to be empty Ziploc bags and Tupperware, eating utensils, and other random odds and ends.

"It's the supplies Bigfoot stole from us!" Lixi whispered.

"Oh, great, Bigfoot," I said. "Let's go get the others."

"No way," Lixi said. "Let's check this out."

"But the last time I investigated a cave, it ended in total disaster."

"Did it?"

"Yeah, I incited the Troll attack," I said. "Which resulted in three of our Sentry warriors dying, and probably also my friend Stoney . . ."

"But it brought us back together," Lixi countered with a grim smile. "Come on, we got this. Don't worry, I'm a much better fighter than you. This time will go better."

I knew she was kidding, but it did comfort me some. A bow and arrow in the hands of a fully trained Elf could be silent and deadly and way more effective than other weapons in a covert situation such as this.

I followed Lixi into the cave.

The moonlight illuminated the inside of it surprisingly well, the pale light reflecting off quartz-crystal walls. This cave had a smaller entrance than the Trolls' den and was also a lot neater and less macabre. Aside from the scattered Elven supplies, the only other objects immediately noticeable were some loose rocks and leaves. There definitely wasn't bloody armor and old bones and skulls littering the floor. And the place smelled piney and fresh, and not like rotting flesh, urine, and Troll farts.

Already, this was off to a much better start than the last time I'd invaded a cave.

But then I saw Stoney.

He lay motionless on a bed of pine boughs, his lone arm folded across his chest like he was in a coffin.

Like he was dead.

I took a step forward, not really wanting to find out if the worst was true.

Before I made it halfway to the makeshift pine bed, I was shoved to the side by something large and powerful. Lixi landed with a grunt on the cave floor next to me as a huge, hairy beast brushed past us.

The creature was at least seven feet tall, with shaggy brown-and-gray fur covering its entire body. It walked upright like a Human, but with a slight stoop. The form in front of us, standing between me and Stoney, was unmistakable: a Bigfoot, a Yeti, or whatever you wanted to call it, looking just like it did in all those suspiciously grainy YouTube videos of days past.

The beast roared at us.

I raised my knife, but Lixi put a hand on my arm.

"Just wait, Greg," she whispered. "He could have killed us both just now if he wanted. I actually think he's trying to . . . *protect* your friend."

I lowered Blackout slowly, making sure Bigfoot saw that I meant no harm.

He stared at us for several moments. Two surprisingly expressive eyes peered out from under a mass of stringy hair on his face. Then he grunted and turned around and put a hand gently on Stoney's chest. Bigfoot removed a primitive wood-and-leather flask from somewhere inside his fur and held it to Stoney's mouth.

"I think he's trying to help him," Lixi whispered.

I hoped desperately that she was right. Not because it would mean Bigfoot wasn't a threat (though that would also be nice to know), but more so because it would mean Stoney was still alive, even if seriously injured.

"My friend," I said to Bigfoot, gesturing toward Stoney. "*Friend.*"

I expected Bigfoot to respond with another primal grunt or growl. Or a cocked head. But instead Bigfoot turned, stood to his full height, and spoke in perfect English (or Plain Tongue as it's apparently called around here), in a voice so soft and gentle it was like he was coaxing a baby to sleep.

"Some friend, indeed," Bigfoot said. "He's missing an arm, has a broken rib, *and* a concussion, and all because *you* led those Forest Trolls right into your camp. You're lucky Rock Troll blood is too thick for him to bleed to death."

"Stoney came along of his own volition," I shot back. "I never forced him to lead this mission."

Bigfoot, who'd clearly been following us for some time, must have known this was true because he merely shrugged his massive, hairy shoulders.

"Is he going to be okay?" I asked.

Bigfoot glanced back at Stoney and then sighed.

"I think so," he finally said. "With some rest."

"Well, he can rest at our camp," I said. "We can take him from here."

"No, you won't," Bigfoot said. "He's staying right here."

"He's not some possession to be fought over!" Lixi argued.

"I know that," Bigfoot said, his voice remaining soft and calm and surprisingly soothing. "It's not even what I *want*, but it's what *he needs*. We can't risk moving him right now. He needs rest. I'm afraid he won't be going anywhere for at least a week or two. Unless you want to risk killing him?"

I shook my head slowly.

"But we don't have two weeks," Lixi said.

"Listen, uh, Bigfoot," I started. "We . . ."

"Bigfoot?" Bigfoot interrupted. "Who or what is a bigfoot?"

I suddenly remembered that we were in a magical forest realm that had been separated from our own modern world for millennia. Of course he wouldn't know what modern society called his mythological existence.

"It's, uh, well, what we call creatures like you where we're from," I explained.

Bigfoot (or Not Bigfoot) scoffed and shook his head.

"Why in the Pineshire's fire would they call me that?"

"Because of how huge your feet . . ." I stopped, because as I spoke, my eyes finally found his surprisingly tiny feet.

They were bizarrely small, relative to his size. In fact, this seven-foot-five humanoid gorilla had feet that were barely bigger than mine (and let me remind you that I'm pretty short, even for a thirteen-year-old).

Bigfoot/Not Bigfoot looked down at his feet and then laughed.

"These *are* big feet," he said. "For an Iluyaru."

"Iluyaru?" I said, not recognizing that word from any of our Monsterology texts or Dwarven stories or folklore.

"You've never heard of Iluyaru?" Lixi asked me. "We've been learning about them in Elven school since we were three!"

I shrugged sheepishly.

If Elves knew about a whole race of Separate Earth creatures that Dwarves didn't, then I couldn't help but wonder what knowledge we might possess in our old texts that wasn't in theirs. And if that were the case, how much more knowledge could everyone have if Elves and Dwarves stopped all this squabbling and finally put their heads together for the greater good?

"Well, anyway," the Iluyaru said. "My name in my native tongue is Johhangaggzorc Groggenzoggen. But you guys can just call me John."

"Um, okay," I said. "Nice to meet you, uh, John."

"I'm Lixi," Lixi said. "And this is Greggdroule."

"Yeah, I know," John said.

"So how long *have* you been tracking us?" I asked.

"Long enough to know you're never going to find what you're looking for."

How could John possibly know that? Then again, I admitted to myself, he lived in these woods. A forest that I hadn't even known existed at all until like three months ago. So he likely knew better than we did what we would or wouldn't find.

"Well," Lixi said, "then maybe you can *help us* find what we're looking for?"

"No, I can't," John said. "No one can. Because it doesn't exist."

That was now two locals who had said as much. It was certainly getting harder and harder to remain hopeful that our mission had any real chance at success. But we couldn't be on this long, treacherous, action-packed quest all for nothing, right? *Right?*

"Are you sure we're even referring to the same thing?" I asked him.

"The Faranlegt Amulet of Sahar?" John said drily. "Yup, I think so."

I sighed.

"Well, *dyffro*," Lixi said, using what I assumed was an Elven curse word to express how we both felt.

"Can you at least help us find the cave it's supposedly hidden in?" I asked. "So we can see for ourselves that it's not there?"

"Stoney was our navigator," Lixi added, motioning toward my unconscious friend. "We can't find it without him. And since you say he needs to stay here and rest, maybe you can help us. Since you seem to know so much about what is or isn't in this forest . . ."

John considered this for some time. He looked at Stoney and then at Lixi, and then back to me, then back to Stoney, and on and on like that for at least a few cycles.

"Okay." He finally nodded. "I'll help. But first you must do something for me."

An involuntary groan escaped from my lips.

Seriously? A side quest? How many more fantasy things was I going to have to do to complete this mission and save the world?

But it turned out that John didn't have a side quest for us. Instead, he unleashed an even bigger and lamer fantasy trope.

"I'll help you find the cave you seek," John said in a singsongy voice. "Though brave you be, it won't be free. First you must answer me these riddles three!"

CHAPTER 27

A Sublime Cup of Tea Threatens the Entire Mission

Y ou have got to be kidding me!" I nearly shouted. "A riddling Bigfoot? What's next, a magical sorting hat?"

"I am," John said calmly.

"Am what?"

"Kidding you."

A long silence followed as Lixi and I processed exactly what he was saying. Then we both offered weak, nervous laughs.

"I know, not that funny," John said. "*Of course* you don't need to answer any riddles. That'd be lame. I actually just need a few petals of pigeon thistle. I know the older Elven gentleman, Rhistel, has some in his pack. Bring four petals back to me. I need them to make more medicine to keep treating your friend. In exchange, I will tell you how to get to the cave you seek."

"Deal," I said. "That seems very fair, perhaps even generous."

"Yeah, well, don't thank me just yet," John said, scratching his hairy cheek. "I feel I must warn you again: The journey to this cave will be dangerous. And in the end, you *will not* find what you're looking for. The amulet is a myth."

⚊⚬⚊

Everyone was relieved Stoney was still alive.

Well, everyone except Rhistel.

"What do you mean, you need my pigeon thistle?" he snapped, clutching his satchel closer to his chest.

"Bigfoot, er, I mean, John says he needs it," I said. "To keep treating Stoney."

"So? He can go find his own."

I sighed. "If we bring him the pigeon thistle now, he'll tell us how to find the cave where the amulet is supposedly hidden."

"The amulet he says doesn't exist?" Rhistel sneered back. "How convenient."

"It is suspicious," Edwin chimed in. "And disheartening." I was about to protest, but then Edwin continued. "*However*, we must at least try. And this appears to be the fastest way to find out where we need to go. So just give him the flower petals, Rhistel."

It was odd to see my thirteen-year-old friend giving an order to a middle-aged man who was once the CEO of a massive company in the Human world. But Rhistel didn't argue. He made a big fuss of digging through his bag, but he did end up removing several bright purple-and-green flower petals and throwing them in my general direction.

I scooped them up (they were remarkably soft) and put them in my pocket.

"Why did you even bring those?" Edwin asked him.

"Pigeon thistle makes sublime tea," Rhistel said with his chest puffed out like a royal.

168

"All that fuss over tea?" Lixi scoffed.

"If you ever tried it, you'd have fought it, too," Rhistel said.

———✦———

Fifteen minutes later, we were back inside Bigfoot John's cave.

"The cave you're looking for is just another day's hike from here," he said, as he used two stones to mash the petals of pigeon thistle into a paste. "Maybe two. Follow the creek below deeper into the valley. Eventually, it will disappear as it flows into a crevice where the bases of Dryatos Peak and the Empty Mountain collide. Once there, you will find a boulder formation that looks like a two-headed turtle. The cave's entrance is behind them."

He finished making the pigeon thistle paste and began smearing it over Stoney's arm stump.

"Supposedly, anyway," John added as he worked. "Nobody has ever actually managed to set foot inside the cave."

"Why not?" I asked.

"You'll see."

We let his cryptic answer sink in for a moment.

"Wait a second," Lixi said. "If nobody has ever set foot inside this cave, then how do you know we won't find the amulet there?"

"Because," John explained, "the amulet is simply not real. Everyone knows the story about the Fairies using and hiding a powerful amulet is totally made up."

"Apparently not *everyone*," I muttered, remembering that at least half the Dwarven Council had believed the story to be true.

"Either way, I must admit I do not know exactly what you will find inside the cave," John said, turning back to face us, his eyes dark with fear and sadness. "But knowing these woods, whatever it is will surely be horrible and dangerous."

CHAPTER 28

❖

The Rain and Blob Show

ey, my sword!"
I rushed over toward what looked like a *Ficus benjamina* tree at the edge of the clearing. It was the next morning. After sleeping a few hours, we'd risen with the sun and begun preparing for our journey into the valley formed by the large creek. As the Elves packed up their tents, the Dwarves scrounged the forest, looking for the rest of our weapons and supplies that had been scattered in the Troll attack.

That's when I spotted my sword tangled up in the tree's exposed roots.

I grasped the handle and pulled it free.

"I found my sword!" I said, holding it up as I rejoined the others.

Five shocked gasps erupted from the group. Specifically, from Edwin, Lixi, Foxflame, Wrecking Ball, and Rhistel.

"What is it?" Ari asked, drawing her ax, looking around for whatever had startled the Elves.

"It's . . . it's the Sword of Anduril," Edwin said, gawking at the weapon in my hand.

"The *what?*" Glam asked, confirming that I wasn't the only one who had no idea what Edwin was talking about.

"The Sword of Anduril," Foxflame said. "Also known as the Oathbreaker, the Jaws of the Sun, the Willsmasher, the Bringer of the Prince, the Gutrender, and the Pledge of Suffering's End."

"Okay, so?" Glam sneered. "Other than having a thousand names, what makes this sword so special?"

"Well, for one, we all thought it was a myth," Foxflame said, his awed gaze still fixed on the sword. "A legend our elders told us for pure entertainment."

"I can't believe it's actually real," Lixi whispered, transfixed by the old, perfectly ordinary-looking sword with a makeshift hilt clutched awkwardly in my hand.

"It's supposedly one of the most powerful Elven swords ever crafted," Edwin said, clearly seeing that we still weren't getting how or why this sword was special. "At least, according to the old legend."

"It was once owned by Elf Lord Tarron Valrynn, the seventeenth Ordained Elf Lord," Foxflame added. "So I'm sure that tells you how old it is."

Though I didn't know much about the history and succession of Elf Lords, especially going back to Separate Earth, the fact that Elf Lord Valrynn had been just the seventeenth Elf Lord *ever* did indicate, in a very basic way, that this sword was exceptionally ancient. (If it was in fact the same sword—I still wasn't at all convinced.) If it *was* the same sword, then it was possibly even older than the Bloodletter.

"In the right hands, the sword is peerless," Foxflame continued. "Indestructible and devastating in battle. It also supposedly possesses a magical prowess unparalleled by any other weapon ever made, Elven, Dwarven, Orcish, Human, or of any other origin. The Sword of Anduril is said to have been forged by Agis Balynore, a renowned Elven blacksmith who was frequently contracted to make weapons and other objects for the ancient god Bitrix, the Lord and Keeper of Death. Anyway, after Bitrix became bored with our planet, and moved on to others in the universe, she gifted the sword to Elf Lord Valrynn. For many years, the powerful weapon helped Lord Valrynn rule the United Elven Kingdoms, restore order, and keep the peace. But it was stolen one night after a particularly raucous royal party. Stolen by a *Human* knight, of all things, named Sir Neel the Jackal. After that, all record of it is lost. Neither the sword nor Sir Neel were ever seen or heard from again."

"Master!" Blob shouted, so excitedly that an air bubble in his blobby goo popped, releasing a particularly pungent waft of his horrible odor.

We all covered our noses.

"Your master was Sir Neel the Jackal?" Ari asked through her sleeve.

"Yes!" Blob said. "Well, I mean, he changed his name, of course, to avoid capture. Stealing *anything* from an Elf Lord is punishable by death, you know. But stealing his prized sword would have been punishable by a long, torturous death, spanning several agonizing decades. So when he found me, he was no longer Sir Neel the Jackal, but instead went by the name Nobleman Rainaldus the Honest. But I just called him Rain. Yeah, Rain and Blob, we were a real pair, we were."

The fact that we'd found Blob with this sword certainly lent some credence to the Elves' story. That is, if we could believe

Blob. But so far, he'd given me no reason not to trust the many, many, many, many (etc.) things he said.

I examined the sword again, expecting to see it differently now that it had some context. But to me it still just looked like an old sword, despite being remarkably well preserved (especially if it was as old as they said it was).

"What happened to Rain?" Ari asked.

"Master Rain?" Blob replied slowly and sadly. "I must confess I do not know. He cut a hole in the stone and told me to go inside to see what I could find. I, being a dutiful friend and servant, happily obliged. The next thing I knew, the entrance was sealed, and I was stuck inside the stone for many, many years. Until you lot came along and finally let me out again."

The clearing fell silent as the Elves ogled my new sword like they were watching a star go supernova or something.

"It just looks like a regular sword to me," I said. "How can you be so sure this is the Sword of Anduril? It doesn't even have any markings or anything."

"What do you mean, it 'looks like a regular sword'?" Edwin asked, clearly stunned by my comment. "Do you not see that?"

If anything, his awe only made the sword look even more unremarkable.

"See *what*?"

"The blade," Lixi said softly.

"The way it shimmers and sparkles like liquid diamonds," Foxflame continued.

"Like purple gemstones in the sun," Wrecking Ball added.

"It's the most beautiful and magical-looking weapon I've ever seen," Edwin said. "You really don't see that?"

I looked again at the cold, unpolished steel of the blade.

"Nope," I said, then turned to my Dwarven companions. "Do you guys see any of this?"

They all shook their heads, clearly as confused as I was.

I shrugged finally and sheathed the sword, breaking the bizarre spell it had cast over our Elven companions. They were still looking at the hilt sticking up from the scabbard, but they now looked more envious than transfixed.

The nice thing to do would have been to offer them this supposedly magical sword in exchange for a different weapon, since it clearly had so much value to them. But at the same time, it made more sense for me to hang on to it for now. As a sort of bargaining chip I could maybe use later, once we found the amulet.

I'm sure Edwin understood this logic, because he finally looked up from the sword and nodded at me.

"Okay, then," he said. "Let's get going—let's go find the amulet."

CHAPTER 29

◆—➤❂◀—◆

Glam, Ari, Tiki, and I
Bury Ourselves in Sand

W ell, it does look a lot like a two-headed turtle," Edwin said. "I'll give Bigfoot that much credit."

We were all standing at the end of the ravine, where the creek flowed into the crevice where Dryatos Peak and the Empty Mountain seemed to converge. And just as Bigfoot John had described, where the water drained into the rock wall towering above, there was a formation of boulders that looked remarkably like a massive turtle with two heads.*

"I told you he wasn't lying," I said.

"Just because this is here doesn't mean Bigfoot wasn't lying about what's behind it," Edwin replied.

"Well, I almost hope he *was* lying!" I countered. "Since he

---

* I should mention here that the day and a half of hiking to get there had not been uneventful or easy. In fact, we'd had to battle past a Hulking Gragglebrax and several swarms of Lacridous Whettle Wasps. But those are stories for another time, perhaps.

pretty clearly stated we would not only *not* find the amulet, but also that perilous dangers lie past these boulders."

Edwin considered this for a moment and then finally said, "Touché."

"But John also said," Ari added, "that nobody has ever managed to make it into the cave itself."

We nodded thoughtfully.

Bigfoot John had been pretty cryptic about that part, refusing to expound on what he meant. Which was weird. It certainly looked like moving these boulders would be as simple as casting a basic Dwarven spell or two.

"Stand aside," Glam said, shoving her way to the front of the group. "I think I got this."

Everyone gathered around her as she stepped closer to the massive turtle-shaped boulder formation. She closed her eyes and raised a hand, summoning a spell to move the boulders. But instead of the large rocks being blown aside by magical winds or shoved out of the way by enchanted vines from the earth, or even disintegrating into piles of gravel, they shifted and rumbled as if coming to life.

Which, we found out seconds later, was precisely what was happening.

The huge boulder that made up the turtle's left head rose like it was waking from a nap. A mouth suddenly formed in the rock. It opened wide and lunged at Glam. She dove out of the way, narrowly avoiding getting snapped in half by the powerful stone jaws of the rock turtle.

The right head came to life as well. It also snapped at Glam as she rolled away. And it would have gotten her if Foxflame hadn't swooped in with grace and balance and pulled her out of the way.

The turtle's boulder heads dipped and bobbed, and its boulder legs shook, but its body did not move from its spot, anchored in front of the supposed cave entrance.

"I guess this is what John was referring to when he said nobody has ever gotten past the boulders," I said, as Glam and Foxflame scampered back toward the group.

"If we can get past Forest Trolls and a Gragglebrax and Whettle Wasps, then I think we can take out a stationary two-headed rock turtle without much trouble," Edwin said.

I doubted this would be that easy. Because why would it be? But I hoped he was right.

"Okay, then," I said. "Do your thing."

Edwin nodded at Wrecking Ball and Rhistel (the only other Elves with the Ability to perform magic). They approached the two-headed rock turtle, Edwin with his sword drawn, Wrecking Ball with a glowing fist raised, charged with Elven magic, and Rhistel with his staff, the medallion on the end ablaze with purple-and-red fire.

Then they launched their attack.

Streams, jets, bursts, and orbs of glowing Elven magic fired at the rock turtle from Wrecking Ball's hand, Edwin's sword, and Rhistel's staff. It was like a fireworks display up close. Elven energy erupted across the necks and heads of the boulder turtle.

The creature lurched but did not move.

The energy dissipated and steam drifted up from an entirely unharmed and intact boulder turtle.

The twin heads opened their mouths at the same time, and an ear-piercing shriek dropped us to our knees. The wailing screech was so intense it felt like someone was trying to push my head apart from the inside, like it was an exploding watermelon.

We writhed in pain as the turtle shrieked. Even Blob sloshed about, feeling every bit as much displeasure as the rest of us. After an agonizing ten seconds, the noise finally faded. The twin turtle heads bobbed up and down as if to taunt us, or maybe even to warn us not to make it do that again.

"Egads!" Blob cried out. "It felt like I was melting! What *was* that?"

Edwin raised his sword as if to launch another attack, but Ari put her hand on his arm.

"Don't!" she said. "Your magic clearly won't have any effect on this thing."

Edwin hesitated, but then nodded and lowered his weapon.

"What do we do?" Lixi asked.

"How can we get past this jonky murm of a thing?" Tiki added.

Nobody had an answer.

This couldn't be it. This couldn't be how our quest ended, could it? Stopped by a stationary two-headed turtle made from rocks? Then again, the turtle, however enchanted it might be, was clearly still made of stone, a natural element of the earth that Dwarven magic should theoretically be able to manipulate.

"Let's try Dwarven magic again," I suggested. "From a safer distance than Glam tried."

"Together, all four of us," Ari agreed.

And so Glam, Ari, Tiki, and I faced the turtle, well out of range of its snapping boulder heads.

"What are we going for?" I asked. "Uprooting the rocks? Turning them into gravel? Summoning a mini-earthquake?"

"I agree we should all focus on the same sort of spell," Ari said.

"Let's pulverize them into sand," Glam said, punching her fist into her palm.

"That *should* work," I said. "After all, sand is just a huge boulder that has been finely divided again and again by the elements and weathering and stuff, down to tiny mineral particles. So Dwarven magic should have no problem speeding that up, right?"

Ari nodded slowly.

"Sounds right to me," Tiki said. "Let's give it a plorping shot."

"Okay, so on the count of three, we all give everything we've got to reducing this turtle to piles of sand," I said. "One . . . two . . . three!"

On three, I put every ounce of my magical will into dissolving this turtle-shaped pile of boulders into a formless mound of sand. I thought about all the fine sand along the sixteen miles of the Lake Michigan beaches in Chicago. I thought about the feeling of the tiny grains under my bare feet and the processes by which rock and stone eroded. I thought about the destruction of rocks and stone and just how much sand had developed over time on this planet.

And then I opened my eyes, almost expecting to see piles of gray and brown sand in front of me. But I knew better. We were Dwarves after all. Success didn't come that easily to us.

What I actually saw was the turtle opening both of its mouths, its heads steadying in front of us.

I winced, anticipating more of that terrible shrieking.

But this time the turtle did not make a sound. Instead it began barfing up streams of sand all over us.

At first, I wanted to laugh, thinking our spells had worked after all. But then I quickly realized the turtles were mocking us. They spewed out so much sand that I was already buried up to my waist and could no longer move my legs after just a few seconds. Even as my brain processed this, the sand reached my chest, pinning my arms to my sides, crushing the breath right out of me.

Glam, Tiki, and Ari were shouting as we struggled against the fountains of sand.

The last thing I saw before the sand engulfed me whole was Ari's desperate face as sand covered it up and buried her alive.

Then I was being crushed by darkness, unable to breathe or see.

But at least I would die like a Dwarf, having my own spell backfire while fighting a magical two-headed turtle.

What more could I have hoped for?

CHAPTER 30

Riddle Me This (For Real This Time)

I should have known better.

Of course our friends weren't going to let us die in a pile of sand. I might have been a spectacularly epic failure, but that didn't mean everyone else was. After just a few seconds, hands grabbed my hair and pulled. I would have screamed but opening my mouth would have meant swallowing more sand, and so I merely winced as the hands let go and then eventually found my armpits.

Moments later, I was being pulled from the sandpile, even as I summoned a wind spell to help disperse it.

Ari, Glam, Tiki, and I choked and wheezed as we rolled down the huge mound of sand piled in front of the very much intact boulder turtle.

There'd now be sand stuck in my underwear forever, it seemed, but at least I was still alive. I shook as much sand free from my hair and clothes as I could, spitting grainy, muddy bits of rock onto the ground. Someone handed me a flagon of water, and I drank greedily, trying to clear my mouth and throat. Glam, Tiki, and Ari did the same.

The turtle resumed bobbing its heads up and down, as if dancing to a beat. Once again, I got the distinct impression it was a warning to stop trying to physically move it. It was almost as if the turtle didn't actually *want* to harm us, but it would do whatever it had to in order to protect what lay behind it.

"Now what?" I finally managed to ask.

"We could try other spells?" Ari suggested.

"No, no way," Edwin said. "I think it should be obvious by now that magic is not going to help us get past this thing."

"There has to be a way past it somehow, though, right?" Lixi said.

"Not if whatever is behind it was never intended to be found," Froggy said ominously.

This was something none of us had considered yet, and it cast the whole group into a defeated silence as the turtle loomed above us, still bobbing its heads. Now seemingly as if to say: *Yeah, kid, you got it. That's exactly what's happening. You will never get past us!*

"So that's it, then?" Tiki said after a healthy silence. "We're just giving up like a bunch of purbogging plorbies?"

"Hey, I'm not a plorby, you Gwinty refuse bag!" Rhistel shot back.

Tiki and Glam stood up as if to take the insult to blows. Rhistel reached for his staff, but Edwin quickly stepped between them.

"Guys, stop this!" he commanded, and both sides immediately fell silent. "Arguing among ourselves won't solve *anything!*"

"He's right," Foxflame added. "We need to work together to find a solution—"

"Hey!" Ari suddenly shouted in a panic. "Where's Lake?"

We all looked around, realizing that her twin brother was nowhere in sight. My first thought was that perhaps he'd been inadvertently buried in the massive sandpile. I clearly wasn't alone, as we all turned toward it in a panic. But then Froggy stepped forward and pointed up at the rocky slope to the left of the boulder turtle.

"There he is."

Lake was steadily climbing up the slope toward the back end of the largest boulder, the one that formed the turtle's "shell." It was a huge, slightly flattened, oval stone about the size of two school buses parked side by side. It probably wouldn't have looked much like a turtle shell, aside from sharing the same general shape, were it not for the dozen or so other boulders attached to it, that made up the turtle's tail, four limbs, two necks, and two heads.

"Lake, what are you doing?" Ari shouted.

Lake, still clutching at some rocks on the steep slope, merely glanced back at us with a grin. Then he went back to work, shimmying his way across the cliff face, toward the turtle's shell. Once he was positioned nearly above it, we all realized what he was going to do.

"Lake, don't!" Ari yelled.

But Lake jumped anyway.

And he wouldn't have made it, were it not for me casting a quick spell that sent a burst of wind whipping behind the turtle and funneling up between it and the side of the mountain. The gust of wind caught Lake just as he was falling and lifted him onto the back of the boulder turtle.

He still landed pretty hard and went sprawling across the boulder, tumbling nearly off the other side. But he managed to find a few handholds and stayed on top of the shell.

Lake gingerly climbed to his feet and grinned down at us from behind the turtle's twin heads, which, though the mouths were opening and closing, didn't ultimately seem too concerned with his presence on their shared back.

"What are you doing up there?" Ari demanded.

"Whence sand spewed forth betwixt ye turtle's mouths," Lake yelled back down, "thyne peepers beseeched nary emblems marking solution. What hath doth presented itself but glimpses ye carvings in ye shell!"

"What the heck did he just say?" Edwin asked.

"When the turtle was shooting sand at us," Ari translated, "he thought he saw some carvings on the turtle's shell."

We waited as Lake crawled around on top of the boulder and out of sight.

"Well?" Lixi finally yelled up after a few minutes. "Are there markings?"

"Aye!" Lake yelled back down. "Thee be'est ruination symbolic of ye ancient tongue."

"Can you read it?" Glam shouted up.

"Aye!"

"I can't believe his obsession with ancient languages might actually be anything other than annoying for once," his sister said with a hopeful grin.

We all waited silently for Lake to read the ancient inscriptions. It felt like nobody was even breathing for the better part of several minutes.

Then, finally, Lake's smiling face appeared above us, and he sat down on the edge of the turtle shell just to the right of the heads, which were still bobbing slightly, but much slower than before.

"So what does it say?" I asked.

"An ancient riddle!" he shouted, holding up a piece of parchment that he'd apparently used to transcribe the translation.

I sighed.

I had thought perhaps we'd actually be able to make it through this quest without having to answer some lame riddle. But at the same time, I was extremely grateful and encouraged that we might have found a solution that didn't involve futilely battling a stone turtle until the end of time.

"Well, okay, then!" Edwin said with a grin. "Let's hear it!"

Lake cleared his throat and began reading:

"'You, dear traveler, of noble spirit and soul, are on a quest. Your journey is nearly over, and from this point forward, there can be no going back. You have arrived at a fork in the road, and the goal you seek lies at the end of one of these two paths. Down the other, a fate even worse than death awaits. At this crossroads sits a mystical turtle god. It is known that there are two turtle gods who rule this realm. One, Abraxis, is evil; he *always* lies and always means you harm. The other, Sixarba, is good, means you well, and *always* speaks the truth. However, these turtle gods are twins and cannot be told apart. Therefore, you have no way of knowing which one sits before you. But legend says the turtle god is permitted to answer one solitary question from a traveler such as yourself. One lone question can lead you to either your goal . . . or endless pain. What question do you ask this turtle?'"

A few seconds of silence allowed his words to sink in (and also the fact that this was the first time I'd ever heard him speak "normally," which was likely due to the direct translation of the riddle).

"What the heck?" Glam yelled.

"Yeah!" Tiki added. "This is bloggurgin stupid!"

"But it's clearly our only way past this thing," Edwin said.

"And also symbolic," Foxflame said.

We all turned toward him.

"I suspect," he elaborated, "that this is more than a simple riddle. I suspect that the fate of the traveler in the riddle will match our own. If we ask the correct question to solve the riddle, then we will be shown to the path we seek. If we ask the wrong question . . . well . . . you heard where the other path leads . . . ."

As he spoke, the boulder-turtle heads nodded again, much faster than they had before, as if confirming this was true.

We all considered Foxflame's words. We had no reason to believe his theory wasn't true. All the symbolism matched up. The bobbing of the two turtle heads only cemented this in our minds.

Which meant we were now literally trying to solve a riddle to save our lives.

CHAPTER 31

Is It *the* Red Sea or *a* Red Sea?

So what's the answer?" Glam asked, breaking the somber silence. "Come on, Greg, you and your friend are the smart ones. What do we need to ask this stupid turtle?"

I shook my head, at a total loss.

"It's tricky . . ." Edwin said, thinking aloud. "The turtle could either be Abraxis, in which case anything he says will be a lie. Or it could be Sixarba, which would mean the answer is the truth. But how will we know which one we are talking to?"

"We could simply ask which turtle it is," Wrecking Ball suggested.

"No, because we still wouldn't know if it's telling the truth or not," Edwin countered. "If it's Abraxis, it will say it's Sixarba since it always lies. And if it is Sixarba, it will say Sixarba since it always tells the truth. So, either way, it's going to answer Sixarba. But we still wouldn't know which turtle it really is, and also we wouldn't know what path to take, which is what we're really trying to find out."

We all fell silent again as we brainstormed.

"What about if we ask it something we already know the answer to," Ari eventually suggested. "Like, we could ask it: Are you a turtle? Then if it says yes, we know it's Sixarba. If it says no, we know it's Abraxis."

There were several people nodding in agreement, but Edwin shook his head vigorously.

"No, that still doesn't help," he said. "Knowing which turtle it is still won't tell us which way to go. And remember: we only get to ask it *one* question."

"Well, dang," Ari said.

After another short silence, Lixi jumped to her feet.

"I think I got it!" she said. "We could ask it: Am I going to die if I take the left path?"

"Okay . . ." Edwin said, as he worked it out in his head.

"Think about it," Lixi explained. "If the left path is the good way, and the turtle is Abraxis, he's going to lie and say yes. But if it's Sixarba, he'll tell the truth and say no. So if it's the bad path, Abraxis will say no, and Sixarba will say yes . . ."

But even as she spoke, we could see that saying it aloud was helping her see the fundamental flaw in the question: it was a way to get a different answer, sure, but it still wouldn't tell us which way was *correct*, because we still wouldn't know which turtle we were speaking to. So that question would only work if we knew which turtle god it was to begin with. Nobody even needed to explain this to Lixi. She trailed off, realizing it on her own.

"Oh," she said, her head dropping. "Oh, yeah, okay, I see now why that still doesn't work."

We all went back to our own thoughts.

At some point, I stopped thinking about the riddle itself, and started thinking about my dad. He was always very good at riddles. I remembered this one time when I was seven or eight, and we went to this old diner called Cozy Corner. They had place mats with puzzles and mazes and riddles on them. That day there was this riddle:

If you throw a white stone into a red sea, what will happen to it?

I could tell from my dad's wry grin that he knew the answer right away. But he stayed quiet and let me work on the question for a while. After three or four incorrect guesses, in which I tried to figure out if they meant the actual Red Sea or just a sea that was red, and what type of white rock we were dealing with, I finally gave up.

"So what's the answer, Dad?"

"The rock will get wet," he said.

I scoffed at such a stupidly simple solution. It *had* to be cleverer than that, right? But then I checked the answer key on the back of the place mat, and sure enough there it was: *It will get wet!*

It almost seemed like the exclamation point in the answer key was its own way of laughing at itself. And at you, for not being able to figure out a question so simple that it was actually stupid.

"Riddles have a very basic mechanism for fooling people," my dad explained as he shoveled a gargantuan twelve-egg bacon-and-sausage omelet into his mouth in massive bites. "They trick you into overthinking the problem or question. The answer is usually so simple and direct that most people overlook it right away. The riddle outsmarts people by allowing people to outsmart the riddle. Solving a riddle is like solving most of any of life's problems. You just need to find the simplest, most direct way to answer the question."

My dad applied that logic to almost everything in life, not just solving lame riddles. When the air conditioner broke one summer, we just wore fewer clothes around the house (and we were fine). When our car got a flat tire once, and we couldn't afford a new one, we simply sold it and rode the bus more often. When he set dinner on fire, we just ate around the burned parts. When trying to figure out what lamp to buy for our living room, he chose the one that required no assembly.

So what's the most direct way to the solution, keeping in mind that it might even be to ignore the problem altogether?

In this case, all we needed to know was which way to go. Which path was right, and which path was wrong. So the most direct, simple question would be . . . No. No way could that be correct. It was, after all, so easy.

So simple.

"I think I got it," I said suddenly.

The whole group looked at me.

"We ask the turtle: *Which way should I go?*"

"Pfft, come on!" Rhistel said. "It's got to have a cleverer answer than that!"

"Yeah, doesn't that end up with the same problem, where we would get two different answers?" Ari said. "If left is correct, Abraxis will say right. And Sixarba would say left. And so we still wouldn't know which—"

"No, Greg's right!" Edwin interrupted quickly, speaking fast like he always did when he was excited. "Or at least he's *very* close. We just need to alter his question slightly, since we're forgetting about a key detail: one is evil, and one is good. That detail is in there for a reason. So what we really need to ask is: *Which way do you WANT me to go?*"

"That's a pretty purboggingly small difference," Tiki said.

"But it will make all the difference in the answer," Edwin said, pausing so we could all figure it out on our own.

And he was right; that subtle change fixed everything.

Asking which way the turtle *wanted* you to go factored in both that they always lied or told the truth, *and* their good or evil intentions. For instance, let's say the left path was the good path. If the turtle was Abraxis, he would want you to go right so you would die, but since he always lied, he would say to go left. If the turtle was Sixarba, he would want you to go left so you would succeed, and since he always told the truth, he would say to go left. So either way, you would be told the correct way to go. You'd get the same answer, the correct answer, even without ever finding out which turtle god was in front of you.

Once it was clear that each of us had figured this out, we huddled up in front of the sandpile.

Lake climbed down to join us.

"We're all in agreement, then?" Edwin confirmed. "Because if Foxflame is correct about this riddle being symbolic of our actual fates, and this answer is wrong, then it means certain death for all of us."

One by one, we all nodded, including Blob, whose version of a nod was to mold himself a sort of head protruding from his mass and wag it up and down.

"Okay, then," Edwin said. "Who wants to do the honors?"

"You should, since you figured it out," Ari said.

Edwin shook his head.

"Not without Greg's original question, I wouldn't have," he said.

"Let's do it together, then," I suggested. "Me and you."

Edwin nodded.

We broke our huddle, and Edwin and I both stepped forward in front of the boulder turtle.

"We have the answer to your riddle," I shouted up at the turtle's heads, which slowly turned so that it seemed like they were looking at us. "We would ask the turtle at the fork in the road . . ." I stopped, pausing so Edwin could join me. *"Which way do you want me to go?"*

Almost immediately, the turtle's heads dove toward us, mouths wide open. The right head went for Edwin and the left for me.

We were too stunned to react, and they swallowed us whole.

CHAPTER 32

——— ✦※✦ ———

The Moment You Find Out I Won't Die, at Least Not Until the Very End (Though I Hope You Already Knew That)

O kay, so, clearly you know I didn't die.

How else would I be telling you all this, and how would you still be reading? After enough false deaths to fill three books, I'd hope you'd have learned by now that I somehow ended up surviving at least most of this whole ordeal.

I did, in fact, survive being eaten alive by the huge rock turtle. And so did Edwin.

For one thing, the turtle's heads did not have teeth. Secondly, they did not clamp down with the intent to crush us, but instead scooped us up and tilted back so we tumbled down a pair of parallel tunnels in the stone, which I suppose were like their esophagus.

Unlike when the Kraken swallowed me whole, I did not end up in the belly of a beast. This time I slid down a narrow tunnel of stone and into a dank cavern lit by glowing green crystals embedded in the walls. I could only assume, as Edwin plopped down next to me, from his own neck chute, that we were now inside the boulder that comprised the turtle's "shell." The ceiling was domed, and there was an open doorway at the far end, where the turtle's tail connected to the mountainside.

Beyond it: the unknown darkness of more caves and tunnels.

"Dude, I think we got it right," Edwin said, helping me to my feet.

"Yeah, we really beat that turtle by a *hare*," I said.

Edwin actually guffawed at my unexpected and terrible pun.

"Yeah, yeah," he said, still laughing. "I'm shell-shocked we survived. We should really have a *shell*ebration!"

I laughed, and then we both quickly fell silent a moment later.

"They're all going to think we just got eaten and are now dead," Edwin said.

"Maybe not?" I suggested.

But in the brief silence that followed, we could actually hear our friends outside. Their voices were faint, as if halfway across the world instead of ten feet away, but they were screaming and wailing at the loss of their friends and supposed "leaders." It was pretty awful to listen to.

"We have to let them know we're okay," Edwin said. "If we can hear them, then surely they could hear us?"

I nodded, and we both began shouting and screaming, trying to let them know we were okay. But after yelling for several minutes, until our throats were sore, I stopped him.

"Wait, if all they hear is us screaming, they're probably assuming we're getting, like, slowly and painfully digested or something?"

"Oh, yeah, good point," Edwin said with a grim smile. "What do you suggest, then?"

I quickly pulled Blackout from my belt and cut off a small chunk of my shirt.

"Got anything in there to write with?" I asked, nodding at Edwin's satchel.

"No . . ." he said, quickly plucking my knife from my hand. "But there's always this."

He made a shallow cut on his arm.

"Dude!" I gasped.

"Pretty gross, but blood is the oldest form of ink," he said.

"Is that really true?"

Edwin shrugged.

"I don't know, probably," he said. "It sounds true. Now come on, hurry up. Elven flesh wounds clot and heal very quickly."

"Is *that* true?" I asked, pretty shocked that nobody had told me that before.

"Yeah, man," he said. "You got the strong bones, but we got the strong fleshy parts. Now what do you want me to write?"

He took the cloth from me and placed it against the wall. Then he ran a finger along his cut.

"'We're okay,'" I said. "'Give the turtle the same answer.'"

Edwin quickly scrawled the message in blood with his finger on the scrap of my shirt. When he was done, he handed it back to me.

"So how did you plan to get it to them?"

"The same way we'll be doing lots of things going forward," I said. *"Magic."*

I threw the chunk of cloth up toward the left turtle neck tunnel and then summoned a wind spell. A gust of fresh mountain air blasted down through the right tunnel and then swooped up the cloth, carrying it deep into the left tunnel and (hopefully) out through the rock turtle's mouth.

"Neat," Edwin said.

I nodded.

And then we waited.

I could only imagine the turtle's head gagging and spitting up a bloody piece of my shirt. Only imagine my friends at first thinking this confirmed the turtle had indeed devoured me and was now just burping up the leftovers. Only imagine the moment Glam grabbed it and clutched it to her face, finally seeing Edwin's writing. Only imagine half of them getting excited and the other half nervously certain this was some sort of trick. Only imagine the debate that ensued. Only imagine the first of them to throw up their hands and step forward and recite the same riddle answer that we had. And I could only imagine that person would be Ari.

Several long, agonizing minutes went by as I imagined all these things.

"Do you think it even made it out?" Edwin finally asked. "Maybe we should just press on alone?"

"A few more minutes," I said.

Edwin nodded.

As if on cue, several seconds later, we heard a girl screaming. It got louder and then Ari flew from the left tunnel and landed softly on her feet between us. She grinned at me and pushed us out of the way as two more howls echoed down the tunnels. Glam and Lixi both emerged and landed on the ground moments later.

One by one, our companions arrived, sliding down the chute after being swallowed by the massive turtle's heads outside. The last one down was Rhistel. Based on his expression, as he landed on the ground, I figured he was not the sort of person that enjoyed carnival rides.

"What about Blob?" I asked, once Rhistel confirmed he was the last.

"He wanted to stay out there," Glam said. "Made up some story about patrolling the perimeter or something."

"Well, I gotta say," Edwin said, "I'm sort of relieved. Can you guys even imagine what he'd smell like inside a confined space like this?"

We all laughed uncomfortably, then turned to face the passageway opposite the neck tunnels. It was roughly carved into an uneven oval. Beyond the opening, a few feet of tunnel could be seen by the glowing light from the green crystals embedded in the walls. After that, it was pitch-black.

"Between you and me, Greg," Ari whispered as she stood beside me, "I think Blob was scared. Being trapped alone inside of a rock for so long definitely had some sort of psychological effect on him."

I nodded, realizing she was probably right. Blob didn't seem like the sort to be afraid of much. But it was hard to argue that he might think twice about being coaxed into a confined space in a rock again.

"Well," Edwin said as we all stood at the entrance of the unknown caverns within the mountains, "I suppose I can lead the way this time."

He drew his sword, and the blade ignited with magical blue fire, like it had when we fought on Navy Pier. Even though that had only been roughly six months ago, it felt like years with everything else that had happened.

Edwin held up his makeshift torch and stepped into the tunnel.

CHAPTER 33

※※

We Find Out Our Existence Is Insignificant and Meaningless and Nothing Really Matters Anyway

I bet you expect we encountered a maze—a labyrinth of impossible tunnels straight from an M. C. Escher drawing, complex and impossible to navigate.

Or perhaps a long-dormant dragon, sleeping in his chambers.

Or maybe a booby-trapped floor, into which one of the lesser-known people from our group, like perhaps Wrecking Ball, falls to his death.

Or maybe a mutated Gollum-like creature with glowing eyes and shiny, slick gray skin and sharp teeth covered in rotting flesh.

Well, sorry to disappoint, but this time there was no maze. No monsters. No booby traps.

The tunnel extended several hundred feet straight ahead, along an uneven but surprisingly accommodating floor. Edwin's flaming sword lit up the whole thing, what with the highly reflective green crystals in the walls. Eventually, the tunnel led to a huge cavern filled with stuff, such as: a treasure trove of, well, treasure (including gold coins, gems, jewelry, and more), old books, scrolls, weapons, pottery, cups, chalices, crowns, scepters, chairs, tables, couches, and almost anything else you could imagine.

The cavern was the size of a massive sports stadium, and it was literally piled, nearly wall to wall, with *stuff*. Some of the stacks of books were thirty feet high or more. Other piles (like one particular mound of old bronze coins near the back) towered even higher than that, so high that the light cast from all the burning torches on the walls didn't even reach the top of it.

But the cavern was large enough that plenty of it was not covered in stuff. There were walkways and rows and spaces among all the junk, almost as if it were some sort of library or antique store (and not just a storage facility), where people could walk around and browse at will.

It almost looked like one of the huge flea markets my dad used to take me to as a kid, the ones that took place inside college football domes, or on commercial parking lots. Except, unlike those, where hundreds or thousands of shoppers picked through the junk and haggled with the vendors, there were *no* people here. And most of this stuff was not junk. Even the old books and scrolls almost certainly contained some valuable history or information or records. Most people probably wouldn't stash meaningless books alongside piles of treasure and fancy weapons inlaid with gold and gemstones.

Nearly everything inside this cavern held at least *some* value.

"How are we going to find the amulet among all this crap?" Glam asked.

"We start digging, I guess . . ." Edwin said softly.

"But it will take years!" Ari said, even as she admired a well-crafted lance resting on a weapon rack to her right, near the door.

"Oh, so you think if you find a room full of items, you can just take whatever you like without asking?" a voice boomed, echoing off the walls as if it was coming from everywhere and nowhere all at once.

The voice had natural authority, yet still sounded old and worn, as if it hadn't been used in hundreds of years. It was also prickly and angry and sent chills down into my bones.

"Is that normal where you come from?" the voice demanded. We looked around, trying to find the source. "Simply taking what doesn't belong to you!"

I wanted to defensively lie and claim that we weren't going to "just take" anything. But Dwarves don't lie, at least as much as we can help it. And so I tried to think of another way to reason with this person, whoever it was. But Edwin beat me to it, having no trouble lying at all.

"We had no plans to take anything without asking," he said, looking around the huge room. "We seek an amulet, and we will pay handsomely for it."

"You cannot *lie* to me, boy!" the voice seethed, not getting louder, but certainly more ferocious. "I *know all*!"

"But we *will* pay for it!" I countered. "We'll give you anything and everything we have. Please? The world depends on it."

"Oh, does it, now?" the voice asked, calmer, almost mocking. "And how do you know this?"

"Well, because . . ." I started, but then stopped, realizing I wasn't sure I did really *know* anything.

"There's a group of Elves amassing an army," Edwin began. "They go by the name of—"

"Verumque Genus?" the voice interrupted. "Oh, yes, I know all about them."

"Well, then you must know what they're up to," Edwin said. "That's why we seek the amulet! It's the only way to stop them from unleashing their army of monsters on the world."

The voice didn't respond at first. And I figured maybe we had gotten to it, maybe it was actually considering what we were saying. But then it finally spoke again and dashed those hopes.

"Well?" the voice sneered.

"Well, what?" Edwin shot back.

"I'm still waiting for you to tell me how *the world* depends on you stopping the Verumque Genus," the voice said.

We looked at one another, flabbergasted. If it knew so much, how could this thing not see the harm the Verumque Genus Elves and their army of monsters posed?

"Their army will kill millions in their quest for power, maybe even billions," Edwin finally said. "How is that not clear?"

The voice laughed, cold and bitter.

The laughter stopped abruptly as a figure came walking into view from around a pile of fancy wooden chairs. It was a lanky old man, perhaps Human or Elven, hunched, limping, and wearing a faded brown robe. His hood was up over his head, but wisps of white hair and the edges of a beard were visible, poking out near the neck. Glimpses of wrinkled and worn skin could be seen by the torchlight if you looked closely enough.

He stopped thirty feet away and then looked up, his face still mostly obscured by shadows and the hood.

"It's quite clear that the Verumque Genus's plan would indeed result in the deaths of many," the old man finally agreed. "But what is less clear is how that would affect the larger world, as a whole, to the point where it would *end*."

"Billions of people will die!" Edwin nearly yelled. "I would call that affecting the world in a *major* way!"

"Yes, the deaths of billions of creatures would surely be tragic, but the world would not *end*," the old man said calmly. "Far from it. I assure you the world will go on either way. Damaged? Yes. Scorched? Perhaps. Bursting with tragedy? Surely. But it *will* continue to exist. And eventually the Verumque Genus and their monsters will die themselves, or be unseated, and then another group will take over. Perhaps this group will rule with even more terror and destruction than those before them. Or perhaps they will pretend their society is peaceful. Either way, the world *will go on*. Even once this planet is a shell of itself, and no longer suitable to host most living beings, the world itself *will* continue. So to say the world depends on anything is, frankly, just incorrect.

"Life in this universe has spanned billions of years before this, and it will span billions more, no matter what any of you do or say. Do not be so self-centered as to think the very nature of existence revolves around *you*! It does not know you or care about you. Existence is merely that, a metaphysical continuation of events, bound by all life everywhere. One person, one race, one planet, one galaxy, none of these individual parts matters; only the whole matters. So *no*. The world, *literally*, does not depend on you finding or retrieving *anything* from this room."

The old man finished ranting, having taken several more steps toward us in the process.

We were stunned into silence, perhaps knowing that, ultimately, he was right.

Theoretically.

But to reduce our existence to something so insignificant was unfair, even if it was technically true. Because to us it wasn't true. We only knew and experienced our own lives, and we should not, by definition, know or do or see anything beyond that scope.

"But you're disregarding the *experience* of our *own* existence," I finally said. "The heartache and pain that people on this, or any other, planet feel matters. It's real to us, and it's all we have. It *is* our world. Your nihilism shouldn't justify allowing evil to prevail! Even if we are but one small part of the world. It's the only part we know and—"

The old man silenced me with a savage snarl and a wave of his hand.

"What you say matters not!" he hissed. "When you have been stuck in here for as long as I have, the mortality of individual life becomes meaningless. If you were to live this long, and see the things I've seen, you'd have the very same beliefs I do, trust me. But all of this is beside the point; for you see, nothing in here is for sale. Nothing can be taken or removed without permission. And I do not grant it! In fact, you are all trespassing!" The old man's voice was rising to near thunderous levels, which didn't seem possible from such a frail form. "And trespassers, according to ancient Thurian Law, can be killed on sight!"

The man lifted both hands then, and suddenly the old chairs in the pile next to him were flying toward us at impossible speeds, a tornado of twirling wooden legs and backrests.

Before I had a chance to react, or even think about casting a spell, one of the heavy wooden chairs collided with my face, and I dropped to the ground like dead weight.

CHAPTER 34

What Do Sir Neel the Jackal, Nobleman Rainaldus the Honest, and Ranellewellenar Lightmaster Have in Common?

Thankfully, because Dwarven bones are so strong, my face did not shatter on impact with the hard chair.

But that didn't mean it hadn't hurt (it really had). Or that the cartilage in my nose wasn't broken (it definitely was). Or that I wasn't completely dazed for several seconds as blood ran down my chin (I don't really remember).

Then the inside of the cavern exploded with Elven magic and arrows.

I looked up just in time to see every single spell cast and arrow fired miss the old man by a wide margin. It had to be defensive magic of some sort. I'd seen Edwin and his Elves in battle before, and their aim was deadly accurate.

The old man reacted to the attacks as if he were sipping hot tea. His movements were slow, almost bored, yet graceful and probably a lot quicker than they appeared.

He countered our attack by sending hundreds of bronze coins from a nearby pile whizzing at us. They zipped past like little bullets. One coin splintered a chair in half next to me, as if it was made of balsa wood and not varnished walnut.

I quickly transformed myself into stone as more coins pelted the area. Several bounced off my granite exterior.

I turned back to flesh-and-blood Dwarf and climbed to my feet just in time to see an entire ten-person dining room table hurtling toward us, spinning end over end.

I dove behind a pile of books as the table crashed down onto the stone floor with a horrible screech.

I peeked around the corner.

The old man was still exactly where he'd been standing when the attack began, totally unconcerned by the arrows clattering to the ground around him.

I quickly summoned a wind spell.

A burst of air rushed past me from the entrance of the cavern, so powerful that it toppled a stack of books nearby.

My wind spell collided with the area where the old man stood. Debris and junk went flying behind him in all directions.

Yet he remained totally unmoved and unaffected.

He looked right at me, and beneath the shadow of his hood, I saw an amused smirk.

Was this *funny* to him?

My nose was broken!

Then I saw Glam and Lake emerge from behind piles of old chalices and sacks of coins and charge toward the man from both flanks. Glam had her ax at the ready, and Lake was pinwheeling his own around his head like a propeller.

The old man, still looking right at me, casually flicked a hand in each of their directions. Glam and Lake both went sprawling backward as if hit by an invisible fist. Their weapons clattered to the floor.

I was about to pull my new sword free and charge him when Blob suddenly appeared to my right, at the mouth of the cavern.

"Hey, guys!" he said, his unfortunate stench following him inside. "I got lonely waiting outside, so I finally decided to answer the riddle and . . . Hey! What's going on in here?"

Everyone stopped and stared at the smelly blob that had just stumbled into the middle of our battle. Even the old man. In fact, he hadn't just stopped fighting, but had also finally taken a few steps forward and pulled down his hood.

A strange expression formed on his gaunt and ancient face, framed by that long wispy white hair and long white beard.

At first I assumed the old man was just shocked to see a talking, sentient blob. But then I saw recognition in his eyes.

"Blob," the old man said in a hoarse whisper.

"Master?" Blob responded, sounding shocked.

"This is your old master?" Ari asked, peeking out from her hiding spot behind a pile of parchment scrolls. "The one who enslaved you and was always so mean?"

"Well, I did sort of deserve it," Blob said, rolling slowly toward the old man.

"You did," the old man confirmed, taking a cautious step forward himself.

Which meant this nihilistic, ancient (yet undeniably powerful) old man was really Blob's old master. The Human knight once known as Sir Neel the Jackal, then later known by the name Nobleman Rainaldus the Honest. Which, if he really had just been performing magic, meant that some Humans could apparently perform magic as well. But that couldn't be right either. If this was the same guy, then he'd be like a gazillion years old, and Humans didn't live that long.

"Why did you trap me in that rock, Master?" Blob asked, still rolling toward him. "I know I was a failure, but I always tried my best."

"Ah, my dear old friend, Blob," Sir Neel or Rainaldus or whatever his name was said. "How many times do I have to tell you to stop calling me Master? I never owned you . . . You were my, well, my friend, I suppose. My traveling companion at the very least."

If blobs could cry, Blob was doing it, as little streams of funky-smelling liquid ran down his curved sides.

"Then why were you always ordering me around?" Blob asked.

"Because you were always telling stories I'd already heard so many times!" the old man said. "Giving you jobs gave you something to do, something to shut you up for a while."

The words themselves were a little mean, but the man said them with fondness—and I think Blob recognized that.

"But why did you seal me inside a stone?"

"For your own protection," the old man said. "I had a duty to uphold. A new mission to embark on, given to me by the Fairies, that would change everything. Had you not been protected by the power of the Sword of Anduril, you likely would not have survived."

I put my hand on the hilt of the sword—so it really was the powerful sword of Elven legend.

"Thank you, Master, thank you!" Blob said, rolling to within a few feet of the old man, who, having not smelled Blob in eons, put a hand to his nose.

"Please don't call me Master, my friend," the old man said. "And I am sorry it took so long for someone to unearth you. I had no way of knowing so much time would pass before magic returned to the outside realm."

I noticed then that everyone had lowered their weapons. Whatever tensions had fueled the battle before seemed to be gone now that Blob was reuniting with his old traveling companion. Also, I had the distinct feeling that the old man had just been toying with us anyway, that he could have killed us all quite easily within seconds had he really wanted to.

As the silence settled, Tiki began making the rounds, casting spells to help heal our injuries.

"So you *are* Sir Neel the Jackal, then?" I asked, stepping forward.

"No," the old man said. "Not anymore. Nobody has called me that in a long time."

"But you *were* him?"

He nodded slowly. "Once upon a time, yes."

"So Humans can perform magic?" I said, leaning my head back as Tiki cast a spell to help mend the broken cartilage in my nose.

"Well, of course they can!" the old man formerly known as Sir Neel the Jackal said. "Some of them, anyway. Did you really think that only fantastical creatures such as Elves, Dwarves, and the like were special? Humans originally came from Separate Earth, too, you know."

I shrugged.

The old man seemed to find my ignorance rather amusing.

"*Of course* there are Human Wizards and Witches," he said. "But alas, I *was not* one back then. Wizards are not allowed to become knights. I could not perform magic when I was Sir Neel the Jackal."

"So only once you became the, uh, Nobleman Rainaldus, then?" I asked, clearly very confused.

The old man laughed, shaking his head.

"No, no, that was nothing more than a simple name change," he said. "To hide my identity! I was the same person. Either way, both of those men, those names, died a long, long time ago. I am something else entirely different now. Which is why I can perform *magic*, as you call it."

"So what are you now, then?" Edwin asked.

"Well, officially, my new given name is Ranellewellenar Lightmaster," the old man said. "But I sort of prefer to go by Kreych. Though of course that's a rather amusing sentiment in itself, since you're the first living creatures I've spoken to in many thousands of years."

I grunted as a sharp elbow hit me in the ribs. It was Ari, and her eyes were wide with excitement.

"Greg, that's him!" she whispered. "Just like the Fairy legend! Ranellewellenar Lightmaster is the name of the guardian of the Faranlegt Amulet of Sahar!"

CHAPTER 35

The True Tale of Ranellewellenar Lightmaster: Guardian of the Faranlegt Amulet of Sahar

So you're really him?" I blurted out. "*The* Ranellewellenar Lightmaster?"

"Kreych, please," he said. "Call me Kreych. I never liked that name . . . *Ranellewellenar Lightmaster*. Yeecchh!"

"But you *are* the guardian of the Faranlegt Amulet of Sahar?"

Kreych laughed and then shrugged.

"No," he said. "The reality is I am so much *more* than that now."

"What does that mean?" Glam asked. "I'm tired of all these riddles!"

"It's no riddle, child!" Kreych said. "A long story, yes, but surely tis no riddle. Come, then, let me tell you my tale, so you will fully understand and can stop all your fussing."

We gathered around the old man as he lifted a stool upright to sit on.

Up close, I realized just how old he really looked. His skin was so saggy and wrinkled and pocked with warts and moles and spots that he almost looked inhuman. Like a skull covered in a soggy dishcloth and a cheap white wig.

Blob rolled up to Kreych's side, and the old man placed a hand affectionately on the smelly mound of ooze.

"Now then, where to start?" he said. "Oh, yes! Why not with meeting the Fairies in a small village called Thornpond in the northernmost reaches of the Troyon Province in the Rozen Kingdom. The Fairies had summoned me there for a job. Why me? To this day, I still do not fully know, but I do know I am forever cursed because they chose me! Regardless, the Fairies offered a pretty considerable sum of gold just for the meeting itself, so of course I agreed. But I had no intention of accepting whatever silly mission they were going to offer.

"Anyway, we met in a dingy tavern called the Nimble Salt on the edge of town. Just the Fairy Mother, whose name was Tangy Neverbees, and me. Blob and her Fairy Warrior escorts waited outside and kept watch. It is quite odd for a Fairy and a Human to be seen together, especially in a region like Troyon. And so certain precautions had to be taken, such as her assuming the form of a Human. And we also met late, well past the rise of the moon, nearly to its fall, in order to avoid drawing unwanted attention. Even when disguised in 'Human' form, Fairies still emit a faint ethereal glow that would be easily noticeable to a keen observer."

And then the old man told his tale.

"Nobleman Rainaldus the Honest," Fairy Mother Neverbees began. "Or should I say: Sir Neel the Jackal, disgraced knight, thief, confidence man, most-wanted outlaw in the Amalgamated Kingdoms, and all around scalawag?"

I hesitated before answering, she having so fully and accurately called me out.

"Perhaps," I said.

"There's no need to pretend around me," Mother Neverbees scoffed. "Fairies are clairvoyant. Were you not aware?"

I nodded—I had heard that, but of course as with most things, hearing that something is true does not make it true.

But she knew who I really was. If anyone else around there were privy to such information, they'd be clamoring to behead me so they could take my ugly mug to the Elf Lord and collect the substantial bounty he'd placed on me for having stolen his prized sword. Then again, if the Fairy Mother wanted to collect a bounty on me, I would already be dead or incapacitated. Even a wily, conniving Human such as I was no match for the Fairy Mother. It was often said she was the most powerful single living creature in this world. Besides, Fairies had long been known for their spritely benevolence. And not for violence, greed, or lawful righteousness.

"Okay, so you know me," I finally said. "What now?"

"Now," Mother Neverbees said with a patient smile, "you will listen to me."

I nodded.

"This planet is going to change," she began, using a word which at that time I was not yet familiar with. Back then, I still had no idea our Earth was just one of a gazillion others like it, spread throughout this universe. "Not the planet itself, but the nature of its civilizations, the governing rules behind the way energies interact. Many species will go extinct, or rather, will virtually disappear, becoming as dormant as the magical energies that breathe life into them at present."

I still didn't have any real clue what was going on, but I essentially got the meaning of what she was telling me.

"How do you know all of this?" I asked in a low voice. "Fairies are clairvoyant, sure, but even you cannot see the future. Nobody can."

"You are right," Mother Neverbees confirmed. "I am not seeing the future. But I know these things will happen, because we, the Fairies, are the ones who are going to instigate the change."

"What? Why would you want to do that?"

"We must, in order to save the world from certain destruction."

"Well, see, now you've really lost me," I said, shaking my head and downing the rest of my tankard of ale.

Mother Neverbees continued to smile patiently, the subtle glow around her face making my eyes water.

"You're aware that the Elven and Dwarven kingdoms, and their allies, are at war, yes?" she asked.

"Yeah, of course," I said. "But the fighting is happening halfway around the world in Thiess, in the Elven Realm of Efferion and the Dwarven Kingdom of Voldor, mostly. That's partially why I fled that region and came over here. So what's that got to do with me now?"

"Their petty squabble is growing," she explained softly. "Their number of allies is growing. Their armies are growing. They are learning new ways to harness the powers of magic and are using it in unspeakable ways. It won't be long before our whole planet, our very existence, becomes a casualty of this war."

"Okay," I said uneasily.

That certainly seemed plausible to me. But I had never feared death. When I died, I would simply be dead and gone. I probably wouldn't even know it had happened. My own death was of no concern to me—it would happen eventually and could not be stopped. It would be what it would be. No more and no less.

"So what?" I finally added after a long pause. "If that happens, it happens. How could you even stop their war anyway?"

"We are going to purge this world of magic," Mother Neverbees said, her tone dark and ominous (for a Fairy). "Banish it to the depths of the Earth. We believe this will diffuse their battles. Or, at the very least, keep them from destroying the rest of us while they attempt to destroy each other."

I knew the power of Fairies, but still didn't believe they were capable of something like that.

"I suppose how you plan to do this isn't something you can share, right?" I asked.

Mother Neverbees nodded.

"That is indeed none of your concern," she confirmed. "But we do need your help with an ancillary matter. One of the utmost importance."

"I'm listening . . ."

"We need you to travel to the Dedmouth Forest," Mother Neverbees said. "There you will take up residence inside a cave at the base of Dryatos Peak and the Empty Mountain. You will become the Immortal Prophet Ranellewellenar Lightmaster, Keeper of All Time and Existence, Recorder of Life, Guardian of the Earthly Vaults, Warden of the—"

"Whoa, whoa, wait just a second," I interrupted. "What in the name of Goodricke's Beard are you talking about? You want me to become some sort of immortal prophet?"

Fairy Mother Neverbees nodded.

"I mean, that's . . ." I started, but then I stopped since I didn't really know where to go from there. I took a breath, collected my spinning thoughts, and tried again. "Even beyond the insanity of what you're saying, why me?"

"I cannot explain it in a way you could fully comprehend," she said. "But your spirit is pure, and your heart is noble, and—"

"What!?" I interrupted again. "You said yourself I was a thief, a liar, a confidence man, and an all-around scalawag. And you weren't wrong! I'm a mercenary. I do unlawful, sometimes terrible and cruel things for money. That sounds like the opposite of a pure spirit and noble heart to me!"

Mother Neverbees laughed.

"You Humans have always viewed everything so . . . superficially," she said. "The true nature of who we really are goes so much deeper than a mere collection of actions. A person's deeds are sometimes accurate. Other times, they are wholly deceptive."

"Okay, whatever, maybe I'm not so bad deep down," I said, waving my hands around like I was telling a tall tale. "Even still, there have got be purer souls around than me, right?"

"They have other purposes in this realm, and the next."

I was a bit miffed. This lady was basically telling me I had no other purpose than to help them somehow banish magic by moving into a cave and becoming some sort of immortal prophet or some such nonsense. But I must admit now, even back then I knew she was right. I wasn't happy with my life. Never had been. I was always chasing a coin, or a woman, or a drink. Searching for a sort of fulfillment I'd never find. Lying to myself that being a vagabond, that not having a care or purpose in this world, was true freedom and what I always wanted.

"Okay," I said slowly, carefully, so as not to make it sound like I was accepting her job just yet. "So, what does being this prophet entail?"

"You will first cease to exist as you do now," Mother Neverbees said. "You will no longer be Human, but rather a Laresombie: an undead entity trapped between the spirit world and the physical world. You will be immortally tied to this Earth, until either you find a replacement, or the very planet itself is destroyed. You will know everything that has ever happened on this world. Though nobody can see the future, you will become a keeper and knower of the past and present, of our very existence. You will monitor the planet, become a record of all that happens, so others that come later may learn from our mistakes. And in time, should the Fairies find a way to come back to this realm, we will need *a record. We will need a keeper of things, a warden of history, natural and civil, and—"*

"Hold on," I interrupted again. "What do you mean *if* you find a way to come back? Where are the Fairies going?"

"As I said," she explained softly, ever kind and patient, "certain beings will cease to exist once we do what we must."

"You're going to destroy yourselves to save the world?"

"Some sacrifices are worthy," Mother Neverbees said. "So be content in knowing you will not be the only one making a sacrifice for the greater good."

I nodded then, not needing to hear anything more.

I already knew what I must do.

—•⚹•—

"And so," Kreych said, finishing his story, "the next day Blob and I set off on our journey toward the Dedmouth Forest."

"So that's it?" Ari said. "You accepted her offer just like that? You gave up your own life on a whim?"

"Hardly!" Kreych said, standing up suddenly and leaning back. His spine cracked loudly several times as he groaned in relief. "I took the rest of that night to think it over while downing a dozen more tankards of ale. Then I did the same all over again for nearly a fortnight while on our journey. But, in the end, the Fairy Mother knew me better than I knew myself. She had offered me a purpose. Finally. It is sort of ironic how a guy with a death wish, who truly didn't care about the value of his own life, somehow then became immortal. Hah. But such are the stories of life. Believe me, I know them all now. More crazy things, including many that were never recorded or written down, have happened in this world than any of you can possibly imagine."

"Why couldn't Blob come with you?" I asked. "If all you're doing down here is, like, ruminating on the stuff happening in the world?"

Kreych actually smirked slyly at me, as if laughing along at my own cynical breakdown of his new job.

"Being the Prophet, the Keeper of Existence, is meant to be a solitary duty," he said. "It's why the Fairies needed someone who had formed very few personal connections with others. Someone like me. Back then, Blob was truly my only friend, and even then it was because he simply wouldn't go away."

"I would not!" Blob confirmed, and then laughed. "I was like feces stuck to your boot, as you so often told me!"

Kreych smiled fondly at this memory and nodded.

"Indeed I did," he said, patting Blob like a pet.

"So if you're like a keeper of knowledge or whatever," Wrecking Ball, who I knew was a neat freak, asked, "then what's with all this stuff in here? Aside from the books, this is just *stuff*. Chairs? Goblets? I mean, is that a pile of spoons over there? I would hardly call all of this a real record of life and existence."

Kreych laughed, surprising us all.

"It is indeed mostly junk!" he said. "Fairies may be benevolent, noble, altruistic, kind, playful, et cetera, et cetera, but they are also super vain. I mean, I'll be frank: Fairies *really* like *pretty things*." Kreych motioned around him at the piles of stuff. "And they find beauty in *everything*."

Some of our group chuckled.

But I was anxious to get back on track. I was more sure than ever that the amulet was here in this very room. And I wanted to get my hands on it before Edwin did.

"You must know then how the Fairies banished magic," I said. "Since you're now the Keeper of the World or whatever. The guardian of the amulet."

"I already told you, I'm not the guardian of the amulet," Kreych said. "I have many titles, but that is not among them."

"Okay, so guardian may not be one of your many titles," Edwin pressed, likely thinking the same as me: that he wanted to get to the amulet first. "But surely the amulet must be down here. The Fairy legend has long said as much."

"No, I'm not the guardian of the amulet because it simply doesn't exist," Kreych said. "The Faranlegt Amulet of Sahar is nothing but a myth. A simple story made up by the Fairies and nothing more. It is not real."

CHAPTER 36

◆—◆—

I Find Out That Failing Brilliantly Is Not a Dwarven Thing at All, but Rather Something Purely Unique to Greggdroule Stormbelly

The silence in the cavern said it all.

We had come all this way, battled through so much, to find the amulet. An amulet that didn't exist and never had. Just like Bigfoot John had said. Just like the old Elf in Chumikan had said. Just like nearly half the Dwarven Council had said.

We'd been warned so many times that the story was hogwash, and we'd dismissed them all.

"But . . . but that's impossible," Edwin finally said weakly, clearly as shocked and discouraged as I was. "How else did the Fairies manage to suppress magic for so long?"

"To this day, I am not entirely sure," Kreych admitted. "That is a secret only they know. Consider it a tiny hole in my canvas of knowledge, so to speak. But they did warn me that travelers might end up here in the future, like you are now, searching for a fabled amulet. They told me they would make up a story to throw anyone in search of the truth behind their powers off the trail. Sorry to disappoint you . . ."

I slumped to the ground, sitting on the floor like I might never get up. Edwin began pacing and swearing. As did a few of the others. All of us were upset, angry, defeated, and left feeling hopeless and empty.

"How can we defeat the Verumque Genus now?" Rhistel asked.

"Like I said before," Kreych said, "that's not my concern. Wars and battles come and go. Come and go. They're all objectively terrible in the moment. But in the end, none of them *really* matter."

"How can you say that knowing what the Fairies did to stop this war the last time it was ongoing?" Edwin asked.

"Because I now know more than *they* did about the true nature of our world," Kreych said coolly. "Fairies were clairvoyant, powerful creatures. But even their knowledge had its limits. Plus, they were mortal. They *would* care about such things as *life and death*, and the fate of a single planet among a billion-trillion-gazillion others. I, however, do not. In fact, if this Earth dies, then I will finally get to die along with it myself. Something I have longed for for at least the past thousand years. I'm sorry."

Which meant we now faced a full war with the Verumque Genus and their army of monsters. There was no way to subvert the violence. No way to magically suck the wind from their sails before anyone else had to die. Furthermore, we now had to fight them without an object so powerful it would have ensured our victory. And beyond all of that, I now felt almost completely hopeless about my dad's vision to bring peace to the world with magic. I had actually begun believing that something as powerful as the amulet was the key to his vision.

But now I knew it wasn't.

Because there was no such thing as the Faranlegt Amulet of Sahar.

"But Stoney couldn't have been wrong, could he?" Ari asked, as she sat down next to me. "He *knew* it was real. He knows *everything* about minerals . . . I mean, what about Rock One?"

"Stoney never claimed to know about the amulet," I reminded her. "He only cared about the *heart* of the fabled amulet. A rare and enchanted gemstone known as *Corurak*."

"Right," Ari said, lowering her voice. "And it was supposedly the only quantity of the mineral in existence."

"Yeah," I said. "Maybe that's real, maybe not, but it doesn't matter now, since—"

Ari stood up, not listening to me anymore.

"What about the gemstone known as *Corurak*?" she asked Kreych. "The rock said to lie at the heart of the amulet? Is *that* real?"

"Oh, that? Yeah, sure," Kreych said, as if he was talking about a chunk of coal, instead of an object so rare there was only one in the entire universe. "That's very much real. In fact, it's around here somewhere, among all this junk."

"It is?" I asked, getting back to my feet now, too. "Maybe that has some importance?"

"But how will we find it?" Tiki asked, looking around. "It'll be like trying to find a purbogging hanklebump among a heap of plorping flembaggers!"

"Oh, goodness!" Kreych said with a laugh. "The language on this one! Ha-ha! But do not fret, my new acquaintances, for you forget how powerful I am."

Kreych held up an open hand.

A rattling noise echoed inside the chamber, then there was a clattering of gems as they fell to the floor from a huge mound near the far wall. Something stirred within the gemstone pile. A rock roughly the size of a flattened golf ball burst free, showering us in a rain of diamonds, emeralds, rubies, and other precious gems.

The *Corurak* landed gently in Kreych's palm a second later.

The gem glittered and sparkled in ever-shifting tones of yellows, reds, and blues that dazzled so brilliantly I couldn't look at it for longer than a few seconds at a time. Now I knew why Stoney was so enamored with tales of its brilliance.

I had no idea if it had any real powers, but I wanted it now just the same.

"So, uh, what kind of quest or mission must we go on for you to give that to us?" I asked. "What kind of crazy riddle or puzzle do we need to solve?"

Kreych laughed again.

"Here, you can just have it," he said, tossing me the stone. "It's quite useless without its companion anyway."

"Companion?" I said, looking at the brilliant stone in my hand.

It was semi-translucent, cold to the touch, and quite heavy. Up close, it almost seemed to be moving inside as it shimmered and constantly changed colors.

"Yes, well, this stone does indeed have substantial powers," Kreych said. "But only when paired with its enchanted counterpart can it harness them. A weapon was constructed specifically for this stone long ago. When they were together, they were a symbiotic force of nature, a powerful duo that had no rival, capable of winning wars all on their own. But they were separated many thousands of years ago. Since then, this has become just another rock. A remarkably pretty rock, but still just a rock."

"What, uh, what weapon was it made for?" I asked, having a very bad feeling I already knew the answer.

"That piece of *Corurak* is an ancient Rune that should fit perfectly inside a legendary Dwarven ax called the Bloodletter," Kreych said with a smug grin. "A weapon with which you are already *quite* familiar."

I felt like I was going to be sick.

I'd had part of the solution the entire time, and I'd thrown it into the San Francisco Bay. Like a Dwarf. But actually, most Dwarves would have killed to own that ax. So perhaps I should instead say: I had failed, yet again, in a way that *only* Gregg-droule Stormbelly could.

"But even if it's reunited with the Bloodletter," Edwin said, looking more upset than I'd ever seen him, "it wouldn't have the power to harness and control magic like the fabled amulet was said to be able to?"

I'd forgotten that his whole plan to save the world* was crumbling right before him.

"Well, the true powers of the Rune and the Bloodletter are not fully known," Kreych admitted. "Not even by me. However, I am fairly certain they would *not* have the powers to harness magic like that. No earthly objects can control magic the way the Fairies once did."

Edwin's head dropped in defeat, his master plan all but confirmed as impossible.

"But it would be powerful enough to help us defeat the Ver-umque Genus and their monsters, right?" Glam asked.

---

* Which, in case you forgot, was to take away magic from everyone but him and his closest allies, so they could then essentially take over and "police" the world into peace.

"Yeah, probably," Kreych said with a shrug. "I guess."

"Great!" Glam said, standing to leave. "Then let's get out of here! Let's get back to the real world, find Greg's missing ax, and then go smash some evil Elves!"

While I wasn't as psyched about going to war with a faction of Elves and their savage army of monsters, I did have to admit I felt a surge of relief that we had some hope back on our side. After all, that had been one of our goals in finding the amulet: we wanted to use it to stop the Verumque Genus. Of course, we had hoped to use it to *prevent* a battle in the first place. But either way, I felt a lot better knowing we could probably at least defeat them in the battle that now seemed inevitable.

All of this, of course, was dependent on me being able to find the powerful ax I had foolishly thrown away.

"I'm with Glam," Ari said, motioning for everyone to get up. "We're wasting time. We need to get the Bloodletter and this Rune back to the Council."

We turned to face the passageway of the cavern, but it was no longer there.

In its place was the solid rock wall of a sealed cave.

"You're right: you don't have much time," Kreych said ominously. "The Verumque Genus are gathering their army outside Chicago right now, as we speak, to begin their final assault. But it doesn't matter. Since, and I do sincerely apologize for this, I can't let you leave."

We spun back around.

Kreych was smiling, but it was a smile filled with a mixture of sorrow, pain, and bitterness.

"I've been down here all alone for a long, long time," he said. "Without any companions, aside from my endless knowledge. Do you know how lonely that can be?"

CHAPTER 37

❖

One of the Real Heroes of This Story
Does Yet Another Quietly Heroic Thing
(And No, of Course It's Not Me)

You *can't* keep us down here forever!" Ari shouted.

"Yeah, you can't *force* us to be your friends," Glam added. "You'll have to kill us first!"

"What?" Kreych said, clearly confused. "No! Oh, no, no, no, you've got it all wrong. I don't want friends. Immortal all-knowing spirit things like me don't need *friends*. You would only bore me further, no offense. No, what I really want is to *die*."

"Die?" Lixi repeated.

"Yes, I want to die," Kreych confirmed. "I want to *finally* die."

"You want us to, like, kill you?" Foxflame asked. *"Plorping bunkle."*

"Ha-ha!" Kreych said. "I wish it were that simple! No, I am immortal; you cannot kill me."

"Then how—" Foxflame started, but the old man cut him off.

"I'm getting to that if you'd let me talk!" Kreych snapped. "Sheesh. The only way I can be freed from my immortality is if someone takes my place. If someone else becomes the Prophet Ranellewellenar Lightmaster, Keeper of All Time and Existence, Recorder of Life, Guardian of the Earthly Vaults, Warden of the blah, blah, blah. Only then will I finally be released from this curse and able to die in peace!"

"No, Master!" Blob cried out, sending a new wave of his putrid stench wafting up into the cavern.

"Yes, dear friend," Kreych said, covering his nose. "It is finally, mercifully, my time. Now, then, which one of you will take my place as the prophet?"

Nobody spoke for several long, agonizing seconds.

"And we'd have to, like, live here in this cave?" Lixi asked.

"Yes, indeed," Kreych said. "You would not physically be able to leave ever again. Though, I must say, you will be outside of it, in essence, *always*, as an all-knowing being. Even right now, as I'm speaking to you, I'm simultaneously witnessing and knowing and seeing everything that is happening everywhere on this planet. It's kind of a neat trick, really."

"And it will be forever?" Foxflame asked.

"Yes," Kreych said. "But do not be alarmed. It will only be *forever* in the sense that it will be for as long as life on this planet remains. Which, at the current rate, probably won't be for much longer. Perhaps even as few as several hundred years. Even if you solve the planet's environmental issues, the sun has only about four to five billion years left before it burns out. So in this particular scenario, *forever* can be only five billion years, maximum. But as I said, it will probably be far, far less than that. See? Not so bad!"

We all looked around at one another—that sounded like an awful long time to a group of kids who had been alive for an average of fourteen years. It was even a very long time to the three adults: Rhistel, Foxflame, and Wrecking Ball.

"Let's draw straws," Edwin finally suggested. "It's the only fair way."

There was some nodding among the group, as Edwin began looking around for something we could use to either draw straws or pull a random name from a hat.

But seconds later, another voice spoke softly from the corner: "I'll do it."

Everyone fell silent and turned toward the voice.

"I'll volunteer to take his place," Froggy said, stepping forward.

"No," Ari gasped. "You don't have to do that for us."

"Yeah!" Glam added, panic in her eyes. "We can draw straws like this Pointer suggested."

"No, it's okay," Froggy said with a thin smile. "I *want* to. I can't stomach the thought of more battles and wars. Of killing anything, whether in self-defense, or in the name of the greater good, or otherwise. It simply isn't in my nature. Also, I've never been, like, a very social person. I *enjoy* being alone with my thoughts. Here, I can live alone in peace, with all the world's knowledge, knowing I saved every one of you from a terrible fate . . . at least from your perspectives."

The room was silent as the reality of what was about to happen set in.

Froggy made some good arguments. If this was what he wanted, then it wasn't our place to try to talk him out of it.

"You must be *sure* this is what you want," Kreych said, though he couldn't hide the zealous excitement in his eyes. "You acknowledge that it means you must stay in this cave and guard the knowledge and history of this world. Never to leave. Never to see family or friends again."

"I understand," Froggy said quietly, more somber now, but still resolute. "I *want* to do this. It's important and worth the sacrifice."

"Good, good," Kreych cooed. "While I'm quite anxious to get on with this so I can finally be done with this wretched life, I shall grant you a few moments to say goodbye to your friends. I know you've been through a lot together. The Troll attack on your Underground several months ago was particularly harrowing, I must say!"

Froggy nodded and faced the group.

His goodbye to the Elves was short and sweet, since he barely knew them. It consisted mostly of them thanking him profusely for his sacrifice. Edwin took the longest, since they had known each other for years during their time at our old school, the PEE. Edwin leaned in and whispered something to Froggy, who listened and said nothing in return. They shared another short moment, exchanged a small nod, and then Froggy moved on to the Dwarves.

His goodbye to Lake was brief but meaningful, with both of them smiling over some shared inside joke.

Froggy hadn't known Tiki Woodjaw too well. But he appeared to share some bit of advice with her. She nodded, then hugged him and cursed so vulgarly that the Elves flinched.

Glam told Froggy he was the finest, noblest Dwarf—half, full, or otherwise—that she'd ever had the pleasure of knowing. Or, well, that's my paraphrased version. What she actually said was gruntier, louder, and far less eloquent as she struggled to not break down crying.

Froggy spent perhaps the most time saying goodbye to Ari. They both cried and hugged and shared a number of words that I didn't hear—nor should I have. What was said between Froggy and each individual friend was meant to be between them and only them, and I think we all understood that.

"Greg," Froggy said as he faced me last, his eyes already wet and his cheeks streaked with tears. "You'll never know how much it meant that you were kind to me at the PEE. That you sat with me at lunch, accepted me for who I was, even defended me at times."

"Even though me defending you sort of caused all this?" I said, meaning it as a joke, but the words came out choked as a tear ran down to my chin, robbing them of any levity.

But Froggy chuckled anyway as he wiped his eyes.

"Please don't feel bad for me, or think of me as anything but happy," he said. "I truly want to do this. I'm only crying because I'll miss talking to you guys."

"You mean listening to us talk? And talk. And talk," I said.

Froggy laughed again. "Yeah, exactly."

"Well, Froggy, I will miss you, too," I said. "You might be the smartest, kindest, *purest* kid I've ever met. I think this role suits you."

"Thanks, Greg," he said, nodding. "And so does yours. I know you don't want to be a hero. Or a leader. Or have a destiny or legacy or any of that. But sometimes your fate isn't fate at all. Sometimes it's merely the choice you know you have to make because you're a good person and want to do the right thing. You will rise up, Greg, and save us all. I know it. Even if you do it reluctantly, or even if it's an accident, or even if you fail so spectacularly that you unwittingly save the day in the process."

This time it was my turn to laugh and cry at the same time. "However it happens, it will happen."

I nodded, unable to tell him he was wrong, and not wanting to in that moment, no matter what I actually believed.

"One last thing," Froggy said. "Can you please pass along a message to my dad? I want him to hear in my words why he's losing his son a second time . . ."

"Of course," I said.

I still have the message Froggy gave me for his dad. I wrote it down, and read it and read it again and again so I had it memorized even though it was also on paper. I wanted to be able to pass it on even if I lost the paper. But I cannot share it with you. I don't have that right. It's a sacred, private moment between a father and his long-estranged son, and it's only for them.

"Okay, then?" Kreych said somewhat impatiently. "Are we all done now? Can I finally go die in peace like I've been dreaming about for the better part of a millennium?"

"Yes," Froggy said, facing the old man. "I'm ready. Now what?"

"Come over here, child," Kreych said.

As Froggy approached, Kreych reached out a bony, veiny hand. To his credit, Froggy didn't step back or even flinch as the old man placed the wrinkled hand on Froggy's head.

The prophet then closed his eyes and began speaking an incantation in a low voice. A faint glow appeared between his palm and Froggy's forehead. He spoke in a language I didn't recognize. After a short time, Froggy began repeating some of the same words back.

Then Kreych pulled his hand away, and it was all over.

A cold silence fell over the cavern as Kreych grinned like he'd had to pee for days and finally just now got to go.

"That's it?" Froggy said. "I don't feel any different at all. Are you sure it worked?"

"Of course you don't feel different!" Kreych said with a laugh. "You're still you!"

"I don't understand . . ."

"That was just the oath," Kreych said. "Your binding pledge to take my place. You won't actually become the prophet until I die, which won't be long now. I can feel it happening already; my immortality is fading. Which is also why I must go. Go back to my bed to die alone in peace."

"How will I know when the change happens?" Froggy asked, looking scared for the first time.

"Trust me, you'll know," Kreych said ominously. Then perhaps seeing Froggy's fear and anxiety, he let a smile spread across his face. "Don't worry, it doesn't hurt. Quite the opposite, in fact."

Froggy nodded, looking reassured.

"Farewell, then," Kreych said to us all. "I'm off to die now. Thankfully. Finally. But my last bit of advice: Whatever you're going to do, you better do it fast. The Verumque Genus are now in Naperville. They will attack the Dwarven front lines gathered there when the full moon is at its peak, which is in just five or six hours. Without the Rune and the Bloodletter, or a unified Dwarven and Elven army, it will almost certainly be a massacre. So don't dally about here if you really care so much about all these lives that don't really matter."

With that, he began laughing and slowly limped toward the back of the cavern. Blob, who had been remarkably silent all this time, rolled after him.

"Blob, where are you going?" I called out. "We're leaving now!"

"I'm going to stay," Blob said, causing Kreych to stop and turn back. "I want to die with Master. My first and best master."

"I'm not your . . ." Kreych started, but then grinned and sighed. "You may come with me *only* if you call me by my name for once, and not Master."

Blob actually hesitated, his oozing green-brown goo vibrating with emotion.

"Okay, Rain," he finally said. "Let me die with you. The Rain and Blob show should end together."

"Can you even die?" I asked.

"Indeed I can!" Blob said. "It's hard to kill me, but I can choose to cease my bodily functions anytime I please."

"Then why on earth did you stay alive in that rock all this time?" Kreych asked. "You must have been going mad! When I sealed you inside, I never thought it would take thousands of years for you to be freed or I wouldn't have done it!"

"I was waiting," Blob said. "For you to come back. For the chance to see you again."

For the first time since we got there, perhaps because he was turning Human again, Kreych showed a hint of real feelings. He took a deep, shaking breath, said nothing, and then nodded, once again placing a hand on Blob's exterior.

"Thank you, Greggdroule and companions," Blob said. "For letting me come on your adventures. You were good friends. I will see you again, perhaps, in another life."

Most of us said goodbye.

All I could do was wave, too emotionally, physically, and mentally exhausted to even dare try to speak.

Without another word, Kreych and Blob disappeared out of view, heading somewhere toward the back of the massive vault-like cave.

The rest of us stood by the cave's entrance, which had re-appeared at some point during all the goodbyes. Froggy stood several feet away, watching us intently, and dare I say, even looking a bit excited. He was, after all, about to acquire all the world's knowledge and history. There would literally be no mystery he would not know the answer to: Have aliens really visited Earth? Who assassinated JFK? Is the lost city of Atlantis real and where is it? Who built Stonehenge? What killed the dinosaurs? Who shot Tupac? Was Shakespeare a real person? And on and on and on.

Part of me was even sort of jealous.

"Go on, you guys," Froggy finally said. "I'll be fine. Get out of here. You heard him; you only have hours before the Verumque Genus attack, and you're still halfway around the world, inside a totally separate magical realm!"

I nodded and put the Rune, aka Rock One, aka the *Corurak*, aka the Bloodletter's power booster, into my pocket.

We all waved goodbye a final time.

"For Waldwick the Wizard's sake, *go!*" Froggy said with joking impatience. "Go save the day already!"

CHAPTER 38

I Make Edwin the Most Powerful Person on the Planet

I need to find the Bloodletter," I said to the group once we were back outside.* "That's obviously my first step."

"We don't have time!" Glam said, her fists becoming boulders. "Besides, we don't need that stupid ax; you said so yourself back when you threw it away! We can smash the Verumque Genus Elves by ourselves!"

"She's right," Ari said. "We don't have time. I mean, it took us four weeks to sail here to begin with. And we don't even have a boat anymore."

"Whoa, wait a second!" Edwin said, stepping between us. "You took a *boat* here?"

Ari, Glam, Lake, Tiki, and I looked at one another, wondering why this was so shocking. Planes didn't work anymore. What other way *was* there to get here?

---

* Getting out had been much easier than getting in. A new doorway had appeared beneath the twin turtle heads, which then promptly sealed shut once again after we had all made it out.

"Um, yeah . . ." I said slowly.

Edwin exchanged a smug grin with Lixi, Wrecking Ball, Foxflame, and Rhistel, all of whom could barely hold back their laughter.

"Man, that's so . . . well, *Dwarven* of you," Edwin said. "No offense."

"No wonder we got here before you guys did," Foxflame added.

"Wait, so how in the name of smidgy kunk did *you* travel here, then?" Tiki demanded, not liking being the butt of a joke.

The Elves looked at one another as if they were unsure exactly how to respond. As if they'd just been asked to explain computers to a caveman.

"Can't Dwarves travel by telemobility spells?" Foxflame finally asked.

"Tele-what?" Glam said.

"Traveling from one place to another using magic," Edwin explained. "There are actually a number of different ways to do it, including the Nym spell, Aymon's Proxy, and all the various Luvanaar spells in the Joydark branch of Elven magic."

I had no idea what he was talking about, but Ari was nodding as he spoke, clearly having done some reading on the topic.

"We do have travel spells," she confirmed when he was done. "They're different from yours, simpler in the same way all Dwarven magic is simpler than Elven magic. But we can travel by magic . . . *theoretically*."

"We can?" I asked.

"Yeah, how did *I* not know this?" Glam added.

"And why did we take a purbogging boat, then?" Tiki demanded.

Ari held up her hands as if to ward off an attack, then quickly began answering all our questions.

"Yes," she said, nodding at me, before turning to Glam. "Because it's not common knowledge. I only know because Eagan told me the Council had discussed this option during a closed session." Finally, she faced Tiki. "That's complicated to answer. For one thing, Dwarves believe that using magic to travel is mystically *unethical*. It's considered, well, *cheating*, in a sense. Sort of like stealing, but obviously not quite exactly the same. Even back in Separate Earth, it was only allowed during life-or-death emergencies, like most Dwarven magic."

"That's so bizarre," Rhistel said. "If something is available that can make your life better or easier, why not use it? Why not take every advantage you can get in life?"

"It's fascinating," Foxflame added.

"This is the fundamental difference between us," Ari said. "Dwarves don't live for the sole purpose of bettering their own situation as easily as they can. We value hard work and accomplishment and preserving the energies of the world for everyone and everything. We take only what we need, nothing more. Traditionally."

The Elves were about to counter this with some other argument, but I stopped them.

"Look, just stop, everyone!" I said. "We don't need to get into another fight right now about whose culture is better. What I still want to know is why the Council didn't consider our mission a life-or-death emergency. We could have saved so many lives by not taking that boat."

"Yes," Ari said, nodding. "According to Eagan, the Council did consider this. But you're forgetting a larger complication: Stoney. Even though some spells can include Dwarves without the Ability, our two or three known transportation spells would not transfer to a Rock Troll."

I nodded.

If that was true, then the Council had made the right decision since Stoney had been a vital part of this mission. Poor Stoney. I wondered if he was awake yet and wondering where we were? Even if he was, we'd have to leave him behind for now. But I'd come back for him. *If* I survived our fight with the Verumque Genus, that is.

"Either way, we're wasting more time we don't have," Edwin said. "We can help you travel by magic, if you don't know how. It's not instantaneous, but it is remarkably fast. Getting back to America will take maybe twenty minutes, at least via Elven spells. Which means you *do* have time to get back before the Verumque Genus launches their attack. The real question is: What now? What are we doing right now?"

A moment of silence followed.

"Well, I need to get the Bloodletter—" I started.

"Yeah, we know that," Edwin interrupted. "And we can discuss specifics later. What I meant was: What are we doing *together*? Elves and Dwarves as a whole? We all came for the amulet. We joined up to retrieve it, but now we know it doesn't exist. And you have a Rune that when combined with the Bloodletter will be a game changer. And we're left with . . . well, *nothing*. Our journey—the people we lost coming here—was all for nothing."

Glam stepped forward to argue with him, but he silenced her with a single wave of his hand. "I'm not just being petty," he said. "It's not the score of a game, I know that. But I *am* trying to look out for my people. I am the Elf Lord, responsible for the well-being of millions of Elves globally. Including those who have joined the Verumque Genus. Many of them will return to our ranks eventually. What can I take away from this to ensure we're protected? Why should I pledge my soldiers to help you battle the Verumque Genus outside Chicago?"

"He's right," Rhistel chimed in. "The smart move for us would be to let you and the Verumque Genus fight it out for a while. Both sides will be weakened, and we would have a much easier time defeating whoever emerges the winner."

Edwin shot an annoyed glance at his dad's old adviser. His colder, shrewder take on the situation was clearly not quite what Edwin wanted vocalized. But at the same time, Edwin said nothing more. He did not correct Rhistel or add anything to his statement. Which meant, though Edwin would have phrased it more diplomatically, what Rhistel had said was technically true.

"You make a solid point," I said to them, drawing my new weapon, the legendary Sword of Anduril. The Elves flinched, but the tension eased when I merely rested the sword on my open palms like I was holding a serving tray. "I'd like to offer you this sword as a token of our trust. A peace offering, I guess. It's useless to me anyway. I don't see the power in it that you do."

Edwin stared at the blade with wide eyes full of awe, wonder, and surprise. He was being offered the most powerful weapon in the history of Elven lore. And a supposed mortal enemy of his race was giving it to him.

He reached for the sword, but I pulled it back slightly.

"Wait," I said. "This isn't free. There are conditions. Consider my offer of this sword a contract, an unwritten promise that you will help us defeat the Verumque Genus. That you'll stand alongside us, right now, in the battle at Naperville. Afterward, assuming our side wins, we will do our best to convince the Dwarven Council to open up peace talks with you. To have discussions and not just resume fighting like Elves and Dwarves did the last time magic existed on this planet. And I think, if you help us save our capital city, the Council *will* agree. They will see your intentions are pure. And your insurance policy is this sword. If it's as powerful as you say it is . . . well, then even if the Council doesn't agree to acknowledge or reward your assistance, you'll have gotten this out of it. A weapon that, if you decide to betray me, could be the end of us all."

I held up the sword again.

Edwin reached for it, knowing he was pledging an oath to help us defeat the Verumque Genus, to defend the Dwarven Capital and home of our Council.

"We're in this together now," Edwin said, nodding, as he took the sword from my hands.

Once the hilt was in his grasp, I suddenly saw what the Elves had seen all along: the blade lit up, glowing unnaturally purple and sparkling, moving like it was made of liquid and not metal. The sudden infusion of power into the weapon was visceral, almost like you could *feel* the crackling of electricity coming from it.

For a brief second, I wondered if I'd perhaps made my biggest mistake yet. Edwin could now easily cut us all down where we stood, take the Rune, find the Bloodletter, and become a force to be reckoned with. He could take over the world here and now if he wanted.

But I hoped I knew him better than that.

This was still Edwin, my former best friend. And he was still a good person. He seemed to be past the bitter, corrupting anger of his parents' death, just like I had finally moved past what had happened to my own dad. I was no longer trying to ascribe blame for it, but rather had merely accepted that it had happened.

And though I knew my friends Glam, Ari, Lake, and Tiki must have been even more nervous and apprehensive than I was, they surprisingly said nothing. They had not protested when I offered Edwin the most powerful Elven weapon ever made. And I could only assume it was because they trusted me, and by proxy, trusted Edwin.

"We need all the help we can get to defeat the Verumque Genus," I said. "You will join us?"

"Yes," Edwin said as he replaced his old sword in his sheath with his new one. "We *must* help you. We will need to work together to defeat them. Though we both wanted slightly different outcomes from the amulet, our one shared goal was stopping the Verumque Genus. And that remains. So we must hurry and leave now. Does everyone agree?"

All ten of us, five Elves and five Dwarves, nodded.

"Okay, good," Edwin said. "Who's going where?"

"I need to go find my ax," I said. "After that, I'll meet up with you all on the battlefields of Naperville."

"I'm going with Greg," Ari announced. "I helped him dispose of the ax, and so I should help him retrieve it."

I shot her a grateful nod.

"Lake, Tiki, and I will head back to Chicago to get the Council up to speed and help our armies get prepped for battle," Glam said.

"I will go with them," Foxflame announced. "To be the Elven envoy, there to assure the Dwarven Council that we share the same goal: defeating the Verumque Genus and their army of monsters."

"Yes, good," Edwin said. "And Lixi, Wrecking Ball, Rhistel and I will return to our headquarters. We will assemble our own armies and then rendezvous with your Dwarven forces just outside Naperville in a few hours. Greg, hopefully you'll find your ax in time to return to Illinois early enough to see Elves and Dwarves actually working together!"

"Yeah, I hope so," I said. "Now then, who wants to explain to us how we can travel by magic?"

CHAPTER 39

There Are No Free Movies
When Traveling by Magic

We crashed down into the San Francisco Bay so hard we'd have broken every bone in our bodies had we been cursed with brittle Human skeletons.

Traveling by magic was indeed fast, but that didn't mean it was comfortable. There definitely weren't flight attendants to bring you pretzels and sodas while you sat back and watched free movies on your phone. Instead, the journey had been loud, cold, scary, and disorienting.

Perhaps it was better for Elves. It sounded like their travel spells worked a lot differently from our own. The more common Elven travel spells used magical energy to create ripples in the atmosphere, kind of like theoretical wormholes, that transported people from one place to another quickly, safely, and with minimal interaction with the elements.

But Dwarven magic worked differently, of course. Rather than using energy to create something new, or to totally alter a natural law of physics, our magic could only manipulate the natural elements as they currently existed. Which meant there were two known options for Dwarves. The trickier spell was to pass right through the Earth via a magical tunnel. But it was believed this method could cause rippling disturbances, such as earthquakes and volcanic eruptions, across the globe if not done properly. And so the easiest, simplest, and safest spell was merely a variation of the very same wind spell I had so often used before. The travel version created a sort of wind tunnel, like a long, thin tornado, that carried you from your starting spot to your destination.

This was how Ari and I traveled from eastern Russia to the San Francisco Bay: twirling, spinning, and hurtling through a cold, harsh, violent tornado that spanned the Pacific Ocean like a huge, gray, hollow spaghetti noodle.

We were deposited rather rudely (finessing this spell apparently took some practice) into the middle of the San Francisco Bay as if fired from a cannon pointed directly down into the water.

As we swam desperately back up toward the surface, I was struck by how warm the water felt compared to the sea I'd spent time in the week before while battling sea monsters off the coast of Russia.

"Well, that was *fun*," Ari said, as our heads bobbed on the surface of the relatively calm water.

I couldn't tell how sarcastic she was being and so I merely nodded, my head still spinning from having literally just been tumbled about inside a tornado for the better part of what felt like an hour.

"What now?" Ari asked, treading water. "How will we find the Bloodletter?"

"I suppose I could just ask him where he's at," I said, "if we're close enough . . ."

You don't even need to be close to me right now to speak to me. The Bloodletter's voice suddenly filled my head.

Huh? I thought back. *Is it really you this time?*

I'd basically concluded that the last few times I'd heard his voice back in the Sea of Okhotsk, I had been hallucinating.

Of course it's really me! he snapped. *And it was the last time, too. You mean to tell me you still haven't figured it out?*

Um, I guess not?

The Bloodletter sighed loudly inside my head.

What do the last few times we spoke have in common? he asked.

I thought about it for a second, still so disoriented from traveling via tornado that I couldn't possibly imagine what he might be getting at. At least, that is, until I accidentally swallowed a gulp of salty water and realized the answer was obvious.

I was in water, I finally replied.

That's right! the Bloodletter said. *Water is a natural conduit for magical telepathy. So even halfway around the world, we can still be linked. Which means I really did witness your blundering attempts to save yourself off the coast of Russia.*

"What's wrong, Greg?" Ari interjected.

"Huh?"

"You're just sort of staring off into space."

"Oh, sorry," I said, treading water, my clothes feeling heavy. "I'm talking to the ax now . . . well, telepathically talking, anyway."

Ari nodded.

"Okay, but please hurry," she said. "I've got a bad feeling there are more than just fish, dolphins, and small, harmless sharks in these waters now that magic is back."

I nodded and returned to my thoughtversation with the Bloodletter.

Where are you, Carl?

Oh, so now you've come crawling back, eh? he sneered. *And I suppose you just expect me to forgive you for what you did?*

No, I don't expect anything, but I'm hoping you will forgive me anyway, I thought. *I was wrong; I admit that now. Your power scared me, but I realize now that you were right. That I still needed you. That we weren't finished yet, fulfilling our destiny and all.*

Of course, I still wasn't sure I believed in destiny, but I was trying to get my ax back, and so I was saying what I thought he needed to hear. As much as I could without outright lying, that is.[*]

Good, he said. *Not what you just said, but that you're not expecting forgiveness. Because you won't get it!*

That's fair, I admitted. *But can you at least tell me where you are? So we can talk, uh, face-to-face?*

I'm still at the bottom of the sea, right where you threw me away! he shouted angrily in my brain. *I'm an ax with no fins, arms, or legs. How could I be anywhere else, you dolt?*

He was right, but I still didn't think name-calling was necessary.

"He says he's still right where we left him," I said to Ari. "Do you remember where we were?"

Don't you mean "DUMPED"? the Bloodletter interjected. I did my best to ignore him. *You abandoned me, threw me away like garbage, tossed me overboard like a dead body, discarded me like rubbish, deserted, forsook, ditched, rejected, disowned . . .*

"Ummm . . ." Ari said as she swam around in a circle, looking at the noticeable landmarks: the Golden Gate Bridge (lined with hundreds of dead, abandoned vehicles), Alcatraz (topped with scorched piles of rubble from the Elven battle), and the

---

[*]   Because remember: Dwarves don't lie, not even to their psychopathic magical axes.

eerily dark San Francisco skyline (dotted with small fires burning inside several office buildings and houses). "I think it was over that way."

She pointed to a spot closer to the shore along the city—a spot somewhere between Alcatraz and the place where our boat had eventually made landfall shortly after we'd ditched my ax.

I nodded, and we began swimming in that direction.

Using magic to aid us, we swam at Olympic-record-shattering speed. But even still, finding an ax at the bottom of a bay, hundreds of feet deep in some places, in the relative darkness of the coming dusk, was going to be nearly impossible without the Bloodletter's assistance.

Please help me find you, Carl, I thought as we swam.

No. And I hope you drown looking for me.

Come on, you don't mean that.

I do, Greggdroule. I really do.

"I think we're roughly there, Greg," Ari said, stopping to tread water. "But unless we know exactly where to dive down, we'll never find it."

"I know. I'm trying," I said.

"I'm going to start looking," she said, pulling free her dagger.

The blade began glowing* and Ari dove under the surface, using the illuminated knife as a sort of flashlight. Watching her descend slowly into the darkness, I knew that even with magic to help us swim, to help equalize the pressure of the deep, and to help us breathe, it might take hours, even days, to find the ax.

I had to think of another angle.

What did the Bloodletter want more anything?

What could I use to get him excited?

---

* One of her dagger Lightbringer's inherent magical traits, along with being able to expand and contract several inches as needed.

The answer was easy. It was the very same thing that had made me want to get rid of him in the first place: *power*.

My ax craved power—he was a tool created purely for destruction, after all.

I have the Corurak *Rune*, I thought. *YOUR Rune. If you tell me where you are, I can finally reunite the two of you.*

At first I took his long silence for confusion, or perhaps more anger. But when he finally "spoke" again, I realized what the silence had really been: reluctantly excited awe.

It can't be, he said. *You're lying.*

Dwarves don't lie, remember?

Greggdroule, don't be silly. Everyone lies, even Dwarves.

Okay, fine, I gave in. *But I'm not lying now. I have the* Corurak *in my pocket. The same stone you were custom designed for. You know, I'd always just thought that small indentation near the junction of your shoulder and your langet was purely decorative. But now I know better. Now I know what really belongs there. Surely you can feel its presence.*

There was another pause and then: *Where did you find it? It has been missing for so long, I assumed it had been destroyed.*

It doesn't matter, I said. *What matters is you can be together again, after all these years, if you simply help me find you.*

There was another long silence while the ax debated what to do. But I think we both knew that an ax that craved power above all else wouldn't be able to resist a reunion with a magical, enchanted stone that supposedly amplified its power exponentially.

Okay, fine, the Bloodletter finally said. *But this doesn't mean I have forgiven you.*

Fair enough, I thought back, just as Ari finally resurfaced.

"It's no use, Greg," she said. "You can barely see anything down there, even with magical light. We'll never find it."

"It's okay, he's going to help now."

I will guide you toward me, Greggdroule, the Bloodletter said. *Start swimming toward the bridge and go deep.*

"Stay with me," I said to Ari. "I'll need your dagger's light to see."

She nodded and followed as I dove down, swimming toward the bridge and the bottom of the bay.

As we swam, I finally saw what Ari had meant. Though her dagger shone quite brightly with magical luminescence, the water itself was murky, cloudy, dark, and full of algae. No matter how bright the light, visibility was only ten or twelve feet at most.

But the Bloodletter continued guiding me, telling me when to turn slightly right or left as we swam deeper and deeper into the depths of the bay with the aid of magic. Finally, at about seventy feet deep, I saw the bottom below us, gently sloping deeper as it ran toward the bridge.

Keep going, the Bloodletter hissed, sounding somewhat panicked. *They're coming for you now.*

Who is?

Just hurry!

I quickly motioned for Ari to keep an eye out, pointing two fingers at my eyes and then all around us. She nodded that she understood, and we continued swimming, descending farther toward the bottom at a rate that would have been impossible without Dwarven spells helping us along.

Hurry, Greggdroule! the ax hissed again, sounding terrified. *They're almost to you now.*

Who is? I thought back. *I don't see anything!*

But then I did see something.

Not a monster. Not a sea creature.

I saw the Bloodletter.

He was lying mostly buried in sand and silt just ahead of me in the darkness, perhaps another fifty or sixty feet away. Visibility had cleared somewhat this deep, closer to the bridge. But I still wouldn't have been able to see the ax if it wasn't glowing blue, illuminating the seaweed around it like neon tentacles.

I see you! I said. *I'm almost there!*

It's too late, Greggdroule, he replied somberly. Defeated. *They've found you.*

Who?! I screamed back in my mind.

But there was no need to wait for a reply.

The shapes of several Drenchers appeared in front of me, cutting off my view of the Bloodletter and the path to my weapon, which was now just ten agonizingly close feet away.

All I saw now were gaunt, ghoulish faces, red glowing eyes, and thin pointy teeth.

CHAPTER 40

It All Checks Out: I'm About to Get Eaten Alive by Slimy Sea People

D renchers were pretty easy to recognize.

We'd learned in Monsterology class that there were only four known humanoid creatures that dwelled in large bodies of water: Mermaids/Mermen, Sirens, Amphibanoids, and Drenchers.

Real Mermaids and Mermen supposedly looked less like what you might have seen as a kid in the old cartoon *The Little Mermaid*, and more like an actual fish/Human hybrid should look—scalier and slimier. But they were still generally gentle and cautious, and avoided investigating intruders in the sea, let alone attacking them.

Sirens technically lived in bodies of water, but though they were excellent swimmers, they spent most of their time flying *above* the surface of lakes or seas. Their attacks usually began from the air, where their horrifying screeches would incapacitate helpless victims nearby.

Amphibanoids looked similar to the creatures closing in on me now, in that they were truly humanoid in shape—with two legs, two arms, and a head—and were covered in scales and had fins propped up by bony spikes. But they, like Mermaids and Mermen, were known to be shy and unaggressive. They did not have sharp teeth (instead they swallowed smaller prey whole, like a largemouth bass), nor did they have glowing red eyes or a desire to rip apart and eat a small Dwarf.

Drenchers, however, had several distinct features, all of which I was seeing on my attackers: Red, bottomless eyes that never blinked and that dazed you into a motionless stupor if you looked directly into them?

Check.

Big, bony, scaly, grabby hands that clutched at your limbs and tried to drown you and tear you apart at the same time?

Check.

Feet that looked more like spiky flippers than anything resembling feet, which, when combined with their pliable, flexible leg bones, allowed them ridiculously nimble, quick, and precise swimming movements that could not be escaped?

Check.

Thin, pointy teeth that were brittle enough to break off, but long and sharp enough to pierce a heart, or pass all the way through your head before they snapped away from their gaping, fishy mouths?

Check.

Yep, definitely Drenchers.

I knew from class that they always traveled in packs of twenty-four. Why twenty-four exactly? Well, nobody really knew, since as of the latest edition of our Monsterology textbook, the

Drenchers' language (a series of wails and clicks similar to those of both dolphins and whales, but more shrieky) had yet to be decoded or translated. Drenchers also usually conglomerated on one victim at a time, ensuring that they'd all have at least a small snack, rather than risk losing it all by each going after a separate feast and possibly losing a one-on-one battle with their prey.

And given that I was being grabbed and pulled and ripped at by what felt like dozens of hands, it seemed I was their chosen prey, and not Ari.

She must have recognized this. Instead of going for the ax, or fleeing in terror, Ari began chopping and hacking and slashing at the Drenchers with her dagger, trying to get them to come after her instead of me.

I attempted to use magic to break free, but there were only a very limited number of offensive spells I could even try underwater, and the Drenchers seemed unaffected by all of them. Which wasn't surprising, given that they lived in the sea. What could I do to manipulate the water around us that would bother them but not harm Ari in the process?

Nothing.

Blackout fell from my grasp almost as soon as the attack started, after a bony, sharp hand grabbed my arm. Then my biceps felt like it was on fire, as one of them dug its needle teeth into my flesh.

Greggdroule, turn to stone! the Bloodletter screamed in my head.

I instantly turned myself to granite, just seconds before the Drenchers' sinewy muscles and greedy mouths would have literally torn me to shreds.

Suddenly I was sinking. Like, well, like a rock, since, you know, that's technically what I was at that moment.

The Drenchers could no longer hold me up, and so they simply let me go.

As I sank toward the seafloor, I saw the Drenchers' confused faces above me, forty-eight red eyes framed by shadowy, spiky fins in the darkness. They had surely never seen a Dwarf turn to stone, and it completely bewildered them. That was another thing I remembered about Drenchers from class: they were barely smarter than most fish. Yes, they had a language, and yes, they were debatably self-aware, but that was about the extent of it, as far as the ancient Dwarven zoologists who first studied them could tell.

Drenchers operated mostly on the predatory instinct of survival.

Which, in this instance, caused all twenty-four heads to turn around in unison, and fix their hungry stares on Ari.

Turn to stone, Ari! I thought.

But unlike the Bloodletter and I, Ari and I did not share a telepathic link. And so she did not hear me as she turned and began swimming furiously away. But she wouldn't need to hear me to know what to do. Ari was objectively a lot smarter than me. So why was she trying to outswim these things instead of merely turning to stone like I had? She had to know that, even with magic, she stood no chance of getting away from such agile and fast swimmers.

Ari took one last desperate look back at me as she swam out of visibility with a whole pack of Drenchers right behind her.

And I knew then, as the glowing light from her dagger suddenly blinked out in the distance and left me in total darkness, why she had fled instead of turning to stone. She was leading them away from me, creating a diversion, so I could get the Bloodletter and make my escape.

Ari was trying to sacrifice herself for the mission.

You're purbogging right she is! the Bloodletter confirmed. *Now turn back into a Dwarf and get over here and get me off the seafloor so her death is not in vain!*

CHAPTER 41

—◆◆◆—

A Massive Larenuf Is Held to Celebrate the Resurrection of the Bloodletter

The moment my hand closed around the Bloodletter's handle, it felt like a part of me that had died was suddenly resurrected.

Not just resurrected, but welcomed back to life with a massive festival, complete with a buffet of meats and cheeses and cakes, fruity drinks, live music, dancing, fair rides, and thousands of happy partiers in attendance. It was like the opposite of a funeral. An un-funeral. A Larenuf. Either way, it felt like a celebration was going on inside me even as the ax's bloodthirsty ways, the very reasons I wanted to get rid of him to begin with, also flooded back.

I was suddenly filled with anger, bitterness, and resentment over the amulet mission being a near total waste. Regret for having just handed over a weapon—whose power rivaled the Bloodletter's—to Edwin, with no assurances he wouldn't use it against me eventually. In fact, part of me was now longing for a final epic showdown between us, each with his race's most powerful, legendary weapon.

It was almost too perfect *not* to happen.

A battle to end all battles.

But I knew those weren't my real thoughts. Whether the scenario was poetic or not, I truly didn't have any desire to fight my former best friend. And I certainly didn't want to fight him using a pair of weapons rumored to be so powerful that a clash between them would surely destroy everything and anything in between us, and all around us as well. I didn't want to fight him, because I didn't want to win. And with the Bloodletter in my hand again, I felt like I couldn't lose.

I pushed those unnatural thoughts to the side.

Right then my only job was to save Ari.

The ax coursed with energy, still glowing faintly blue as I heaved it up from the sand and silt on the sea floor. Brown clouds billowed around me, shrouding me in darkness as I kicked up and started swimming, needing magic to get off the bottom with a heavy ax now in my grasp.

There's no time to save her, he said. *We need to get back to Chicago and help with the battle.*

There's always time for my friends, I shot back.

Is her life really worth more than all of those in a whole city?

Argh! I actually said in my mind. *I'm not leaving without Ari.*

I willed the ax to glow even brighter as I swam in what I thought was the general direction Ari had been heading when she created a diversion for me. I used magic to help propel me forward as quickly as possible, the osmosis breathing spell still keeping my blood oxygenated. At this depth, with the sun fully gone above us now, my glowing ax provided only ten feet of visibility. But I searched the murky depths around us anyway.

The first sign I saw of Ari was the faint specks of glowing red eyes in the darkness.

Drencher eyes.

Unblinking, uncaring, hungry, and hypnotic.

I swam toward them as fast as I could, the glowing ax held out in front of me. As I neared, I saw that they were all gathered around a lifeless shape lying on the seafloor, among several fluttering entrails of seaweed.

It was Ari's motionless body.

Except it wasn't really her. She had turned to stone. Which meant she was still alive, since the spell required a lot of concentration and effort to hold it for longer than a few seconds. The Drenchers swarmed around her, waiting patiently for their meal to turn back into consumable flesh. Which would happen eventually. During our magic training sessions, the longest anybody had been able to hold this spell was three minutes and eight seconds: a record held by Doral Deepfall, an eighteen-year-old from a family known for their magical prowess. Doral was usually the best at every spell we learned.

Ari had maybe a few minutes, or perhaps even seconds, before she'd finally, unwillingly return to her normal body and be torn to shreds by the pack of Drenchers.

What's worse, Greggdroule, the Bloodletter said, *is that there's another pack coming in. Look to your right. Now come on, let's just get out of here while we can.*

I looked to my right, and my stomach dropped at the sight of another forty-eight glowing eyes approaching steadily from the darkness.

Oh kunk, I thought.

Exactly, the Bloodletter said. *Let's go, Greggdroule! There is no time to save your friend. If we try, you will perish right along with her! I may be powerful, but I can't stop forty-eight Drenchers all at once, and you know it.*

I didn't want to admit it, but he was right.

As I stared desperately down at Ari's motionless form, I knew she would say the same thing as my ax. The larger mission was more important than one Dwarf. Without the Bloodletter and the Rune, we had little hope of defeating the Verumque Genus. Which was more important than her single life.

Just then, Ari finally lost her grip on the spell and turned back into herself. Her eyes opened wide with panic and fear, clearly visible even as she lay helplessly on the murky ocean floor.

The Drenchers immediately swarmed over their meal with a zestful frenzy that would have made a pack of hungry sharks look lazy.

CHAPTER 42

It's That Time in the Story Where I Ask You to Play Some Music (Yes, Really)

One single thought passed through my brain as I watched the Drenchers swarm Ari, even as she desperately slashed with her dagger, even as I knew the other pack of Drenchers was closing in on me, just a few feet away now, their hungry mouths already open.

That single thought consisted of just two words.

The Rune!

It was time to see if this thing was as powerful as Kreych had said it would be when combined with the Bloodletter.

I quickly pulled the stone from my pocket and placed it inside the small indentation at the ax's shoulder, the place where the blade met the handle. The *Corurak* didn't snap into place like a piece of plastic, but rather seemed to instantly become a part of the ax itself, merging with the intricately carved metal as the water rippled with energy all around me.

The Bloodletter's blue glow went from intensely bright to

a strobe light of pure power, a surge of energy that would have blinded anyone looking directly at it. The blast of light erupted from my hands like a shock wave, spreading so far throughout the bay that I was certain anyone camping out on top of the Golden Gate Bridge probably figured the earth had split open and the world was about to end.

The water filled with the horrified shrieks of the Drenchers as they cowered away from me, momentarily blinded or stunned.

I couldn't even look down at the ax in my own hands, it shone so brightly.

But I didn't need to see it to know how powerful it had just become.

I could *feel* it.

It coursed through me like a dam had burst in my heart. But more than that, I suddenly felt like I possessed an extra sense I'd never had before, like clairvoyance. I suddenly *knew* things about the world, and magic, and life and death that I could have only guessed at lying awake in bed before. It's hard to describe, but it almost felt like the Bloodletter and I had merged, becoming a single entity. Like I had just become a different person.

Someone my enemies should fear immensely.

This is the sort of moment where, in movies, the cool song starts playing and you know the hero has finally reached his or her full potential. Maybe it's a cheesy bombastic song from the 1980s, like "The Touch" by Stan Bush, or "Eye of the Tiger" by Survivor. Or maybe it's a bone-shaking modern rock song. Or perhaps it's a softer, beautiful, understated song to contrast with the powerful violence ripping across the screen. I guess it all depends on the sort of movie you're envisioning.

Either way, in your head, that song should be playing right now.*

AAAAAAAIIIYYYYYYYYYEEEEEEE!!!! the Bloodletter howled in my mind. *Let's go save your friend!*

I didn't need him to suggest it twice.

It's hard to adequately describe how easy what I did next actually was. Magic now felt less like an unknown power we were all struggling to harness and get used to and more like something as natural as breathing. Danger no longer felt like something to fear, but something to laugh at. And destroying Drenchers no longer felt scary, improbable, and somber.

Now it was *fun*.

I swung the ax in a quick half circle, and a thin razor of blue light arced out from the blade, quickly slicing a baker's dozen Drenchers cleanly in half where they swam. It looked almost like Elven magic, but I now knew that the two types of magic were actually more similar than different. With the Rune Bloodletter, I suddenly knew I could perform any spell I wanted.

The ax propelled me forward, tearing through the water toward Ari.

Along the way, I spun and twirled, dispatching several more Drenchers as if they weren't even there. I cleaved another in half from the top of its head down the middle to its legs. Then two bursts of blue energy fired from the blades of the ax, vaporizing a couple more that had been pulling at Ari's arms.

---

* Or maybe even do one better. Put down this book and go get a music-playing device of your choice. Go on, I'll wait. Now find that hero song that's in your head, press play, and listen to the song for real while you finish this part of my story.

She swam toward me, eyes wide with a mixture of fear and wonder.

We clasped hands as the remaining Drenchers hesitated around us, suspended in the water, debating whether to keep going after their prey or to simply flee in terror.

I didn't even give them the chance to make a choice.

The Bloodletter was suddenly pinwheeling out of my hand, twirling through the seawater like some kind of self-guided torpedo-boomerang-ninja-star. It did a quick arc in the water, easily taking care of the remaining Drenchers, then returned to my hand as if on a string.

WWHHOOOOOOEEEEE! the ax belted as it killed the Drenchers. And once back in my grasp, he said: *Come on, Greggdroule, let's go win a war!*

CHAPTER 43

Never Tell Me the Odds

It almost scared me how easy magic had become.

Before, when I'd tried to perform a spell, it felt like I was merely hoping for the best. And my efforts were mostly successful. But then there were the times I had accidentally set my own pants on fire and whatnot. But now, with the Bloodletter and Rune united, I knew I could do any spell I wanted. Even a spell as nuanced as turning a single, specific hair on someone's head gray and then back again, took as little effort as merely thinking it into existence.

Transporting Ari and myself back to Chicago had been almost laughably simpler than our trip getting from Russia to the San Francisco Bay, and not just because it was a much shorter distance. We still used the virtual wind tunnel spell, but this time it was more controlled, less violent, more precise, and much faster.

There were still some limitations of Dwarven magic, of course: I couldn't create a new kind of energy or materialize something that wasn't a natural part of the earth or bring a dead person back to life or anything like that. But I did now have a full understanding of how wide open those supposed "limitations" actually were.

Even now, as I stood on the roof of the Hotel Arista, just outside of Naperville, Illinois, looking out across a horizon filled with armies, monsters, weapons—*certain destruction*—I was confident I would survive, knowing all the new power the Rune Bloodletter would bring me. But I still felt devastated that the battle needed to occur at all, and far less certain our side would win.

The Hotel Arista had been a natural choice for a forward base of operations. It was twelve stories high and sat in a relatively undeveloped area, aside from a few clusters of housing developments and office complexes. It provided sprawling views of the region just north of Naperville. Plus, the hotel was large enough to house most of the Dwarven and Elven leadership. The armies themselves were staying in tents and RVs spread out across the fields and parking lots below. Perhaps most fitting of all, the Hotel Arista was just half a mile away from where the Verumque Genus Elves and their massive army had set up camp. They were resting, after decimating most of Aurora, parts of Naperville, and several other western suburbs on their warpath toward Chicago: Capital City for the entire Dwarven nation.

The view from the roof was quite a sight.

While the size of our allied armies was impressive, it paled when compared to that of the Verumque Genus Elves and their monsters.

To the south and east of the hotel was the entirety of the Midwestern Alliance Dwarven Army, a camp holding some 20,000 trained soldiers, including 2,000 Sentry Elite Guard special forces warriors. Joining us were several smaller Dwarven armies from across the globe, including 1,500 soldiers from

Kimmy Bitterspine's NOLA faction, 8,000 from the West Coast, another 10,000+ from East Coast factions, several thousand more from Canada, and just fewer than 5,000 from the rest of the world. We'd hoped for a lot more, as our Council was the ruling governmental body for the entire Dwarven world, but the reality was that many of the smaller factions just couldn't get their armies here in time. Or else were simply too busy dealing with more immediate threats in their own regions. So as it stood, the fate of the civil foundations of the entire Dwarven race (millions globally), came down to an army of roughly 45,000 soldiers, along with close to 2,000 monsters and fantastical creatures that we had pacified and allied with during Monster Pacification Missions over the past several months.

To the south of the hotel sprawled a much smaller camp containing the allied Elven armies Edwin had brought with him. Though numbering a solid 17,000, plus another several hundred monsters and creatures, their army was admittedly a lot smaller than any of us had expected. Edwin had explained to our Council that the Elven kingdom was still quite fractured, with a vast majority of Elves either in hiding, on their own, or simply not willing to choose a side until they saw who prevailed between Edwin's forces and the Verumque Genus. But, he had promised, those present would fight valiantly until the end. And I knew he was right. His people were good fighters, well trained and well equipped, even more so than our own Dwarven armies.

The collective army of 65,000 Elven and Dwarven* soldiers

---

* Some consideration was given to including Humans, but it was decided that they would likely cause more harm than good, being so poorly prepared to deal with foes like Orcs and Dragons, and with the majority of their weapons now dead and useless.

and monsters surrounded the Hotel Arista to the east, north, and south.

But to the west, the army of Verumque Genus Elves and their monsters dwarfed us, if you'll forgive my pun. Literally, their army spanned the entire western horizon. An ocean of black dots, tents, wings, horns, and all manner of shapes, cries, and growls, lit up by moonlight and the residual fires of the burning wasteland that was once Aurora and parts of Naperville. The sight of it was breathtaking. And horrifying. Their forces were confirmed to contain whole legions of Orcs, masses of Goblins, hordes of Manticores, flocks of Harpies and Wyverns, several dozen full-blown Dragons of a wide variety of species, packs of Werewolves, and many, many other creatures. Plus, they had at least 15,000 Verumque Genus Elven soldiers. All in all, their forces topped 300,000. And when our military commander, Debelle Blackarmor, factored in the weighted fighting forces of monsters (for instance: one Manticore equaled 6 trained Dwarves), she said their forces were actually equivalent to a Dwarven army of over 1,000,000.

Those were our odds: 1,000,000 to 65,000.

We weren't simply outnumbered; we were facing near certain defeat, at least on paper. But we had no choice. Standing aside and fleeing, allowing them to devastate and destroy a city containing close to 8,000,000 hapless Humans, Dwarves, and Elves was not an option. Besides, none of the Dwarven commanders or Council seemed to fully understand the incalculable power of the Bloodletter now that it had been reunited with the *Corurak*, even after I'd tried to explain it to them. Nor did they understand the powers the Sword of Anduril would bring Edwin. None of us did, for that matter.

But the point is: with those two weapons on our side, anything was possible.

The prophet Kreych had said as much.

The Verumque Genus were expected to attack in just a few hours, at the peak of the full moon, when their three divisions of Werewolves would fully transform, and their Moonwraiths and other Specters would be at full power.

So I decided to use that time to go back downstairs into the hotel and say my goodbyes, should we succumb to the odds in the end.

CHAPTER 44

Non-Goodbye Goodbyes

Glam was in her room with her parents.

All of us who'd gone on the mission to find the amulet had been appointed a guest room inside the Hotel Arista with our families. The rest of the rooms housed nearly half of our Council members, high-ranking Sentry officers, and Regional Dwarven Committee officials representing the visiting armies. The other half of our Council—along with Dwarves not trained in combat—were back in Chicago, in the Underground, hoping for the best.

But the vast majority of Dwarves in Chicagoland had received at least some combat training, and so were here, ready to defend the city, camped outside along with the other regular soldiers, and the full force of the Sentry. It was all hands on deck. No holding back. In fact, just a single squad of twelve Sentry had been left behind to guard the Underground.

Glam smiled when she saw me at her hotel door.

"Ari told me you and the Bloodletter are like . . . well, pretty fierce now," she said. "I'm a little jealous."

"Well, the good news is *you* don't need an ancient enchanted weapon and powerful Rune to be fierce."

Her smile widened and she shrugged. "So what brings you to our room at the dawn of battle?"

"Nothing specific, just—uh—you know . . ." I stammered, struggling to find a nonmorbid way to explain that I was potentially saying goodbye forever. "Doing the rounds . . ."

"In case we all die tonight, you mean?"

"Well, umm . . ."

Glam laughed.

"We all gotta die someday, Greg," she said. "I'd rather it be defending our city, defending the moral high ground, fighting for innocents, than sick in bed someday. Or in some pointless car accident, not that that's really possible anymore, but you know what I mean."

"Yeah, I do," I said, surprised by how much her point of view comforted me. "I suppose you're probably just excited to finally smash some Elves?"

Her smile slowly faded.

"I wish that were true," she said. "You know I like smashing stuff. And I don't particularly like Elves. But we have been through a lot with your friend Edwin and his people. And I guess, well, I can see that they're not so bad. I mean, I'll still never love them, but I also don't really want to kill them or anything like that. Plus, smashing things is more fun when your whole world isn't on the line."

I nodded solemnly, not wanting to leave already, but also knowing I had limited time to speak to a lot of people.

"Well, thank you for welcoming me as your friend all those months ago," I said, my throat tightening. "And if this is . . ."

"It's not," Glam said so firmly it made me believe her. "I will talk to you on the other side, after the battle is over and we've won."

I nodded again.

"See you then, buttercup," she said with a smile.

Eagan greeted me with a huge bear hug.

It was the first time I'd seen him since Ari and I had returned to Chicago. Which meant it was also the first time we'd seen each other since I departed for Russia on the SVRB *Powerham*.

"You did wonderfully, Greg," Eagan said, inviting me into his room. "I know we didn't get the amulet, but the Council is at least relieved that *nobody* did. Or ever can."

"Thanks," I said, in spite of still feeling as if our mission had ultimately been a failure.

He sat down in a chair next to the desk as I sat on the end of the bed. I noticed his combat armor and weapons lying on the floor near the closet.

"Is that just a precaution?" I asked, pointing at the gear. "Or are you joining the battle?"

"I can't just stand back and watch everyone else fight the battle for me," he said.

"But I thought the Council was barred from taking part in the fighting. To preserve the civil structure and everything."

Eagan nodded slowly and then tilted his head in a half shrug.

"Plans have changed," he said. "Once we finally saw the full fighting force we're facing tonight with our own eyes, anyone with combat experience or training was ordered into action. Council members, Elders, *everyone*. I'm surprised you hadn't heard."

"I literally got back just an hour or two ago," I said. "I only spoke to Dunmor for a few minutes to debrief him on the new powers of the Bloodletter."

"Yeah, Ari told me about that," Eagan said, nodding. "Anyway, yeah. Over half the Council will be taking up arms alongside the rest of you. On the rear flanks, mind you, but we're still likely to see combat. Even Dunmor is suiting up. He insists he's no more or less important than anyone else qualified to fight."

"You don't agree with him?"

"Well, I admire his humility," Eagan said. "But I also can't deny it would prove complicated, chaotic, and possibly structurally fatal to suddenly lose half our government in one single battle."

"To be fair, there will be nothing to preserve or save if we lose the battle outright," I countered with a slight smile.

Eagan nodded and laughed nervously.

"Yeah, that's why my gear is ready," he said, staring at the armor for a second longer, before facing me again. "So what happened to Stoney? Ari said he's still there? In the Hidden Forest?"

I nodded.

Traveling quickly by magic, Ari and I had managed to stop by Bigfoot John's cave before leaving the enchanted realm. I'd insisted it was worth the time to check on Stoney. Since he couldn't travel via magic like we could, he had to stay behind regardless, but I'd at least needed to see him before I left. In case—well, in case I never made it back.

"He was still unconscious when we last saw him," I said, and Eagan made a face. "Don't worry, though," I added quickly. "He's in good hands. Bigfoot John is taking care of him. He assured me he was going to be okay. I'm planning to head back there to get him at some point, after this war is over. Well, assuming we win, that is. I have to go back to the Hidden Forest anyway, because I made a promise to some trees at the entrance. And Dwarves don't break promises."

"You made a promise to . . . *some trees?*" Eagan asked, eyebrows arched.

"Long story," I said with a grin.

Eagan nodded and glanced at his armor again. Unlike Glam, he didn't offer me any brash assurances that we would win. He thought much more like a Dwarf. Much more like me. We knew nothing was assured at this point, except that lots of people and creatures were going to die, regardless of who won.

"Thank you for stopping by, Greg," Eagan said, standing up. "I wish we could sit here all night and talk about the war instead of actually fighting it, but that's not an option. I have to get ready now; I'm due to meet with the Council soon, one final session before the battle."

I sighed and nodded as I stood up.

We hugged again, but this time it was quicker, with a lot of dude-back-slaps, as if we were trying to beat each other's tears back into our heads.

"Thanks for everything, Eagan," I said. And then, not knowing where the confidence was coming from, I added: "You're going to make a great Council Alderman someday. I know it."

"And you're going to be a great hero tonight," he shot back with a playful smile, knowing full well how much I never wanted that for myself. "Because you'll *have* to be."

———◦✦◦———

Ari and Lake met up with me in the hallway near my room a short time later.

"Thanks for meeting us," Ari said.

"Thy parental constituents lest requested ye chamber privacy," Lake added.

"It's okay," I said. "Works better for me, anyway. I have to talk to my dad before it all starts . . ."

They both nodded solemnly as we all sighed.

The full moon was nearing its optimal position in the night sky. It would all begin less than an hour from now.

"Where are the NOLA Dwarves? And Tiki?" I asked. "I haven't seen them."

"They chose to be outside and camp with the NOLA faction army," Ari explained. "They want to be with their own families for the battle."

"Tis nobler than thyne expectations, nary be it for ye Dwarf," Lake said.

I nodded in agreement—that did sound like a Dwarven thing to do.

"Well, thanks for being my friends all these months," I said. "For welcoming me into your group like you did. And for saving my life so many times along the way."

"Greg, stop it," Ari said, wiping her eyes. "This isn't goodbye."

"Thy do'eth describe accurate portrayals yonder events past," Lake joked. "Thee oweth thyne companions thy existence!"

"Well, I'll gladly return the favor tonight as many times as I can," I said to him.

Lake laughed and nodded, then gave me a friendly pat on the arm, before turning and walking away.

"I asked him to give us a moment alone earlier," Ari explained. "I just wanted to . . . well, um . . ."

I stood there uncomfortably. I assumed she was just struggling, like, to get out her true feelings. Since this could be the last time we'd ever speak to each other.

"I know," I finally said. "This is pretty heavy . . ."

"No, that's not what . . ." Ari said, then stopped again to collect herself. "It *is* heavy, but that's not what I'm trying to say. Greg, I'm worried about you."

"Huh?"

"You and the Bloodletter," she said. "I don't think it was wrong for us to go get it. We need it for this fight. Clearly." She motioned toward the west, where the massive, overwhelming army was mobilizing for their attack. "But what I saw in the San Francisco Bay was . . . well, it was awesome. And powerful. And inspiring."

"Okaaay . . ." I said, not seeing the problem.

"But it was also scary, Greg. I mean, the way . . . the way you so easily slaughtered all those Drenchers without hesitating was . . ."

"I was trying to *save you!*" I said defensively.

"I know!" she said. "I know, and I will be forever grateful. That's not what I mean. It's just, it looked like it wasn't even a decision you made. It was automatic, like you were simply taking a breath. I just worry about what that ax does to you. At the end of all this, I just want you to remain *you*. It's almost not worth winning this war if we have to become something we're *not* to do it.

"I know we need the Bloodletter, and we need *you* to wield it. But be careful, is all I'm saying. We need you to be a hero tonight, but . . . well, the slaughter, the power, the death, it all looked too easy back there. I'm actually *less* worried about losing tonight than winning. If we lose, then we'll be dead and we won't know any better. But if we *win*, that's what worries me. You know, specifically what will happen to *you* afterward . . ."

My initial instinct was to launch into my own defensive, abrasive soliloquy on how I'm pretty much our only hope.

The Bloodletter even egged me on.

I told you not to save this one, he said. *Look how ungrateful! She doesn't want you to be powerful! I mean, what kind of friend is she?*

But I fought that urge, because I knew the truth. The real answer to his question was: *a great friend.*

I took a deep breath and nodded.

"I appreciate your concern," I said. "And I promise I will do my best to only use the ax when necessary. To only harness the power for the right reasons. And when it's all over, I will put it away for good."

Ari smiled and nodded, but something in her eyes told me she wasn't fully convinced.

I opened my mouth to say more, but she stopped me.

"Can we just spend this last minute together in silence?"

I nodded, and then suddenly she was hugging me there in the hotel hallway.

We just stood in silence, embracing for nearly a minute. It was quiet. Peaceful. By the end, I was openly crying, and I knew she was, too.

My dad was alone in our room, just sitting at the desk, staring out the window at the armies below.

He would not be joining the battle due to his condition.[*]

---

[*] You know, the one where he would break into a dazed state and spout off nonsensical *Kernels of Truth* for up to ten minutes at a time.

"I can't believe it's come to this," he said quietly.

"Me either," I said, sitting down next to him on the window ledge. "I really thought we'd find a way to avoid a huge battle where thousands will die."

"It wasn't supposed to be like this . . ."

I wasn't sure if he was speaking to me directly or just speaking in general. Either way, this was the most solemn and defeated I'd ever seen my dad. His usual hopefulness, his usual brazen willingness to dive in to anything, sure of failure or otherwise, was gone. He seemed just a shadow, a glimmer of what he once was.

"I'm sorry I never found the ingredients for the potion," I said, referring to the brew that I knew could cure him.

I had intended to look for them in the Hidden Forest, but our mission had just gone wrong in so many ways. And I'd been determined not to make my usual mistakes, not to let my own self-interest interfere with the larger goal. And so I ultimately had spent very little time looking for them.

My dad either hadn't heard me, or didn't care, or was about to have another episode, because he didn't respond. He just sat there, still staring out the window at our armies mobilizing below, forming into their ranks.

As I sat there, looking at my dad, I was surprised at how bitter and angry I was getting. He had always said magic was the answer. Magic would bring us peace. But now magic was back, and we were about to wage the most epic and bloody battle ever fought on American soil (at least since Separate Earth times).

"How could you have wanted magic back, Dad?" I asked suddenly, the bitterness in my own voice surprising me. "It's going to—it already *has* led to so many deaths. Why did you want it back?"

He hung his head for a second. Then finally looked up at me for the first time since I'd entered. His eyes were red and sunken and lost.

"I was probably wrong all along," he said flatly, dashing my hope that he'd have some clever reply that could restore my faith in our future. "But sometimes hope is all you have. You have to believe in it, even when logic tells you otherwise. I just never wanted to let go; I had to believe I was right because the alternative was too bleak."

I breathed in sharply, unable to stay angry with him, but also unable to find any of that hope he'd held on to for so many decades in his life.

"Dad, I . . ." But no words came.

We sat in silence for a few seconds.

"A *Kernel of Truth* for you, then!" he eventually said, his eyes empty as another fit set in. I groaned. "If you want to scare the dog, rubber dinosaur hand puppets work best. But if you want to scare the dinosaur, then—"

WHOOOP! WHOOP! WHOOOOP!

His words were drowned out by the sound of the hotel fire alarm blaring in the rooms and hallways. It was near deafening, but my dad droned on as if nothing was happening.

But something *was* happening.

The Battle of Naperville was about to begin.

CHAPTER 45

A Final Moment with My Former Best Friend

I threw on my armor (only a helmet, a breastplate, and forearm guards), grabbed the Rune Bloodletter, and headed to the roof to get a better sense of how the battle was going to play out.

Since I had arrived at the Hotel Arista so close to the start of the battle, Commander Blackarmor hadn't assigned me a particular squad or division. Rather, while looking at me dubiously, she'd simply said: "Just help out in any way you can, Greg."

I figured I'd get a better sense of how to do that by seeing the battlefield from above. I wanted to identify where I'd be most needed before simply dashing out into the chaotic fray.

Once on the roof, my breath caught in my throat.

The sights and sounds of hundreds of thousands of soldiers mobilizing on both sides—even stretching past my line of sight on the western horizon—was beautiful and terrifying at the same time.

Thousands of Dragons, Wyverns, Sirens, and other flying creatures clouded the dark sky, blotting out the stars to the west.

"It would be pretty if it weren't so scary," a voice said behind me.

Edwin grinned humorlessly, decked out in full Elven armor (which was a lot lighter and sleeker than ours, with fancy carvings and designs all over it).

"It still is," I said, turning back to the battlefield. "Pretty, I mean."

"I suppose it is," he agreed. "It's almost *boo*tifully scary."

I couldn't even force a laugh at his bad pun during a time like this, but I did manage an exaggerated eye roll.

"If we win," I said, "we need to promise we won't start fighting each other right afterward."

"Well, let's just focus on the immediate task at hand first," Edwin said. "Afterward is when I'll figure out how to beat you."

I shot him a dirty look.

"Okay, bad joke," he admitted. "*Of course* I don't want to keep fighting with Dwarves. And now with the amulet out of the picture, I can't even implement my plan, which perhaps would have been the biggest source of conflict between our two sides anyway."

"It *was* a bad plan," I said.

"Whatever, dude. It doesn't matter anymore. Honestly, I have no idea what the future holds for us after this. It will be tricky, and tense, but after what's about to happen here, I'm sure both of our armies will be tired of fighting. At least for a while. Hopefully."

I nodded. "Maybe we can even go back to being best friends in the end."

Edwin laughed, but it sounded genuine and hopeful, and not cynically bitter.

"If sentient talking fart boogers named Blob can be a thing in this new world, then anything is possible," he said. "Anyway, I've got to get back to my command post and speak to the generals directing my armies. But with this thing now in my hands . . ." He paused to pat the hilt of the Sword of Anduril on his belt. "I'll be joining the fray before too long. Maybe I'll even see you out there."

"Maybe," I said. "Goodbye, buddy."

He put an armored hand on my shoulder, gave it a few pats, then turned and headed back toward the door.

My hand was still resting on the Bloodletter's handle, as it leaned up against the short wall on the roof.

It hummed with power and anticipation.

I'm so excited for this, the Bloodletter whispered in my head. *We're going to decimate that army. You and I. Together.*

The Rune Bloodletter was clearly very powerful, unimaginably so. There was no denying it. But I still didn't know exactly what that meant. Or what it could fully do. Regardless, the siege had begun, and so for now the only thing to do was fight. Even though all I had ever wanted was to reject this destiny. Reject this notion that I was the Bloodletter's Chosen One, the Dwarf long foretold to take possession of the powerful ax and restore our race to glory. That because of my bloodline I was supposed to be some heroic and brave warrior.

I had done nearly everything I could to avoid this ending.

To avoid battles, and fighting, and war, and the Bloodletter. But I had failed miserably. Which, if you're still with me this far, you can't really be surprised by.

But I never could have just walked away. Or, I could have, but I never *would* have. All along the way, someone had needed help. Some mission for the greater good had presented itself, and each time my friends and I had been the only ones to rise to the challenge (more or less).

So here I was again.

The war was starting, and I had two choices:

1. Sit back and pretend a war wasn't happening and watch my friends and family perish
2. Get out there and help my friends and family win the war

The way I saw it, there really was no choice at all.

Below me, maybe half a mile away, along the now desolate and unused Interstate 88, armies collided. Orcs crashed into Dwarves. An ocean of Goblins swarmed a small squad of Elves. Manticores, Centaurs, and giant lizard thingies I didn't recognize charged through whole divisions of our soldiers. Fire burst forth from the mouths of several dragons swooping past overhead. Only a Dwarven spell, casting a frost cloud over a division of troops, saved them from getting burned alive.

I grabbed my helmet from the ledge and put it on.

Lifted the Bloodletter with two hands.

Let's get to work, Greggdroule.

I nodded and leaped from the roof of the Hotel Arista. My wind spell easily caught me and carried me right into the center of the battlefield.

CHAPTER 46

The Battle of Naperville

A s I soared toward the action, I magically summoned several bolts of lightning as easily as flipping a light switch.

Three jagged spiderwebs of blue light crackled across the sky and connected with several Dragons. Their sizzling, lifeless forms fell, trailing smoke, back to the earth. As my wind spell carried me gently to the ground, I threw my ax up toward a whole squad of Sirens flying overhead, searching the battlefield for victims. Guided partially by my spell and partially by its own powerful magical will, the Rune Bloodletter swooped through the sky and felled the entire right flank of Sirens, before returning to me just as I leaped onto the shoulders of an unsuspecting Orc.

"URRgHHH?" the Orc cried out, as the bodies of dozens of Sirens fell like winged rain.

I didn't speak Orcish, but I hoped his last word was at least meaningful, and not just a surprised exclamation.

As he fell, I hopped down and took on the rest of the squad of Orcs by myself (fourteen in total), and easily won, the Bloodletter screaming with glee the entire time.

Next I ran into an entire division of Goblins, over three hundred in all. They swarmed me. But a few spells and a full display of the Rune Bloodletter's power later, I was the last one standing.

After that, I freed up a flank of Dwarven warriors that had been pinned down by a pack of ferocious Nekimara (which are basically mischievously deadly, ghoulish vampires). They had a lot of magical powers and very few things could kill them. Thankfully, the Rune Bloodletter was one of them. I wiped out the entire group amid jets of vampire blood and unnatural screeching.

Then I saw a herd of Manticores. Back on Alcatraz, I had fought perhaps a dozen by myself, with the aid of the normal Bloodletter. It was difficult, but I had succeeded. Now, with the Rune Bloodletter, I easily wiped out over a hundred, and it could have been more if there had been more left to kill.

The power of the reunited Bloodletter and *Corurak* Rune was obscene.

Next I turned my attention to ten towering Mountain Trolls who were trying to stomp out a squad of Edwin's Elves. Back in the Underground, when just three Mountain Trolls had attacked, it had taken two full squads of Sentry to take them out. Now all ten of these monsters were eliminated with a simple flick of my wrist and a few effortless spells.

Then a pack of Werewolves came charging at me, savage and snarling, their faces matted with the blood of my fallen comrades. Traditionally, there was only one way to kill a full-moon Werewolf: silver to the brain. Well, now you can add a second way to the list: the *Corurak* Rune Bloodletter. It cut right through them as if they were wisps of fog.

Before long, I looked down at myself and realized I was covered in monster blood of all kinds and colors. I looked like the Jackson Pollock painting that used to hang on the wall in Edwin's parents' mansion.

I had already been fighting nonstop for close to an hour. And with the energy of the Rune Bloodletter spurring me on, I could go for another twenty if that was what it would take.

The battlefield was an epic wasteland. Buildings were leveled; the interstate was covered in bodies, burning cars, and chunks of upturned, crumbling asphalt.

Then I spotted several Council Elders engaged in battle with an Elemental, just to the south of I-88. An Elemental was a huge creature made from dirt. It had no organs or limbs and therefore was nearly impossible to kill as it swarmed its enemies, attempting to smother them with its shapeless, heaving body. The Elemental was essentially a moving mound of soil the size of a small house.

Chunks of Dwarven armor were stuck in its body, indicating it had already taken out quite a few of our soldiers.

Dunmor and another Elder, Dhon Dragonbelly, were desperately running from and dodging around the Elemental. They rolled and dove out of the way as the Elemental thumped down again and again, trying to bury them in its folds of dirt.

As they dodged the attacks, Dhon fired several arrows from a crossbow. They pierced the dirt body of the Elemental, then disappeared inside, causing the creature no pain or damage whatsoever.

Both Dunmor and Dhon looked exhausted.

I ran toward them, ready to easily take care of the beast.

But then I saw my dad.

He came flying in out of nowhere, not even wearing any battle armor. He charged right *into* the back of the Elemental. My dad actually disappeared *inside* the beast, while holding a Dwarven shortsword awkwardly in front of him like a fragile stick.

The Elemental collapsed around my dad, and for a second I feared he was dead.

But then the Elemental howled, a noise so unearthly and bizarre, words cannot describe it.

The beast convulsed as chunks of earth and dirt flew away from it in all directions, almost like it was shedding its skin.

Then the massive creature simply came apart, collapsing into a harmless pile of dirt, with my dad still standing right in the middle, a small black heart—the Elemental's heart—skewered on the end of his sword.

"Trevorthunn!" Dunmor cried. "You were supposed to stay back at the hotel!"

My dad shrugged as they embraced.

"I couldn't sit back and do nothing," he said. "*Condition* or not."

"Well, I'm glad you didn't," Dhon added, clapping my dad on the shoulder. "You saved our lives!"

Then the three of them turned and ran off toward a skirmish near a derelict gas station, where a division of Lykken Ghouls was closing in on a small squad of Elven archers, who were cornered and running low on arrows.

I debated going to help, but seven Sentry Elite warriors fell in behind Dhon, Dunmor, and my dad, and I knew they wouldn't need me.

Instead I turned my attention to the rear flank of the Verumque Genus forces.

I was determined to find their leader: my old school bully, Perry Sharpe. If I ended him, it might just end this battle. We'd been fighting for an hour, and our side was clearly winning. But the VG monster army was so massive that the death toll would be unbearable if we had to literally fight it out until the end.

A quick wind spell lifted me into the air so I could get a better vantage.

I was much closer to the rear flank of their army than I'd suspected. But at the same time, it was clear there was still so much more fighting to be done. As I hovered, held up by magical gusts of wind, I quickly dispatched fifteen or twenty Wyvern with lighting spells.

Killing things was too easy with the power of the Rune Bloodletter coursing through me.

I saw now why Ari had been so concerned.

But my job wasn't done yet, and so I had to continue.

As I searched the ranks for the Verumque Genus leader, several brilliant flashes of purple light caught my attention.

It was Edwin, a hundred yards away, to my left.

He was single-handedly wiping out an entire squad of River Trolls with the Sword of Anduril.

It was clearly as powerful as the Rune Bloodletter, if not more so.

It glowed with purple flames that flowed more like liquid than fire. Edwin was almost floating, he moved so easily with the sword in his hand. As he spun and twirled, the blade passed right through metal, Troll swords, armor, flesh, Troll parts, concrete, *everything*, so easily it was like they were all made of air.

Once Edwin finished off the last of the Trolls, he turned and looked at me.

We locked eyes.

He pointed northwest, and I gazed that way.

A massive Ogre Giant (which is basically like a regular Ogre, except, you know, a lot bigger) lumbered on the darkened horizon, not engaging in the battle, but sort of holding back. Almost as if it was observing the battle and nothing more. But that wouldn't make any sense. Ogre Giants had about as much aptitude for battle strategy as a wooden block. As the largest creature involved in this battle, it would be much more useful simply smashing things.

But that's when I noticed something, or *someone*, sitting on its shoulder.

I flew closer, taking out another Dragon on the way, as Edwin ran in the same direction below me.

Once I was close enough for the moonlight to illuminate the Ogre Giant's features in a strange, ghastly light, I finally saw who was on its shoulder.

Perry Sharpe.

He was surveying the action, shouting out orders, and casting occasional wild spells indiscriminately into the battlefield, almost as if he didn't even care which soldiers they hit, just as long as they hit and killed *something*.

I brought myself back to the ground alongside Edwin.

"Dude, you're *covered* in monster blood," he said.

"How are you not?"

"I guess Elves do everything with a little more grace," he joked. "Apparently even killing monsters in battle."

"This is getting dark," I said, as we both casually engaged several charging Orcs, easily taking them out with a couple of quick spells.

"Yeah, man," he agreed. "Let's go take that jerk Perry out. Maybe if he falls, we can end this before it goes on much longer."

I nodded.

We ran forward, toward the Ogre Giant together.

Surrounding the hulking beast, who was easily seventy tall feet tall, was a whole division of Manticores and a legion of regular Ogres, all guarding their leader, Perry Sharpe. His bodyguard force numbered at least 2,000 Ogres and Manticores combined, possibly more.

But with the Sword of Anduril and the Rune Bloodletter in our hands, we remained unfazed.

Side by side, Edwin and I battled through the Ogres and Manticores.

I wish I could say it was a harrowing struggle for survival, but I can't.

The beasts fell and exploded and came apart as Edwin and I slashed, twirled, and chopped our way through the entire army. Our powers were so heightened that casting multiple spells simultaneously with hand-to-hand combat took almost no effort, a mere afterthought.

Near the end, the remaining several hundred Ogres scampered away in retreat, instead of staying and defending their leader to the death.

Don't let them get away, Greggdroule! the Bloodletter hissed. *They'll only terrorize other innocents if left out on the loose. They eat people, after all.*

I raised the ax, ready to cast a powerful spell that would wipe out all the retreating Ogres in one easy motion, but Edwin put a hand on my shoulder.

"Easy, dude," he said. "Let them go; they're retreating."

"But the Bloodletter said . . ." I started, almost as if in a daze.

"I don't care what your ax said," Edwin insisted. "You don't strike down a fleeing or surrendering enemy. Ever."

Yeah, and I'm totally sure his parents always abided by that rule, the Bloodletter said sarcastically. *The same parents who enslaved and tortured whole races of people.*

My ax made a good point, but I said nothing and merely nodded at Edwin. I let the Ogres make their escape. Because the truth was, Edwin was *not* like his parents. What they would do and what he would do were not the same thing. Nor should they be.

Perry Sharpe must have seen his own personal guards retreating, because he howled with rage from atop the Ogre Giant's shoulder.

"Get back here and protect your master, you lagwaggen cowards!" he screamed. Perry then issued an order to his Ogre Giant. "Kill the deserters!"

The huge beast picked up several long-dormant cars from the road nearby. It half-heartedly chucked them at the retreating Ogres. The cars crashed and tumbled as metal folded and windows shattered, missing their marks badly.

"What kind of throw was that, you moron!" Perry screamed into the Ogre Giant's ear.

It looked to both Edwin and me as if the Ogre Giant was about one or two more insults away from plucking Perry off his shoulder and flicking him into the netherworld of the western burbs like an Elven booger.

"So it's you two again!" Perry shouted down at us. "I should have known."

"Call off your army!" Edwin shouted up. "And we will spare your life."

Perry laughed bitterly.

"Kranklor!" he said. "Smash these two like the bugs they are."

Kranklor the Ogre Giant hesitated.

"Leave that thing out of this," I said.

"We don't want to kill you, too, Kranklor," Edwin said. "We will spare you if you don't attack us."

"Get them!" Perry shrieked. "Or I will kill you myself!"

Kranklor's face scrunched up in a panic.

"Why don't you just come down here and fight us yourself?" Edwin suggested. "And stop getting all these creatures to do your dirty work for you?"

"Hmmm," Perry mocked us. "No. I think I'd rather just have my Ogre Giant kill you both now."

Kranklor took a step toward us, having finally decided to keep its allegiance to its master.

"Last warning!" I shouted. "Please don't, Kranklor!"

"Kill them and I will reward you with riches beyond imagination!" Perry squealed into the Ogre Giant's ear with little semblance of any remaining sanity.

Kranklor roared and stomped toward us.

Again, I wish I could say it was some epic, exciting battle. But the truth was, nothing was a match for the two most powerful weapons on earth, working side by side in unison. Not Perry, not an Ogre Giant, not even a huge army topping 300,000. In fact, the final battle with Perry Sharpe, the leader of the Verumque Genus, lasted an entire two seconds.

Edwin and I both fired streaks of magic from our weapons at the same time.

They struck Kranklor in the chest, and he stumbled backward, stunned. Perry toppled from his shoulder as the Ogre Giant teetered. Perry shrieked during his entire fall, eventually landing on top of an abandoned fuel tanker with a metallic *thud*. Landing on the tanker probably saved Perry's life, at least initially, as he rolled and groaned in pain on top of it.

But then Kranklor the Ogre Giant finally fell.

Perry let out one last shrill whine seconds before the Ogre Giant crashed down on top of him and the old fuel truck, flattening Perry and the truck like an empty soda can. The impact was so deafening, the battle around us suddenly stopped. Well, as much as an epic battle spanning an area the size of a small town could stop, that is.

The Verumque Genus Elves and their monsters clearly were now aware that their leader had fallen. And if they hadn't known before this moment that they were losing this battle, despite still technically outnumbering us, they certainly realized it now.

I still expected the fighting to resume any second.

The Bloodletter was ready for that as well.

Come on, Greggdroule, strike now while they're distracted! he said, sounding wholly unhinged—or as unhinged as an ax can sound. *Use this to your advantage! See that whole squadron of River Trolls? You and I could wipe them out easily while they just stand there scratching their heads. We'll skin them alive and make fashionable raincoats from their hides! AH-HA-HAHAHA!*

But I didn't move.

Because shortly after the Bloodletter spoke, the squad of River Trolls he had referenced turned around and began walking away from the battlefield. One of the Verumque Genus Elven generals ran over as if to stop them. But then he quickly realized none of his troops had followed him.

He looked around desperately, discovering he was the only one who wanted this battle to continue.

Then he saw Edwin and me. His eyes furtively flicked to the Rune Bloodletter and the Sword of Anduril, still alight in rolling purple flames.

The VG Elven general tossed down his sword and joined the Trolls in their retreat.

"We did it, buddy," Edwin said quietly next to me. "We won."

I shook my head in disbelief as the entire Verumque Genus army, and all their monsters, began a slow and steady retreat.

Some of Edwin's men ran after a pack of Goblins trying to make their getaway.

Edwin used a spell to project his voice out over the entire battlefield.

"Stand down," he boomed. "The battle is over. Let them leave in peace."

His soldiers complied immediately.

"Nah!" someone with an Irish accent screamed a few moments later. "They'll only regroup and attack again! We must stop them now! Take them prisoner! Destroy them if they resist!"

I immediately recognized the voice. It was Ooj (O'Shaunnessy O'Hagen Jameson), a particularly nasty Council Elder, and one of the last remaining Leprechauns. He always seemed to take a less generous, more fearful, separatist, nationalist stance on nearly every issue. He pretty much voted the opposite of my dad, always, no matter how minor the topic.

Ooj was leading a whole platoon of Sentry Elite forces. They charged after a retreating division of Verumque Genus archers, fifty or sixty soldiers who clearly had no interest in turning back around and fighting.

"Stand down, Ooj!" Dunmor yelled, running after him. "Stand down!"

My father and Dhon Dragonbelly were close behind.

Edwin and I glanced at each other for a brief moment and then ran toward the fray, as Ooj and his men began firing arrows and launching throwing axes into the ranks of the retreating Verumque Genus Elves.

They completely ignored Dunmor's commands to cease fire.

And then Edwin intervened.

He began casting spells at Ooj and his squad of Sentry Elite. One burst of energy connected with three Dwarven Sentry, killing them instantly.

"Edwin, no!" I shouted, running after him.

I knew there would be many Dwarves who would never be able to forgive his actions, never be able to accept the context in which he had just killed three Dwarven soldiers.

The Sentry then turned their attention from the retreating Verumque Genus Elves toward Edwin. Lixi and several other soldiers were at his side now, all of them looking ready for a fight. Ready to defend their leader to the death if that was what it would take.

"I knew he was a traitor all along!" Ooj yelled. "Kill them all! Kill every Elf still standing!"

As a battle cry erupted from the Sentry, a lone diminutive form ran into the middle of the chaos.

"Please stop!" my dad shouted at Ooj and the Sentry, standing between them and Edwin. "We mustn't let this—"

His words were suddenly cut short.

To this day, nobody really knows (or will admit they know) who fired the fatal arrow.

But as soon as my dad fell, his sentence unfinished, we all knew he was gone.

CHAPTER 47

The Second Battle of Naperville

The trampled field behind the derelict ruins of a suburban gas station was completely still.

Edwin's agonized scream was the first noise, and then suddenly both of us were kneeling at my dad's side. But he was already gone. There was nothing we or anyone else could do. And it was weird; my first thought in that moment was not of how much I had loved and admired my dad, or of any specific moment we'd had together, playing chess, or fishing on the lake, or anything like that. My first thought, strangely, was of Froggy, sitting alone in his cave, seeing and witnessing this from afar. Perhaps he was feeling what I was feeling at that very moment, hoping I wouldn't do what I was about to do, but also knowing he couldn't stop me either way.

Froggy had to simply observe and record what came next.

You know whose fault this is, the Bloodletter seethed. *Now make him pay.*

"You . . ." I said, standing up, looking down at Edwin's tear-streaked face. "You did this!"

He shook his head.

"No . . . I didn't mean . . . I'm so sorry . . ."

The Bloodletter hummed in my hand so ferociously, it felt like my shoulder was going to separate from its socket.

"Why did you have to attack your own allies?" I hissed. "I know they were killing retreating soldiers, but better a retreating enemy than your own allies!"

"It's *wrong* to kill the defenseless," Edwin said, standing up, drawing the Sword of Anduril. "I'm honestly shocked you'd side with your own men, the ones murdering a retreating army! Shooting them in the back with arrows and axes like bloodthirsty savages!"

I shook my head in frustration.

He was twisting my words—of course I wasn't defending their actions. But they also had a right to be upset, after what the Verumque Genus Elves and their army had done over the past few weeks, rampaging across the Midwest toward Chicago, leaving a trail of destruction and death behind them. How could Edwin be so forgiving of *them*, retreating or not?

He doesn't get it, because he's an Elf, Greggdroule, the Bloodletter said. *Always has been, always will be. They think differently. He's so quick to defend his own kind, but the moment a Dwarf steps out of line for a second in the heat of battle, you'd think we'd slaughtered a whole village of kids or something! And now, because of his arrogance, his selective morality and self-righteousness, your dad is dead!*

I realized that, as the Bloodletter was speaking to me, I was saying those very same words aloud to Edwin, as if the ax and I had become one. And only when I'd finished speaking did the true heartbreak, pain, and anguish of losing my dad (without even getting a touching and sweet deathbed moment with him) set in.

Edwin shook his head, his expression changing from sorrow and regret to anger.

"How could you say these things after everything we've—" he started, but I didn't let him finish.

Rage and the Bloodletter had simply taken over.

I launched my first attack, vaguely aware that I was screaming like a lunatic.

Edwin narrowly dodged the blade of energy that fired from the end of my ax.

It whipped past him, the blue light slicing across the sky like a lightning bolt. It struck a small house on the edge of a development across the field, hundreds of yards away. The house exploded into a fireless mushroom cloud, leaving behind a scorched crater surrounded by thousands of chunks of wood framing, splinters of drywall, ceramic-tile dust, misshapen lumps of granite, and deformed kitchen appliances.

Edwin mounted a quick counterattack, lunging forward as if propelled from a cannon, the flaming tip of the Sword of Anduril pointed right at my heart.

I quickly lifted the Bloodletter and deflected the sword at the last second so that it merely grazed my right arm.

When the magical blades connected, even for that short moment, a massive concussion ripped apart the air, like someone breaking the sound barrier.

It momentarily dropped everyone to their knees.

Edwin and I both stood back up and faced each other.

His eyes were wide with fear, shock, and rage, and I didn't doubt that mine probably looked the same.

Everyone else was watching us now, all other tensions forgotten. It was as if we all understood this was a battle by proxy. Whoever won, Edwin or me, the Rune Bloodletter or the Sword of Anduril, would win the whole war. Would take command of everything.

I summoned a wind spell that lifted me off the ground.

I hovered above him.

"I have the high ground!" I yelled, remembering how we both used to make fun of that same cheesy line from some sci-fi movie franchise we watched at his house once. "Don't even try to—"

But his sword was already spewing jets of that swirling, mystical purple fire at me like a flamethrower. The pure force of it blasted me backward and out of the air. I managed to turn to stone just before impacting the ground and skidding thirty feet back across the torn pavement of the gas station's parking lot.

By the time I reanimated and was back on my feet, Edwin was already there, standing over me, swinging down his sword.

I held up the Rune Bloodletter, and the blades clanged together a second time.

The shock wave from the explosion of energy blew us apart by close to a hundred yards, leaving a massive, stadium-size crater between us, nearly as deep as a lake.

The crowd of onlookers, tens of thousands of Dwarven and Elven soldiers, kept taking furtive steps back, away from where our epic battle was laying waste to everything around it.

Edwin and I climbed to our feet again.

We stood on opposite ends of the newly formed crater and stared at each other. Even from a hundred yards away, I could see the determination and anger in his stance.

I lifted the Rune Bloodletter and launched a spell across the void.

Edwin did the same with the Sword of Anduril.

The powerful bursts of energy met in the middle, and another explosion tore through the edges of Naperville. The burst of light was so bright that anyone looking directly at it was instantly blinded (which ended up being several hundred soldiers from both sides). The ground shook, and all the windows in every building in a two-mile radius exploded and shattered into a gazillion pieces so fine they were like powdered sugar dusting the town.

The crater split apart, like we had just literally cracked the Earth open like an egg.

The void was nearly a hundred feet deep, and it pooled with molten lava. The initial burst of heat and steam was so intense it would have killed us both had our powerful weapons not been protecting us.

Everyone else backed even farther away from the lava crater, the place where Edwin and I had literally broken open the planet with our anger and vengeance.

Another wind spell lifted me, and I propelled across the small lake of lava, right toward Edwin.

AAAAAIIIIYYYYEEEEEEE! The Rune Bloodletter howled a gleefully unhinged battle cry.

Edwin's eyes went wide with fear, likely knowing as well as I did that if our legendarily powerful blades connected another time, it might just destroy us all, and maybe even the whole planet.

But I didn't care.

At least if that happened, the pain of losing my dad, of everything turning out this way in spite of all my best efforts, would finally be over.

Edwin used magic to quickly roll out of the way, faster than my eyes could track. My ax connected with the ground where he'd stood, leaving a smoking scorch mark like a scar.

I spun and swung at him again, but he ducked and then swept my feet out from under me; the Rune Bloodletter went flying from my hand.

Edwin saw his moment and lifted his sword to strike.

But I hit him in the chest with a quick burst of wind before he could finish me off, and he flew backward fifteen feet and tumbled across the ground, down the gentle slope on the outside of the lava lake crater.

I stood up and walked toward the Rune Bloodletter, panting, tired, scared, but oddly no longer totally enraged.

Except that wasn't odd at all.

There was a perfectly reasonable, well-established cause for the sudden dissipation of my anger and hatred.

I was no longer holding the Rune Bloodletter.

The ax was at my feet, glowing blue, urging me to pick it up and resume the attack. Not with words anymore; we were past that. Now I felt what it felt.

Who cared what would happen to the people, to the planet. At least I would finally have my revenge. Justice. I would restore Dwarves to all our glory.

I knew if I picked up the ax again, it would all be over. It would take control of me, and I would battle Edwin until either I died, or he died, or we both died, or *we all* died.

This was it, my last moment to decide my own fate for myself. (Well, and also everyone else's fate, too.)

Edwin was standing just below me, where the edge of the lava crater pushed up from the ground. The Sword of Anduril was in his hand, flaming purple, but he did not attack. He stood there and watched, waiting to see what I would do.

Would I pick up the ax and take us back to the very brink the Fairies had hoped to prevent by sacrificing themselves? Or would I leave it there, and finally choose the path I had always claimed I wanted, even if it meant Edwin would be free and clear to do what he saw fit with this world? To either rule or destroy it at his whim.

It was *my* choice.

I stood there for a while, looking down at the Rune Bloodletter. For how long is hard to say now. The ax was so beautiful and powerful, crafted with such care and skill, yet created only for destruction. For causing harm. But also for defending the innocent and protecting the right. For keeping order.

I wasn't sure when exactly I made my decision, but suddenly it had been made. I knew what I was going to do, whether I wanted to or not.

I reached down and picked up the Rune Bloodletter.

CHAPTER 48

The End of the World?
(Or at Least of This Story?)

I could almost feel the collective gasp from the onlooking Elves, Dwarves, and monsters as I picked up the ax.

The tension was hotter than the pools of molten lava behind me.

Edwin's eyes glowed as he stared at me in shock, reflecting the light from his flaming sword, which was raised and ready for the apocalyptic battle to resume.

I raised the Rune Bloodletter.

The blade shimmered in the light and heat from the lava behind me. The immense power of the ax pulsed like it was about to detonate. It sparkled with anticipation, ready for me to deliver a blow so powerful, it might literally kill us all.

But instead of attacking Edwin, I quickly spun around and threw the Rune Bloodletter out into the middle of the lake of lava.

As the blade pinwheeled through the air, a wail of tortured agony exploded in my head.

Greggdroule, NOOOOOOOOOO!

Those were the desperate, final words the Rune Bloodletter managed to scream before he hit the lava. The ax sat on the surface for several long seconds, as bubbles of molten rock splashed onto it. Then the blade began to bleed at the edges like ink running from the pages of a book left out in the rain. The most powerful ax in Dwarven history melted quickly, fusing back with the very earthly elements that had created it.

Gone forever.

I stood on the edge of the crater and faced the thousands of Elves and Dwarves looking up at me in shock.

Edwin was so stunned the Sword of Anduril had fallen to his side, extinguished. Its tip rested on the ground as the sword dangled limply in his right hand.

Then a vision struck me. My dad's vision.

"I urge all of you to do as I have just done," I called out to the crowd of soldiers. "Weapons were made for one thing: killing. You can argue they're for defense. Protection. Upholding law and justice. But I propose this: If no articles of destruction existed in the first place, then what would we need protection from? Why do swords, axes, arrows need to exist at all? They are not tools, but simply articles of devastation!

"This world can be better than that. Yes, we all have personal freedom. We can choose to have weapons, but why would we? *Why* would you choose that if your heart and intentions are pure? We can forge a new existence where we simply live for the greater good. Where magic and metals are used for the advancement of humanity, not the propagation of fear. We can work together for a world filled simply with love. It can be achieved. We will live and let live, and harming others will be a distant memory. In time, we won't even remember what weapons were!

"So please, come forth, rid yourselves of this burden. Join me in a world without weapons, without violence, without war and murder. Throw your weapons into the fire. Create a new existence filled not with hate and fear, but with peace and harmony!"

I finished my speech breathing hard and panting, as I looked out across the crowd.

For an agonizing minute, nobody moved.

But then a solitary figure emerged from the ranks of the soldiers.

Ari walked slowly through the crowd, bleeding, dirty, and wounded. She climbed the crater, smiled at me, and threw her ax (which she had crafted herself years ago) into the lava lake. She took off her armor and tossed it in as well. Then she silently walked back down the slope of the crater.

Lixi climbed up the slope moments later and threw her weapons into the lake. Lake, Eagan, Tiki, and Foxflame followed. Then other soldiers did the same.

Before long, lines were forming, as everyone, Elf and Dwarf, took turns tossing their tools of destruction into the lake of lava. I even saw Dunmor and other Council Elders in line. Many of the Verumque Genus Elves and Orcs and Goblins had returned, and even *they* were throwing their weapons into the lake of fire. And nobody was cutting in line or shoving to get to the front. In fact, people and creatures were *letting* other people and creatures cut in line, and then making jokes about it.

After everyone had come forward, after tens of thousands of instruments of death and destruction had been melted down into liquid metal, only Edwin remained. Still standing there at the bottom of the crater, the Sword of Anduril in his hand.

He looked up at me, and then wordlessly climbed the slope.

Edwin stopped in front me, looked into my eyes, and grinned.

"I guess you really sold us all on the whole *make lava, not war* thing, huh?"

As I laughed at his lame pun, he stepped around me and threw the Sword of Anduril into the lava lake.

The whole crowd cheered.

And that was the beginning of the new world.

One without war or violence or destruction. A place where compassion and peace and kindness reigned supreme.

Where Dwarves and Elves walked arm in arm with Orcs and Goblins and Trolls and Blobs.

And we all lived happily ever after, with the smiling sun shining down on us day after day after day.

The End.*

---

* Well, kinda sorta maybe...

Okay, now here's where you get to decide what sort of person you are.

Yes, that's right, you get to decide. It doesn't matter where you were born, who your parents are, or what your genetic makeup is. You get to take the path you forge.

Got it?

Okay, then.

If you love the way this ended for me, and Edwin, and all of us, close this book right now and put it down and never pick it up again (unless it's to gush to a friend about how good (or bad) it was, or to use it as a coaster or something). If you like where things stand, STOP reading.

It's entirely your right to choose that path.

However, if you view life more like the Dwarves in this story, and you want to know the OTHER ending (or the REAL ending depending on how you want to view it), then by all means keep reading. But I must warn you: Things will not be as pretty, as pleasant, or as hopeful. And so that means if you're the first type of person, and you're still reading this, then I implore you again to stop and go enjoy the rest of your day in peace.

But if you're the type that must continue, if that's your ultimate decision, then I will see you on the next page.

Don't say I didn't warn you.

EPILOGUE

Because Stories Like This Always Have an Epilogue

Of course that's not how things ended.

Life doesn't usually work that way, does it?

I mean, I *did* throw the Bloodletter and the *Corurak* Rune into the lava lake, where they instantly melted out of existence.

And I *did* try to make an impassioned speech.

But things played out a bit differently. The way it really went was a lot more . . . well, *Dwarven*, for lack of a better term.

Here's how it all actually happened: After throwing the Rune Bloodletter into the lava lake, I turned and faced the stunned crowd. I took a deep breath and launched into a bold, heroic speech that would change everything:

"I urge all of you to do as I have just done," I called out to them. "Weapons were made for one thing: killing. You can argue they're for defense—"

"I *will* argue that!" someone cried out. "I mean, the only reason I have this sword at all is to defend my home and my family from monsters. Which is what I'm doing right now!"

I sighed.

"Okay, sure," I said. "But they were *designed* to kill, which is—"

"Yeah, designed to kill someone who's trying to kill *you!*" another voice chimed in. "I mean, I hate to say it, kid, but we'd all be dead right now if it weren't for that weapon you just destroyed."

"I know," I called out, getting frustrated. "But my point is that if no weapons ever existed at all, then I wouldn't have needed mine to begin with!"

A brief silence followed. Then a small Dwarven warrior, not much older than me, stepped forward. At first, I thought he was going to walk up and poignantly throw his sword into the fire, which would start the chain reaction I had envisioned.

But instead he scoffed loudly.

"If I may," he said rather politely, considering he began it all with a scoff. "I like your argument, Greggdroule. *In theory.* But it simply can't apply here. Because, you see, weapons *do* exist. We can't undo that now. You are correct: It would be wonderful to live in a world without them. But that's simply not possible anymore. They're here, and there's no way everyone everywhere will agree to destroy them all. Something like that would take total commitment. What you're asking is simply not possible. Thank you for listening."

His soft-spoken argument was received with a decent smattering of applause from the crowd.

"Okay, I get that, but the world can be *better* than that!" I shouted. "I mean, we can all choose—"

"No, it can't!" someone else interrupted. "I think we've bloody well proven that we are all pretty fallible. Nobody can be perfect, and by proxy, the world can't be either."

"For the love of Odrick's Beard, I'm trying to have a big hero moment here!" I cried out. "Please stop interrupting me!"

But it was too late; the crowd was getting antsy and restless, and several arguments were already breaking out among the soldiers.

Then suddenly Edwin was beside me.

I figured he was there to put me out of my misery. Perhaps a swift beheading would have done nicely. But instead he slammed the tip of the Sword of Anduril into the ground. The magical spark and concussion that followed silenced the rowdy crowd immediately.

"May I remind you all," he boomed in his naturally authoritative voice, "that Greg saved all of your lives here today. He *is* a *hero*. And we owe it to him to hear what he has to say!"

And then I had the massive crowd's full attention once again.

"Thank you," I whispered to Edwin.

"I can't do that again, buddy," he whispered back. "So you better change your game plan and make this good."

I cleared my throat and tried once more.

"Okay, you're right," I said to the crowd. "Destroying all weapons everywhere isn't going to happen. But I want to at least believe it *is* actually possible. And I know you all do, too. If we stop believing our best intentions are achievable, then we may as well stop trying completely. Which is why I just threw my ax into the lava. The most powerful Dwarven weapon ever created. And I don't regret it, even now. As that person down in front just said: *We are all fallible.* Which means no one person, no single weapon, no entity, should ever have that much power. Weapons that can destroy the whole world probably shouldn't exist.

"I won't ask you to destroy your own weapons, but I will ask you this: Why must armaments always be our first recourse when things don't go our way? Or when we feel like we're being cheated? I mean, even if you *are* being cheated, fighting is never the best way to solve it. That's what we're faced with now. How will we react to adversity going forward, knowing that bloody battles like this one can be a possible outcome?

"My answer to that question was to destroy a weapon too powerful for its own good. What will yours be?"

I had the crowd's full attention now. Nobody interrupted. Nobody spoke. Nobody moved.

"This our chance to start anew," I continued. "Right now we can all start making little choices every day to help the world be a better place. And if we can collectively make more kind and empathetic decisions than selfish and fearful ones, I do think that the world can get better. That we can *be* better."

Everyone stood in silence, staring at me and one another uneasily, clutching their weapons to their breastplates, not quite ready to give up on fear entirely. But at least we weren't bashing and maiming one another anymore.

"Greg's right," Edwin said suddenly. "No single person, no single governing body, *nobody* deserves this much power. Weapons as powerful as *this* shouldn't exist."

Edwin turned and held up the Sword of Anduril.

The blade ignited with magical fire again, glowing more brilliantly than ever, almost as if begging him not to do what he was about to do. Almost as if it were speaking to him, trying to remind him that many horrors still remained in this world. And maybe it even *was* speaking to him the same way the Bloodletter spoke to me?

And Edwin hesitated then, the blazing purple flames on his sword reflecting little fires in his eyes. I thought for a moment that he was going to change his mind. That he couldn't actually go through with it. That the safety the sword provided outweighed the idea that nobody should have this much power.

But I knew him better than that. This was still the same kind, funny, generous kid who had been my best friend for the past three years. The same kid who loved lame puns and playing chess.

That kid would always try to do the right thing.

Edwin sighed, then turned and threw the sword out into the lava lake.

The crowd gasped as the flaming blade spun through the air. It somehow sounded fearful, shocked, and hopeful all at once.

The Sword of Anduril landed in the thick molten lava with a searing *hiss* of steam.

Then it was gone.

Of course I wish I could have found a way to end all wars forever, like in the other ending. But unfortunately, nothing, not even magic, will ever stop people from making bad decisions, from doing bad things. From unfortunate circumstances leading to unfortunate events, and so on and so forth.

You simply can't *force* everyone to *be good* all the time.

Which means this war is far from over.

But at least Edwin and I spared us all the worst possible outcome this time around. By destroying the two most powerful weapons in existence, we'd at least assured we would not find a way to destroy the whole planet just yet. And we had, for a moment, actually united Elves and Dwarves—something that had seemed totally unfathomable to many Elves and Dwarves for thousands of generations—to defeat a common enemy, the Verumque Genus. And we did it together, as real friends. Like we even joked about way back when I first discovered the true nature of my past.

And so my dad's vision turned out to be more complicated than simply: *We all lived in peace and harmony forever and ever.*

But that doesn't mean any of us are giving up. Just the opposite. If anything, this battle has made all of us—Elves, Dwarves, Humans, monsters of all kinds—realize just how much of a difference we can actually make. Maybe not always on our own, but especially when united with our friends, family, allies, and sometimes even our enemies.

We've now experienced firsthand that when people and creatures, no matter who or what they are, truly work together for a common goal, good and sometimes great things *can* be achieved.

Things *can* get better.

And so that's what we're going to keep trying to do going forward. One day, one problem, at a time.

I know. I know. This is all really cheesy.

But why should that make us uncomfortable?

Isn't that what we should all *want*?

Of course, finding a more peaceful existence is going to be a very slow process. The future will continue to be messy, complicated, violent, trying, challenging, and all those other words nobody likes in their lives. But as long as Edwin and I, and Elves, Dwarves, Humans, Werewolves, Orcs, etc., etc., keep doing our best to work together, I am confident* that we will, at the very least, make the world a better place to live during our lifetime.

And *that* was my dad's true vision.

Even though he's gone now, and even though I will die (not at the hands of some Troll, but no doubt from something ironically random like a freak lightning strike, or choking on a chicken wing), before seeing his full vision come to fruition, I will at

---

* Ha-ha! A Dwarf confident and optimistic, imagine that!

least die satisfied, knowing me and my friends did the best we could for the world.

There's still more work ahead, of course. There will be other threats. But at least now I take comfort in knowing that whatever we may face in the future, me and my friends—and a hopefully united alliance of Elves and Dwarves and whoever else wants to join us—will be ready to handle them.

Together.

Because peace will always have its enemies.

And this new magical world really is just beginning.

ACKNOWLEDGMENTS

—✦—

I'd like to thank all the people who played a role in bringing this series to life. All the copy editors, editors, agents, publicists, designers, illustrators, everyone at Temple Hill and Putnam, and more. If I missed your name specifically, please forgive me: Pete Harris, Stephanie Pitts, Jennifer Besser, Katherine Perkins, Kate Meltzer, Steve Malk, Brian Miller, Alli Dyer, Cecilia de la Campa, Wyck Godfrey.

Last, thanks to my epic beard for giving me all my powers.